SNAP SHOT

Julia McAllister Mysteries
Book One

Marilyn Todd

SAPERE
BOOKS

SNAP SHOT

Published by Sapere Books.

20 Windermere Drive, Leeds, England, LS17 7UZ,
United Kingdom

saperebooks.com

ISBN: 978-1-913028-59-6

To my agent, Bea Corlett —
don't know what I'd do without her.
(25 to life, probably)

Chapter 1

'This —' The owner of the house cleared his throat and tried again. 'This is highly irregular.' He tapped the letter from Whitmore Photographic. 'The proprietor assures me that he will personally be taking Flora's portrait.'

Julia McAllister glanced at the four-year-old, sitting bolt upright in her best pink taffeta dress. A froth of ringlets cascaded over her shoulders, and the silver locket round her neck twinkled in the meagre light. With her favourite dolls cradled in her arms, three of them in each, you could be forgiven for thinking the little mite was still alive.

'My employer, poor man, his health took a turn for the worse.' Julia flashed a tortured smile. 'His heart, I'm afraid. Notoriously unreliable.'

'Yes, but even so.' Her client's eyebrows met when he frowned. 'A woman?'

Julia slotted the plate holder into her camera. She bit her lip, and reminded herself that this was just a job, another routine portrait — that she should knuckle down, take the picture, forget the subject was a baby.

'Mr. Whitmore would not have entrusted me with such a sensitive task,' she assured the grieving father, 'unless he had every confidence in my ability.'

'For my part —' his wife's voice was little more than a croak — 'I'm comforted that a member of my own sex is looking after Flora. Women,' she added shakily, 'are infinitely more sympathetic, so come, dear.' She pulled her husband's sleeve. 'Let us leave Miss McAllister in peace.'

Mrs., Julia wanted to correct. *It's Mrs. McAllister.* But the death of their only child was testing the couple's strength, their marriage and, judging from the cross on the mantelpiece that had been laid flat, their faith in Jesus Christ. Like families everywhere, too much in life had been taken for granted. It was only when the flame was snuffed, in this case without warning, that it was driven home how little they had to remind them of their loved ones. They wanted this picture to cling to and cherish.

'Rest assured,' she said, 'I will do your daughter proud.'

Alone in the parlour, Julia took a series of deep breaths and forced herself to block out the red flock walls that threatened to close in, the gagging scent of lilies, the silence of the grandfather clock, whose pendulum had been removed and wouldn't be replaced until Flora lay in her grave. How sad. How desperately tragic. When your husband dies, you become a widow. When your parents die, you become an orphan. Yet there's no word to describe someone who loses a child.

To calm her nerves, Julia followed her familiar ritual of running her hand over the Spanish mahogany case of her camera, inhaling the leathery tang of the bellows and fingering the handmade dovetail joints. (None of those factory-made monstrosities, thank you very much.) By the time she'd given the brass fittings one last unnecessary polish, she felt in control, and disappearing under the heavy dark cover, she examined the image. After all this time, she hadn't grown used to seeing the world upside down, but there, now — a quick tweak to the focus, a slight tilt to the left, a touch of back swing and —

Mother of God!

The girl's hand moved.

Nonsense. It must have been a trick of the candles, and that was the problem with having the curtains drawn and the mirrors draped in black. The shadows played havoc.

There! It moved again!

Julia sloughed the sheet from her shoulders and squinted. Impossible. Flora fell downstairs and snapped her neck. In fact, the only thing holding her upright was a metal clamp under her pretty lace collar, and a rope, artfully hidden by dolls, tying the girl to the chair. Julia should know. She'd put them there.

No, no, no. The dead don't —

'Ow!' a voice squealed.

'Were you trying to steal that locket?' Julia grabbed the young boy hiding behind the body.

'Lemme go, you're pinching!'

'Did you think I wouldn't spot a third hand? A third hand, I might add, caked with a six-inch layer of grime.'

'I said lemme go!'

'This will be a double exposure in every sense, if you don't quit squawking.' Julia examined the urchin in front of her. Eight, was he? Nine? 'How did you get in?'

'Door's open, innit.'

Of course. The front door had been left partly open for mourners to enter without jarring the nerves already stretched past breaking point.

'So you thought you'd sneak in and steal the locket that probably contains a clipping of her hair, which is all her mother has to remember her only daughter by?'

The defiance crept out of the boy's face. 'You gonna report me to the rozzers?'

'No.'

'Why not?'

9

'Because these are good people, who don't need to know that some stray urchin crept in their house, defiled their daughter's body and was caught stealing her precious locket. They've suffered tragedy enough, and I won't have you adding to their misery.'

'Wotcha gonna do, then?'

'I am going to take this girl's portrait, that's what I'm going to do, and you, sir, are going to help me.'

'*Me?* I don't know nuffin' about photographs.'

Julia fluffed the girl's lace collar to hide the mucky handprint on the taffeta. 'You don't need to. Just hold the curtain open — the left one if you please — to throw some decent light in the room.'

'Like that?'

'Exactly like that.' She pressed the shutter release, changed the plate, took another, then another, then another.

'Why d'you take so many?' He sniffed, and wiped his nose on his sleeve. 'It's not like she's gonna move and throw the focus out.'

'For someone who professes to know nothing about photography, you seem remarkably well informed. However, your expertise is no longer required, young man. Time for you to leave, preferably in the same covert manner in which you arrived.'

'Can't I —?'

'Shoo.'

Julia packed up her camera, collapsed her tripod and dismantled the contraption that was holding Flora upright, before packing her accessories back in the case and promising the grieving couple that Whitmore Photographic would be giving Flora's portrait the utmost priority.

Outside, Julia felt the weight lift from her. After a month of non-stop drizzle that had combined with the smoke from the factories to form a choking, brown, sulphurous stew, the sun was a welcome sight, and Julia wasn't alone in her joy. Half the population of Oakbourne, it seemed, had turned out to celebrate. The street shimmered with jewel-coloured silks, wide hats festooned with feathers, wasp waists, and shoes with toes so pointed they could put an eye out. Impressive moustaches paraded beneath dark derby hats. Parasols twirled, hansom cabs rattled, and (shock, horror!) could that really be ladies riding bicycles in bloomer suits? Flower girls proffered violets, carnations and stocks a penny a bunch, puppies chased their own tails and a boy played a harp taller than himself to an enraptured audience on the corner.

Stopping at the strawberry barrow, Julia smelled her scrawny assistant before she saw him. 'You again.'

'Seeing as how I helped out back there, I thought you might wanna give me sixpence for me troubles.'

'How about I give you a clip round the ear?'

'Cow,' he muttered. Julia checked her black beaded purse. Strangely, it was still there. 'Threepence, then.'

Dear Lord, give me strength. 'Suppose we say no pence, and I don't call the police?'

'Suppose I went up your chimney and cleaned it?'

'You're too old, you'd get stuck, and by the time you'd starved to death and your skeleton dropped out, I'd have died from frostbite, waiting. Go away.'

'I'll settle for a ha'penny.'

Julia pulled the boy out of the path of a hackney cab and pointed with her strawberry in the opposite direction to which she was headed. 'Go. Now.'

'S'pose I said I wasn't stealing nuffin'. S'pose I told you, I just wanted to see what a pretty girl looks like dead, coz the only corpses I seen are under the bridges by the canal, and them's anything but pretty.'

Against her better judgment, Julia gave him her last strawberry. It disappeared whole, green bits, stalk, and all. 'What's your name?'

'Bug.'

'Bug?'

A grubby shoulder shrugged. 'Short for Bugger Off, which is what most people —'

'No explanation required. In fact, I can well see the attraction in offering that particular piece of advice, but tell me — Bug — when was the last time you took a bath?'

'What's it to you?'

'Personally, very little.' Julia set down her clutter of camera, tripod, cases and clamps. 'In terms of community service, however, I feel it only fair to remedy the situation.'

Grabbing him by the collar with one hand and the seat of his moth-eaten pants with the other, Julia dropped Bug in the horse trough.

The resulting yells were more than satisfactory. Even if the language wasn't.

But it was little Flora's face that stayed with Julia as she pushed through the crush of Cadogan Street and into Westgate Road. Requests for post-mortem photographs — *memento mori*, as they were popularly called — were becoming more and more common, and this was by no means the first that Julia had taken. Some of her subjects were old, well into their eighties, some were children, a few already laid out in their coffin. Rather memorably, one old chap had begun to decay.

For the sake of authenticity, some of her clients she propped standing up, some with their heads in their hands, some leaning back with a newspaper as though they'd nodded off in mid-read. One lady the family had wanted sitting at a table laid with glassware, cutlery and plates, as though waiting for her dinner guests. Many, like little Flora, had their eyes open. With others, she painted their eyelids to make it look like they were posing for the camera. She perched dogs on their laps. (Stuffed, of course — live animals don't sit still long enough for the exposure). Several were arranged with their entire families around them and on one notable occasion, it had been impossible to tell which of the eight was the corpse.

None — not one — of those subjects had affected her like this.

Perhaps it was because Flora was an only child, and the mother was of an age when she was unlikely to conceive again. Perhaps it was the dignity with which the couple bore their grief. Perhaps it was the little girl herself, taken in the blink of an eye. Either way, this morning left a nasty taste in Julia's mouth. One that even the reddest, ripest strawberries couldn't take away.

'Ah. The lady photographer, I presume?'

Julia eyed up the man waiting outside her shop, set down her equipment and proceeded to unlock the door. He didn't look bereaved, was too old to be getting married, and too young to have a daughter needing a wedding recorded for posterity. In fact, in his smart grey lounge suit, derby hat and cocky air, she wouldn't mind betting he wanted to commission a portrait of himself. Recorded for posterity.

'What exactly are you wanting, Mr —?'

'Collingwood.' For all the width of his smile, it didn't reach his eyes. Eyes, the artist in her noted, the same hue as his suit.

'Inspector. Detective Inspector Collingwood, of the Boot Street Police Station. You'd be Miss —?'

'Mrs.' Julia hoped that stacking her equipment would excuse not shaking hands. Shaking being the operative word. 'It's Mrs. McAllister,' she said. 'Now what can I help you with, Inspector? An official police photograph, taken in the station?'

'Not exactly.' He walked slowly round the shop, examining the frames on display, the portraits hanging in the window, the showcase of photos, the little china dogs on sale as a side-line. 'Does the name Eleanor Stern mean anything to you?'

Relief washed over Julia, leeching the strength from her knees — its place instantly taken by a new surge of anxiety. *Nellie, Nellie, what have you done now?*

'Can't say it does.'

'Lily Atkins?'

An image flashed through Julia's head. Black stockings drawn over chubby knees. Enormous breasts. The coquettish twist to Lily's lips as she tweaked her own nipple.

'Again, no, doesn't ring a bell.'

'Hm.' Collingwood paced a bit more. He stared out of the window at the Common, where lovers strolled arm in arm beneath the oaks, ladies of a certain age walked their Pomeranians, and nannies in uniform pushed perambulators as they eyed the soldiers from the corner of their eye. 'Bridget O'Leary, though. Surely you know her?'

'Sorry…' No smile was ever more apologetic. 'Then again, a lot of ladies have their portraits taken, Inspector. I could check the ledger, if you like?'

'That won't be necessary.' The pacing changed from clockwise to anti-clockwise. 'Mr. Whitmore.' He ran his hand across a silver frame with embossed cherubs on the corners. 'He left you this business when he died, is that correct?'

'He did.'

'Yet four years later, you haven't changed the name above the shop, and still pretend to clients that Samuel Whitmore's alive?'

If it had been anyone else, she would have passed that off as respect to her benefactor's generosity. Unfortunately, there are only so many lies you can tell the police.

'Pretend is a strong word, Inspector. As a woman fighting to survive, not only in commerce but in what is very much a man's world, I find it simpler not to disabuse them.'

'Of course.' Collingwood switched his derby from his left hand to his right, then back again. 'And you're not familiar with the names Lily Atkins, Bridget O'Leary and Eleanor, more commonly known as Nellie, Stern?'

'I thought we'd already agreed I am not.'

'Had we? Because these photographs were found in their rooms.'

One by one, he laid them on the walnut counter like a deck of cards. All three were along the lines of the image that had flashed through Julia's mind a moment before. Although in Nellie's case, perhaps a little more so.

'*Inspector!*' Julia swept them off the counter. 'How dare you bring such filth into my premises!'

Something twitched at the side of his mouth as he bent to retrieve them. With luck, it was indigestion. 'My apologies if the content offends you, Mrs. McAllister, but you notice that, on the reverse of these prints, is your stamp.'

Damn. She never put her address on the back of any incriminating — Wait. Whitmore Photographic? In her distinctive purple ink…?

15

'I have no idea how that got there.' And that was the truth. 'But as far as I'm aware, no law has been broken in either posing for pornographic photographs, or taking them.'

'Quite so. The crime lies in the possession and distribution of lewd material, although it piques my interest that you're aware of this fact.'

A trickle of sweat snaked down Julia's backbone. 'You wouldn't believe the requests I receive from certain members of the public.'

'Hm.' Collingwood's grey eyes — wolf's eyes — held hers for what seemed like two days, but was probably only a couple of seconds. She swore she heard the dust motes hitting the ground. 'Your husband.'

'James.'

'Where might I find him?'

'The Sudan.'

One eyebrow rose. 'Fighting in the campaign?'

'Buried there.' Julia smoothed her skirts. 'Now then, Inspector, if you don't mind, a grieving family needs a portrait of their daughter — the only image they will have to remember her by.'

'I understand. You need to get to work.'

'The matter is pressing, and despite my trade plate on the back of these vile photographs, I assure you, I know nothing of their provenance, and to be honest, I'm offended that you think me acquainted with strumpets such as these.' She forced a smile. 'On the other hand, I can see how you made the connection, and — well, far be it for me to tell you your job, but wouldn't it be simpler to ask the girls about the pictures?'

'Strange as it might seem, that thought occurred to me, as well.' Collingwood picked up a china dog, a King Charles Spaniel as it happened, examined the pottery mark, then replaced it in the exact position in which he had found it. 'The problem with that line of enquiry is that all three are dead.'

'I am sorry to hear that.' *Nellie? Lily? Little Birdie...?*

'Murdered,' Collingwood said quietly. 'And from what I can gather, Mrs. McAllister, you work alone on these premises, without an assistant.'

Breathe ... breathe...

'I'm sure there's a point to that observation, Inspector.'

'My point, Mrs. McAllister, is that all roads lead to Rome.' He picked up another china dog, a Skye Terrier, and proceeded to examine it. 'And you, it would seem, are standing in the middle of the Forum.'

Chapter 2

Photographers must be many things. Part-chemist, to hold the silver bromide in a layer of gelatine emulsion to coat the glass plates, then know the difference between chlorohydroquinone, ferrous oxalate, hydroxylamine, ferrous lactate, ferrous citrate, eikonogen, atchecin, antipyrine, amidol and acetanilide when it comes to developing the wretched things. Part-artist, to understand and correlate light, mood and composition. Part-entrepreneur, to know how to display their shop window to attract the right type of client. But most of all, their stock-in-trade is patience.

The perfect photograph is a blend of all these qualities, and more. It captures emotions and feelings in that single and unique moment in time, then freezes it for all eternity, and that needs patience by the bucket load. You cannot allow yourself to be distracted. Not by something that happens in the background when you're taking stuffy wedding portraits, no matter how dangerous or exciting. For the same reason, you train yourself not to jump at a child's scream, an unexpected clap of thunder, a gust of wind that suddenly lifts your skirt and shows the world your ankles. Composure is an art form in itself.

God knows, Julia had experience in that.

'Bosh,' she said levelly, holding Collingwood's gaze. 'Three dirty pictures plus one purple stamp does not equal a hangman's noose.'

'It does not,' he agreed. 'So to that end, I trust you won't object to my taking a look round.'

Hold your nerve, hold your nerve, just a little bit longer…

'Feel free, Inspector.'

Collingwood opened the top left-hand drawer of the desk. 'This would be the stamp which you ink and press on the back of your photographs?'

'It's easy to see how you rose through the ranks.'

He shot her a sideways glance that, with anyone else, might have been construed as amusement. 'Do many of your fellow photographers use purple ink?'

'I sincerely hope none.'

After Sam Whitmore died, she made several changes to the business. Distinctive ink was just the beginning.

'Pretty,' he murmured.

'The ink or the design?'

'Both.' He peered at the elaborate scroll surrounding her name and address. 'The company who manufacture these things —'

'They're based in Greenwich.'

'— inform me that you ordered two trade stamps.'

Did they indeed. 'You'll find the second in the bottom drawer, still in its wrapping.'

That was a precaution, given how shiny silver objects tend to catch the eye of a thief, and not all criminals hail from the rookeries and slums.

'The package, Mrs. McAllister, appears to be empty.'

Damn. No one had keys to the shop apart from herself, and no one else knew it was there. But — he was right. The box was empty.

'Silly me, I have evidently misplaced it.' To suggest someone had stolen it, when she was the only person with access, was tantamount to looping the noose round her neck. Though for one ridiculous moment, it flashed through her mind that someone was framing her — how pathetic was that? 'Is it important?'

'I don't know. Is it?'

If someone had asked her yesterday, even this morning, *what do you imagine detective inspectors from Boot Street are like?*, this man would be as far removed from her notion as it was possible to get. Traditionally, policemen came from unskilled, working-class backgrounds. Not Collingwood. His clothes and his accent smacked of education, along with a solid suburban upbringing. A doctor's son, perhaps, or the son of a lawyer. And his age (hard to say, under that cocky expression, but no more than forty) surely made him one of the youngest inspectors outside the Metropolitan Police.

Which, in turn, made him one of the most dangerous.

'My studio's through here.'

Julia pulled aside the heavy fringed curtain, and his breath came out in a whistle.

'Not what I was expecting.'

'Because it's crammed with scenic backdrops, camera equipment, and lights twice the size of parasols? Or because it doesn't resemble a bordello?'

'Let's just say full-size paintings of train stations wouldn't have been top of my list.'

It was amazing how many sitters — men, usually military types — wanted their portrait taken beside a 1st Class railway carriage. That was in sharp contrast to women, who were invariably happier flanked by elegant drapes or a gentle park view, complete with balustrade and flower-filled urns.

Watching Collingwood inspect the properties boxes (including a bicycle for today's modern, independent young woman), Julia was grateful, more than ever, that she'd had the foresight to lease a separate location for her … let's call them, *alternative* compositions.

In a flash, the girls were right beside her.

Lily, cracking jokes while she posed. Her colossal breasts jiggling like milk puddings when she laughed.

Bridget. Little Birdie, with her springy curls and sparkling eyes, who'd trap earwigs in jam jars and run down four flights of stairs in the middle of the night, rather than kill them.

Oh, and Nellie. Nellie Stern. A face that looked like butter wouldn't melt, but she couldn't resist picking pockets. *Old habits die hard, Mrs. M, it's how us kids was brought up, and I was lucky that bloke in the Queen's Arms didn't call the coppers. Wish he'd smacked me in the ribs, not the mouth, though. Hurt like buggery, it did.* Nellie, Nellie, Nellie. Always talking, always bustling, always in hot water, now the hottest of them all. Why couldn't that bloke have called the bloody coppers!

Collingwood's voice cut through her grief.

'Yours?' In his hand was a scarf of exquisite Flemish lace.

'Rather elegant, don't you agree?'

'I do.' But the smile on his face was the sort a lioness might sport, having circled the herd, picked out her kill and stretched before giving chase. 'Though I can't help noticing it bears a striking resemblance to the scarf in Miss O'Leary's photograph. Having said that —' his mouth twisted — 'I'm not sure the use she's putting it to was quite the original intention.'

Sod that. This wasn't the Serengeti, and Julia wasn't a zebra.

'I believe "resemblance" is the significant word there, Inspector.' She snatched the photograph from his hand. The invitation on Birdie's face, as she teased the scarf between her legs, was blatant. It was the reason her pictures commanded such high prices. 'Given the lighting, I'd say the scarf in this photo is darker, primrose rather than ivory, but even if the colour's identical, these scarves are the height of fashion. Hundreds of women must own the same design. I daresay you can buy them anywhere.'

'Such fine lace? On Miss O'Leary's income?'

'I have no idea what Miss O'Leary's income might be, but I assure you, Inspector, if I knew where this scarf had been, I would have burned it.'

'Of course. My apologies.'

Moving on to her dark room, Collingwood switched on the electric light, and if he was remotely bemused by shelves crammed with bottles and phials, or the pungent smells emanating from the various jugs, tubes and processing baths, it didn't show. Not, Julia decided, a man to play that new American card game of poker with.

Then again, neither was she.

'So then.' He examined the glass plates in the racks. 'This is where the magic is made?'

'No, Mr. Collingwood. It is not.'

Briefly she outlined the elaborate processes involved, from the silver halide crystals in a gelatine base to the bath of diluted acid, and then how, once fixed, the image could be exposed to light, before tapping her heart with her fist.

'*This* is where the magic is made.'

Forget stiff weddings and stuffy portraits, Julia set out to capture individuality through her lens. To add a new and vibrant dimension to every image, encapsulating emotions, rather than simply scenes and people.

'A refreshing philosophy, Mrs. McAllister. Not to mention impressive.' He switched off the light and closed the door behind them. 'If you don't mind my asking, what quality of mine would you encapsulate in your portrait?'

She leaned her elbows on the counter and studied him. Professionally this time. From the high forehead to the dark hair, grey eyes to pointed chin, taking in his lean, runner's build and tailor-made suit, the fact that the shine on his shoes could blind a horse in its blinkers, the spotless starched collar and elaborate tie knot, and, rather unusually for this day and age, that he was clean-shaven.

'I can tell you one thing, Mr. Collingwood. It would not reflect the preening peacock you like to portray. Rather, it would show a man who is meticulous, driven, a little stubborn perhaps, ambitious, and not without guile.'

'Hopefully my devilish good looks will make up the deficit.' His face changed when he laughed. 'Do you always hold back with your sitters?'

'If you want someone to tell you what you want to hear, Inspector, I suggest you visit a fortune teller at one of the fairs.'

'You don't seem unduly concerned that you're my prime suspect in the investigation of three murders.'

'You don't seem unduly concerned that you are mistaken.'

He perched on the edge of the counter, swinging one leg with carefully practised indifference. 'I may have my faults, Mrs. McAllister, but being wrong isn't one of them. These, by the way, are the dates when the girls died.'

While he read aloud from his notebook, her mind whirled. *Why hadn't she read about this in the papers —?*

'I'm sure you can account for your whereabouts on those nights.'

Enough. Julia's nerves were already stretched to the point where you could play a concerto on the damned things. 'I'm a widow, an orphan and an independent businesswoman trying to make a living in a man's world, Mr. Collingwood. Where do you think I would be? Now unless you're going to arrest me, I repeat: a grieving family are desperate for a photograph to commemorate their daughter, and I won't have you risking their precious reminiscences by contaminating the negatives. Good day to you, Inspector.'

Julia bolted the door behind him, turned the Open sign to Closed and pulled the blinds down. Her legs were weak, her stomach was churning, but dammit, that stamp had to be somewhere. Who would take it? More importantly, who *could* take it? Julia had the only key.

It was only after she'd turned out every drawer, gone through every cupboard, upended every box, sack and basket that she had to face facts.

Three girls were dead.

The killer was framing Julia for murder.

And suddenly, it was no longer a question of who was behind this.

It was why.

Chapter 3

Julia paced the bedroom above the shop, punching her fist into the palm of her hand.

Why? *Why* couldn't she have left those girls alone?

Lily in her stinking yellow apron, hawking whelks from a tray slung round her neck. Nellie, back-chatting costermongers in between picking pockets and peddling turnips. Little Birdie, barefoot and shivering, reduced to shouting out for the broom-seller, who'd gone hoarse from barking his wares.

Why couldn't she have simply noted their potential, instead of taking it upon herself to coach it? What arrogance made her think she could give these girls a better life by lifting them out of their poverty?

Vaguely she was aware of the clop of hooves in the street below, the click of boots on the pavement, the hum of conversation interspersed with the squalls of tired infants, of tiny feet pattering to keep up, the yapping of dogs, the clang of a tinker's pans as he passed by.

'Mrs. McAllister? Julia?'

The tap-tap-tap on the glass below made her jump.

'You in there, love?'

She recognised the voice. Rosie Blackstock. Wife of Oliver Blackstock, the man who commissioned Julia's risqué photos, and mother of nine children. Bless her — round as an apple, red as a plum — she was the archetypal mother hen: clucking, fussing, with eyes in the back of her head, and Julia could count the times on one hand when that woman's face wasn't creased up in a smile.

'There's no lights on, so you're either out or in your dark room — *please don't do that, Verity. Daniel, stop pulling your sister's hair* — but I've brought you a pie, love. Goosegogs from the garden, first crop of the year — *yes, Davey, thank you, I do know I'm talking to myself* — I'll leave it on the sill, all right? *Daniel, I won't tell you again.* Anyway, all the pie needs is a dollop of cream, and if you catch it while it's warm, so much the better. Oh, and don't worry about bringing the dish back. Any time you're passing'll do, and don't bother about washing it, neither, I'll sort that out.' Rosie gave her signature tap-tap-tap of goodbye on the glass. 'Night, lovey!'

Julia made no attempt to pull up the sash window or call down her thanks. She didn't want kindness, she didn't want food and she certainly didn't want comfort. Because of her, three girls would never have their own little Veritys to chastise, no Daniels to scold, no goosegog pies to deliver to friends —

She spiked her hands through her hair, knowing she ought to be working, not imitating some wretched caged cheetah. Flora's parents needed that photograph, and they needed it now. *For goodness' sake, take a hold of yourself!* But her mind kept on spinning, her thoughts remained locked in a spiral. A spiral of grief, and anger, and guilt.

All they'd wanted, poor girls, was to fall in love, find a husband, raise a houseful of kids. Now some bastard had robbed them of their lives, their hopes, their dreams and their dignity, and was trying to pin it on her.

Collingwood didn't say how they died. Were they strangled? So the killer could watch the suffering in their eyes? Was that why he made such mention of the scarf? No, no, no. She punched her fist harder and at twice the speed. Strangling's a man's game, he wouldn't associate her with that — unless the killer garrotted them, rather than use his bare hands.

Were they poisoned? That would explain Collingwood's interest in her dark room. All those chemicals. If so, it had to have been a fast-acting substance. Strychnine, perhaps. Cyanide. Otherwise the girls would have called out, run for help, possibly even been saved by swift medical attention.

But fast-acting doesn't mean quick, and it bloody well doesn't mean painless. Julia had worked enough with acids to know that such terms were relative. Cyanide or strychnine, those girls would have died writhing in agony. Burning from the inside out. Did Collingwood — did anyone — imagine Julia capable of such a heinous and cowardly act?

She was lucky not to be rotting in the cells at Boot Street and she knew it. Any other policeman would have dragged his only suspect off in irons, and it was pure luck that Collingwood was a slow-burner, keen to dot his 'i's and cross his 't's. Ambitious detectives build meticulous cases, and he'd want cast iron evidence to put before a jury, or at the very least, a case that was as damning as it could be.

'The sun shall be turned into darkness and the moon into blood, before the great and terrible day of the Lord comes!' Booming out of nowhere, the words caught her off-guard. Echoing so loudly in her head that the man who would quote it at the end of his fist might have been standing behind her. *'They that wait upon the Lord shall renew their strength, and shall mount up with wings like eagles.'*

Oh, yes, Julia knew them all. Acts 2:20 Isaiah 40:3. She knew them backwards, sideways, inside out. Old Testament. New. Mixed and matched to whatever mood her step-father was in. To whatever he'd been drinking —

Julia barely reached the basin before the contents of her stomach ejected.

Blood. Pools of blood. She could see them. Arcing. Splashing. Spreading. Staining. They were the last thing she saw before she fell asleep. The first thing she saw when she woke —

Gripping the dresser, she was sick until there was nothing left to bring up.

Was that what this was? Some twisted act of divine retribution? Sending Julia to the gallows for a crime she didn't commit — *to pay for the one that she did?*

If she believed in God, she might be tempted to think so. But she'd met with the Devil. Looked into his eyes. And knew fine well those eyes would not blink again.

She rinsed out her mouth and wiped the sweat from her face. Sod divine justice. An all-too-human hand was at work here. Only whose?

After twelve years of living under a different name, had an uncle, a cousin, an aunt somehow still recognised her? Then decided to punish her in the worst possible way, by killing innocent girls and laying their deaths on Julia's conscience?

In short, yes. When it came to her step-father's family, the Trevellicks, no grudge was too small, no memory too short, and certainly no vengeance too cruel. Except they were fishermen — why would they be in London? And let's face it, this level of planning was out of their league. Besides, how would they know about Julia's trade stamp? They had no access to her shop, much less the wit to use purple ink — and if, by some quirk, they had spotted her in the street, they might *think* there was a resemblance, but too much time had passed for them to be certain, and Julia had covered her tracks better than well.

So then. If they weren't behind this, who was?

Does Collingwood know about her past? Or at least suspect? If so, how far would an ambitious detective go to make two cases fit?

How far indeed?

With an energy bordering on the hysterical, Julia raced downstairs, scouring every inch of her shop, her dark room, her studio, the properties boxes, and this time, it wasn't the trade stamp she was after. It was anything — any damn thing whatsoever — that was out of the ordinary.

Nothing.

Nothing, nothing, oh thank you God.

Because if there was one advantage of being well organised (which you have to be, if you can't afford servants and assistants poking around), it's that you know exactly where any item is at any given time. Everything was in its customary place. Nothing missing, nothing added.

If Collingwood was prone to planting evidence, it wasn't today.

And realistically, how would Boot Street detectives know about incidents that took place twelve years ago, and three hundred miles away?

She poured herself a shot of Courvoisier, and followed it with another. It was not necessarily the best way to settle a sore, empty stomach, but a sure-fire way to steady her nerves, and maybe that spur to action was just what she'd needed? Because one thing was clear: brooding wouldn't bring those girls back, any more than obsessing about the past would change what had happened.

What Julia could influence, however, was the future.

Being his chief suspect in a series of murders, Collingwood would already have started digging into her background, and so far, he'd only scratched the surface. Her only chance of avoiding the noose was to find the bastard behind the killings, and even *that* wasn't enough. With the finger purposely pointed at her, she'd need to deflect suspicion, as well. How in hell was she supposed to do that? Where, in God's name, would she start?

Nothing's impossible, JJ.

Sam Whitmore's pet phrase booted the biblical echoes into touch. She reached for the frame containing his photo. Everyone mistook Sam's portrait for Buffalo Bill's. Long hair, thin face, same knowing sideways look. That was the reason she took it out of the shop. After Mr. Cody's performance at the Queen's Jubilee, it drew too much attention to a man who wasn't supposed to be dead.

'If you want something badly enough, it's yours for the taking. All you have to do is apply your mind and work hard,' Sam had told her.

Really, Sam? She put the frame back on the dressing table. *Because in the four years since I first laid lilies on your grave, I've been applying my mind until it's worn a hole in my brain, and worked my knuckles down to the bone. Where's that got me, eh?*

'A career you adore and an independence you couldn't have achieved without it,' Sam would have countered. 'New developing techniques make for exciting times, JJ. The world is your oyster bursting with pearls, and it's there, my friend, right in front of you, yours for the taking.'

Fine for a man to say. Sam had had rights, Sam had the vote, Sam never had to contend with the contempt and suspicion that single, independent women were viewed with. Every day of the past four years had been a battle for survival. The reason she'd resorted to smutty photos in the first place.

Julia poured another glass of cognac, except this time she didn't drink.

'On the other hand, Sam, you might just have a point…'

At first glance, the situation looked hopeless, and what she knew about criminal investigation could be written on the back of a halfpenny stamp. And yet — she was not without experience, was she?

'Poacher turned gamekeeper? What do you think, Sam? Reckon I can pull it off?'

Julia knocked the brandy back in one slug. Of course she could. She could do anything she wanted, if she applied her mind and worked hard! All she needed was a clear head and ice cold composure —

'Mother of God!' So much for composure. One bang on the door and her heart all but exploded. It couldn't be Rosie coming back — she'd tap on the glass. And a customer would have seen the Closed sign and moved on.

Her palms were unnaturally clammy as she unlocked the door.

Of all the possibilities, the only one she hadn't considered was a moth-eaten waif, his clothes still damp round the edges.

'Betcha thought I wouldn't find you, eh?'

Chapter 4

'For a small Bug, you have a precociously large appetite.'

Rosie's gooseberry pie was the first casualty of war, even though it was cold by the time Bug wolfed it down, and bereft of dollops of cream. After that, no ham hock or sprat in the pantry was safe. Julia was pretty sure the bread turned itself into crumbs just from quaking.

'Man's gotta keep his strength up,' Bug said, scraping out the last of the meat paste from the jar with his finger. 'Else he'll die on your doorstep and you'll be stuck with the funeral.'

'Man's gotta keep his mouth closed while he eats,' Julia countered, 'or his funeral will come sooner than he imagines.'

'How'm I supposed to talk, then?'

'That isn't talking. That's spraying my table with food.'

Julia had every intention of turning Bug out after she'd fed him. But all that changed when she went into her studio, with Bug hopping behind, his eyes bulging at the painted parks scenes, the seascapes and ships, and especially the railway carriage. (Mind, if he rang that bicycle bell one more time, just once more, so help her, that sound would be the last thing he heard).

'I'll pay.'

'Speak up.' She'd found what she was looking for in the second properties box, but couldn't hear for piling everything back.

'I said, I'll pay for the grub, honest I will. I'll work it off. Anything you want, Missus, I'll do it. I'll clean yer chimney, yer gutters, I'm good with me hands. I was a scavenger in the bike factory, crawling under the machinery to clear the muck out, till me foot got mangled, then no one'd take me —'

Julia swallowed. Why she hadn't connected his hopping to injury, rather than some irritating mannerism? She counted to three. Then breezed on as if nothing had happened. 'I'm sure payment in kind can be arranged in due course, but meanwhile, it's in the interests of everyone in Oakbourne that you secure your trousers with this belt.'

The hundred-mile-an-hour gabbling stopped. Freckles stood out like ink spots on Bug's pale face.

'Those are not the cheeks people want to see on display,' she added firmly.

'You're giving it me?'

'No, Bug, I am giving it *to* you.' The complexities of grammar were undoubtedly wasted on him, but at least she could say she had tried. 'Now take this as well —'

'What is it?'

'In an ideal world, it would be carbolic, but for tonight, Pears will have to suffice.'

'Yeah, but —' He sniffed the bar with suspicion. 'What *is* it?'

'Soap. It is soap, only this time we're going to do things properly, in a tin bath with hot water, and while you scrub that ingrained dirt off with a brush, I'll make up a bed for you in the shop.'

'Why?'

'Because you smell worse than the sewers in Fleet Street.'

'I mean, why are you doin' this?'

Because you're too small for your age? Because it's only one night? 'I'm simply buying time, until I find a way for you to repay me.'

Bug examined the argument for catches and flaws. 'In what case,' he said, 'I'm taking that biscuit barrel to bed.'

***

To say Julia's night was restless was an understatement, and what little sleep she managed was short, and riddled with nightmares.

There was Lily, unbuttoning her camisole for the camera. But as Lily fumbled with the buttons, two hands shot out of nowhere, then a third, smaller and covered with grime. *Lemme go, you bitch,* she was screaming, but the hands clamped round her throat and began strangling her. And when Julia looked down, they were her own hands round her neck... *This is your fault,* Birdie yelled, coming at her with a broom that turned into a knife, then back into a broom, *your fault I'm dead!* — while in the corner, Nellie covered her face with her fishy yellow apron as pools of blood congealed on the floor —

Still. All things must pass, even nightmares, and when Julia opened the curtains to admit a flood of bright sunshine, perspective was, thank God, back on track.

She knew, now, who was behind it.

Well, no. She didn't. Of course not. But the finger-pointing was personal, meaning the killer was in the business, and not simply a fellow photographer. He had to be in the same racy picture trade, someone who'd found a way to satisfy his perverted urges and at the same time use it to drive his only female rival out of business.

Rosie's husband, Oliver, would be able to tell her who else he commissioned these photographs from, then it was merely a question of whittling down a list of suspects to a list of women-haters. How hard could that be?

Warning her models would spread panic and fear, not to mention implicating herself and, worse, alerting the killer. On the other hand, Julia was buggered if she'd let another girl die.

'I have a job for you, young man.'

'Whassat, then?' Bug's little eyes lit up like beacons, and for the first time she saw they were green, and his hair wasn't the colour of wicker after all. His encounter with Pears soap showed it was closer to sand, and several freckles had washed away, too. 'Delivering that photo to the dead kid's house? Coz don't think I didn't hear you creep down in the night to develop it.'

She should have known street Arabs sleep with one eye open.

'I don't need an errand boy.'

'What then?'

'Let's just say it involves you sneaking out through an upstairs window.'

'Cor.'

So excited was Bug by the prospect, that he stuffed an extra slice of bread pudding in the back pocket of trousers, which, Julia was pleased to note, were now firmly secured. God willing, he'd make different associations with belt buckles in future.

Waiting until he'd shinned down the drainpipe without further trauma to his clothes, Julia let herself out through the shop, locked the door, tested it, then set off down the street, swinging her basket without a care in the world. You could bet your life Collingwood set a man to keep watch, with instructions to follow if she left, and sure enough, from the corner of her eye, she saw a constable step out from the doorway of the solicitors, crack the stiffness from his knuckles and nonchalantly follow her through the crowd.

Like shopkeepers up and down the country, the good merchants of Oakbourne opened early and closed late, and the trestle tables outside their shops were already piled high with their wares. Poultry, sugar bowls, confectionery, buns, watering cans, caged songbirds, candles, wallflowers and ribbons.

'Three a penny, nice fat Yarmouth bloaters.'

'Hankies, darlin'? Fine lace hankies?'

'Ho-ho, hi-hi, who wants my nice hot pie?'

She stopped to ask after the butcher's new baby, got an update on her neighbour's bunions, perused the latest fashions (oh, please! if leg o'mutton sleeves got any bigger, they'd never fit through doorways!) and exchanged cheery waves with Blodwen, ladling milk from the churn at the Welsh Dairy. Outside the taxidermist's, Julia paused to admire the latest exhibits where, while leaning forward to pay closer attention to the parrot's blue and yellow plumage, her handkerchief fluttered to the pavement.

The crash that followed made every head turn. As one, dogs yelped, men shouted, women squealed, horses whinnied and children burst into tears as Bug picked up the signal and caused chaos. With the clatter of ironmongery connecting with flagstones, and spades, shovels, buckets and bolts rolling in every direction, no one noticed Julia's basket pass seamlessly to the raggedy cause of the collapsed trestle, much less Julia herself slip down an alley. Especially that poor distracted constable.

Fifteen minutes' walk away, it was a different world. No silks or ostrich feather hats down here. No gentrified parasols, no hansom cabs, no floral buttonholes, often not even shoes, and — looking at the women, old before their time in broken chip bonnets and faded print frocks — it was hard to imagine these very streets were fields until a few years back. Today, that patchwork of berries and vegetables was a faded memory. In their place, brickworks, gasworks, biscuit and bicycle factories glowered down. A brewery here; a boiler maker's there;

virtually every ray of natural light blocked by buildings like the sugar refinery, eight stories high; twin chimneys belching out smoke; and everywhere, eardrums reverberating with the thunder of steam hammers and the pounding of heavy machinery.

If it wasn't careful, she thought, Oakbourne would become the Wolverhampton of London. Its walls covered with so much soot and grime that it, too, would be known as the Black Country.

'Mrs. Mack! What a luvly surprise.' A girl with shining gold hair, and a wholesome smile that dimpled her cheeks beckoned Julia inside, quickly gathering up three pairs of bloomers drying over a chair and stuffing them behind a cushion. 'What d'yer think of me new digs, then? Paradise, I reckon, don't you?'

A room in which a cat being swung would fear for its life wasn't most people's idea of heaven. Or the fact that the furniture shook every time a train rattled past. But compared to sharing a rabbit hutch with three other girls in a fourpenny lodging house, Julia saw her point.

'You've made it beautiful, Daisy.'

Pictures of saints, none of whom Julia recognised, had been pasted above a bed which probably still had a straw mattress, but was spread with a pale pink coverlet and spotless white pillows. A cheap Staffordshire bust of the Queen took pride of place in the corner dresser, and on the table, bluebells from the Common threatened to wilt. A straw bonnet hung on the wall, but the prettiest thing in the room by a long chalk was the baby asleep in the cradle.

'How old is she now?'

'She'll be six months next week, won't you, poppet?' Daisy tickled her daughter under the chin. 'Honest, Mrs. Mack, I can't thank you enough for what you done for me and Minnie.

When you think about that cubbyhole I was in, sharing a bed with a girl who stank of gin and garlic, all that scratching round for work and me five months gone —' She giggled. 'Still can't believe how you took them photos without showing my condition.'

Me neither, Julia thought, giving herself a pat on the back for that one. But from the moment she'd spotted Daisy at the lock gates touting for work — 'any kind of work, sir, so long as it's decent' — her belly swollen with child and destitution written all over her face, she knew she had to step in.

'That's why I called this morning, Daisy. I know you get by well enough with a bit of charring here, a spot of mending there, but I was wondering if you'd be interested in extra modelling work?'

'How many piles of mending d'you see, Mrs. Mack? And do it look like I'm just about to head off charring?' She shook her pretty blonde head. 'The more people that floods into this city, the faster jobs get snaffled up. Three days out of four I can't find work, so you won't hear me turn the offer down, 'specially with what you pay. Tea?'

'Please.'

'So come on, then, what is it?' Daisy spread an embroidered cloth on the table and brought her two best china cups out of the dresser. 'Only you wouldn't have trailed right the way out 'ere, if it wasn't something special.' The last half dozen Garibaldi biscuits in the tin were tipped on to a plate that didn't match the teacups. 'You'd have waited till our next session to ask.'

Should Julia admit there was a sudden shortage of models, and needed Daisy to fill in? Julia was pretty sure none of her models knew each other, so even if Daisy had heard about the girls, it was unlikely she'd make the connection. All the same, it was too big a risk.

'An urgent commission for a flip book —'

'A what book?'

While Daisy poured the tea and added the milk, Julia explained about the sequence of photographs bound together like a book, each shot varying slightly from the one before. 'When you flip the pages, it creates an animation effect.'

'And I'd be what? Taking me clothes off, I suppose?'

'They're thinking of calling it *What the Butler Saw.*'

Daisy blew out her cheeks. 'I'll be honest, Mrs. Mack, I wouldn't do nothing like that in front of a man, but I'm comfortable with you and that's a fact. How many pictures? Half a dozen?'

'Thirty.'

'Thirty!'

'Enough money to get you out of this place, Daisy. More than enough to take you home.'

'Not a chance in hell of that. Not after the names my Pa called me when I told him I was expecting, but I swear, Mrs. Mack, 'ow was I to know Minnie's dad was married? He told me he loved me, swore blind he'd look after me, but if there's one thing I've learned, it's a girl's on her own in this life. She does whatever she has to, to get by, and if posing for mucky photos is what it takes, then so be it. But it don't ever involve going back to Lambeth.'

Fine enough sentiments — while she was young and pretty and still had her health, Daisy could indeed provide for herself and her baby. But how soon before prostitution beckoned? How soon before the workhouse claimed them? Then a pauper's grave…?

'Thanks for helping out,' Julia said, standing up and smoothing her skirts. 'Give Minnie a kiss for me, when she wakes up.' She turned in the doorway, as though it was an afterthought. 'You haven't noticed anything unusual lately, have you? Any admirers hanging round? You're not walking out with a new man friend, perhaps?'

'Believe me, Mrs. Mack, I'm done with men for a long, long — why?' Alarm creased Daisy's face. 'The scum who use these pictures, they don't know me real name, do they?'

'Absolutely not. As far as anyone's concerned, you're "The Swedish Princess". Your identity is perfectly safe.' Julia shot Daisy a reassuring smile, wishing to God that was true. 'I was worried in case you had a man friend who might get upset by your side-line, that's all.'

It was the same with the other two models Julia called on. Anna Chen ("The Rose of Shanghai") and "Scheherazade", better known as Mollie Becks. Both agreed. With life one long, exhausting round of catch-as-catch-can, there were few opportunities for admirers, certainly no men friends, and any break in routine, however trivial, would have been welcomed with wide, open arms.

That did nothing to set Julia's mind at rest. She'd been hoping for a peeping-tom that she could report to the police. Instead, nothing and no one out of the ordinary, and a clot of fear settled in her stomach.

Suppose the killer was following her, not the girls?

Suppose that was how he'd picked out his victims?

What troubled her was why the girls' deaths hadn't made the papers. Oakbourne had long ceased to be a tight-knit rural community, where everyone knew everyone else, meaning they also knew their neighbours' business. The work that attracted thousands of people to the capital had, perversely, served to isolate them, but even so. Someone, somewhere, must have heard something? Seen something? If only the police or the undertaker's cart.

Or were the neighbours so accustomed to crime — burglary, theft, fraud and embezzlement spreading like mould with the march of industrialisation — that they literally thought nothing of it? Did they crave respectability so desperately, that they turned their heads to the wall? Julia knew first-hand how shameful assault was considered. Especially on women. But surely society hadn't reached the point where brutality was ignored in the name of good manners? The point where the veneer must be preserved at all costs? Or was it sheer embarrassment that kept a lid on these crimes —?

Weaving through the crush of costermongers, in their trademark brass-buttoned waistcoats and corduroy bellbottom trousers, hawking everything from potatoes to tin trays to second-hand goods, she was a hundred percent sure no one was trailing her now. Which might simply mean the bastard was careful.

Back among the silks and parasols and ostrich feather hats, Bug was leaning against the wall of the taxidermist, chewing on a straw. At his feet was the basket filled with the shopping she'd despatched him to buy. As well as a fruit cake, a pen knife and a yo-yo that she hadn't, and that she immediately made him take back, since it was clear all three had been stolen.

Whether he returned them or not wasn't her problem.

Wearing a smile any self-respecting member of the acting profession would envy, Julia was confident that the police constable might well be annoyed that he'd lost his suspect in the confusion, but this basket of shopping wouldn't raise even the most sceptical of eyebrows.

It was sod's law, of course, that the most sceptical of eyebrows happened to be leaning against her bloody doorway.

'Well, well, well.' Prising himself off the woodwork, Collingwood tipped his hat in a manner that, with anyone else, might have seemed insolent. 'If it isn't the lady photographer. Do you mind if I take another look around, Mrs. McAllister?'

'We both know that wasn't a question, so please, help yourself.'

Rifling through her cupboards, drawers and boxes as though the search took his full attention didn't fool her. He was well aware of her tipping a paper bag of sugar into the red stone jar, unwrapping two pork chops and placing them on a plate in the pantry, hanging a string of onions from a hook and filling an empty biscuit barrel with lemon creams. Was it bravado, or simply to annoy him, that she piled Granny Smiths on a plate like cannon balls?

'I know why you thumbed through.' He tapped the dog-eared *Oakbourne Chronicle* poking out of her basket. 'But you won't find anything about the murders in the papers. I can't risk sensationalism whipping up panic, so I've put a tight lid on the press.'

Victory loomed. Collingwood had combed the premises top to bottom — shop, studio, dark room, props — he'd been through her ledgers, her papers, her underclothes drawer, and still came up with sod all to connect her to the girls.

'We found a body of a man beside the canal this morning,' he said, chewing his lip. 'Young. Sharply dressed. Early 20s.'

Julia perched on the stool behind the gleaming walnut counter, while he prowled the shop floor. 'But?'

'He'd been beaten so badly, we can't identify the poor chap, and no papers on him to say who he was.'

Why was he telling her this? 'No witnesses, obviously.'

'Bargees lead nomadic lifestyles.' His grey eyes scanned the photographs framed on the walls. 'The bane of Boot Street, given how they bed down at dusk and cast off at first light. Any witness to the murder could be halfway to Paddington or Northampton by now.'

'As could the killer.'

'Exactly. I have officers on the towpaths, questioning the boat people. Someone, somewhere might have heard something, but frankly, I'm not holding my breath. Not because the bargees are uncooperative, but there are precious few locks, and once the water joins the main canal, a boat might take off in any number of directions. Pity there isn't some way to pick up my murder scene and preserve it, so I can examine it later, and at length.'

'You could always go French.'

'Play the accordion and dance the can-can?'

To her surprise, Julia actually laughed. 'Now that, Inspector Collingwood, *would* whip up panic, if it made the newspapers. I was thinking more about how the Parisian police have started using freelance photographers to capture images of both their victims and their scenes of crime from every angle.'

Collingwood stopped pacing. The air turned to ice.

'As to the pictures you were admiring just now —' *Don't stop, keep going, pretend nothing has changed* — 'I'm rather proud of those. This one.' Without so much as a quiver, Julia's index finger tapped the image of four agricultural workers, two men, two women, engaged in conversation either side of a stile. 'That's an amalgam of five images, overlaid one on top the other…'

Overkill perhaps, but while Julia listed, in more detail than was remotely interesting or necessary, the techniques involved in producing another "snap shot of the moment" — this time a blacksmith poised with his hammer above his anvil while a small boy hands him a flagon of ale — she had a feeling Collingwood was pondering what it was, exactly, that he couldn't put *his* finger on.

Chapter 5

'Was it coz of what I done this morning?' Bug lost Julia on that one. 'The rozzer what just left. Was it coz I kicked over all them pots and pans?'

Bug picked up a silver frame. Julia snatched it back and rubbed away his greasy little pawprints.

'No one's brave enough to feel your collar, Bug. Just looking at it makes most people queasy.'

'What's he hanging round for, then?'

Good question. Though Julia wished Bug wouldn't use that word hanging. Why even try to pull the wool over a street Arab's eyes? 'Thirsty?'

'Parched worse than Sarah Dezzard.'

'Sahara Desert.'

A scrawny shoulder shrugged. 'Parched worse than both of 'em, I reckon.'

Glancing at the clock, Julia wished to God panic would stop this nasty habit of creeping up her intestines. As much as she'd have liked to expose the killer as some deranged admirer-cum-prowler, this morning's calls pretty much ruled that out, creating a certain urgency in the need to draw up a list of who else was aware of her involvement in the smutty picture trade.

What she had to remind herself was, urgent doesn't necessarily mean at once.

'Considering you don't hardly have two pence to rub together, why din'cha charge the proper rate for that photo of the dead girl?'

'Flora?'

'How come you put it in a fancy silver frame, then give it 'em for nuffin'?'

There was no point in saying she had plenty of pence to rub together, because when it came to reading people, Bug was sharper than builders' lime.

'Money isn't everything, and freedom has no price.' She swirled tea leaves in the pot. 'How come you're living rough and on your own?'

'Can see why *you're* alone. No bloke'd want a frigid nag like you freezing up his bed.'

Defiance pushed out Bug's jaw. Just waiting for her to grab him by the scruff of the neck, he was, and throw him out, accompanied by a brisk clip round the ear. Julia calmly poured the tea and laid out a plate of sticky buns.

'This is seed cake, that's madeira.'

'What's the other one? That dark thing with the icing?'

'Why don't you try it and find out?'

'No one's ever bin this nice to me.'

'This isn't nice. This is safeguarding my investment, while supporting the sugar industry in the process.' Single-handedly, if Bug kept this pace up. 'But if it helps, I've been where you are now. Living rough and on my own.'

'You pulling me leg?'

'That's what I was doing when Sam Whitmore found me. Called me JJ, because it was neither a boy's name nor a girl's, but a name that put me on an equal footing.'

For several minutes, the only sound was the pendulum from the clock on the wall. Then Bug broke the silence. 'When I was five, my pop said he'd take me fishing. Went out, he did, came home with rods and reels and everythin'. Stuff I'd never seen the likes of. "We'll have a great time, son, just me and you. All boys together, eh?" I ran upstairs, put my best clobber on, would have said ta-ta to my mum, if she'd been sober.

'So off we goes, me and Pop, down to the canal, and all he's talking about is catching trout and cod and salmon for our tea. "This big," he says, holding his arms wide. Then he says, "Gotta call in here a sec, son," which was odd, coz us had never bin in a church in our whole lives.

'Anyways, I follows him up the steps, little hand in big, yer can imagine, and there's this funny bloke in a long brown scratchy dress, who takes my other hand and squeezes it. Then Pop lets go, ruffles me hair, and the next thing I know, the gate's closing behind me with a clang.'

Julia couldn't breathe.

'"Where's Pop?" I goes. "When's he coming back?" And that's when the bloke in the frock tells me, "He ain't. He ain't never coming back," he says. "He entross — *entrus*—"'

'Entrusted?'

'Thassit. Entrusted. "He entrusted you to our care," he said. That was his words. "It's for the best, young feller."'

Silence followed, which Julia didn't dare to break.

'Three months it took. Three months before I believed the buggers about Pop not coming back. That's when I run off. Except when I got home, strangers was living in my house, and none of the neighbours knew where my mum and pop and brothers was, nor any of my sisters. Dunno what I done wrong,' Bug said, tears rolling down his cheeks. 'I wouldn't of done it, if I'd known, but they gotta know, me Ma and Pa, I didn't mean it, honest. Honest, Miss. I didn't mean to be a naughty boy.'

Chapter 6

Unlike Flora's parents, the couple posing for their cabinet portrait could well afford the outlay, the additional copies alone equating to a housemaid's weekly wage. All the same, Julia's reasons to keep the appointment weren't financial. With Collingwood breathing down her neck, it was vital life carried on as normal. Or at least, was seen to.

'Hold still. That's it. Little bit longer, please…'

A retired officer from the 2nd Queen's Dragoon Guards serving in India, the man was typical of the breed. Red jacket, gleaming helmet, stripe down his trousers, he leaned on his sword and fixed his bored eyes at a point over Julia's shoulder. The wife, equally typical, was a peahen. Drab green head to foot, gazing with sickening adoration at a husband who clearly had no time for her. It wasn't Julia's place to judge, though. Just to give them what they wanted. Perhaps, like her, they were also putting on an act.

'Who's T?'

Once again Julia had no idea where Bug's train of thought was headed. Only that it travelled different tracks from everybody else.

'There's an envelope on your desk what says "For T".' Bug was helping pack up her equipment after the couple left. 'I can deliver it, if yer like.'

'Then you're a better man than me, because I've no idea who she is. I was in the churchyard first thing yesterday —'

'Taken up grave robbin', have yer?'

'We all need a hobby, Bug.' His wouldn't hurt to involve baths. 'The thing is, photography isn't recognised as art, but trust me, before too long, it will be.'

'You wanna be an artist?'

'In a sense. You see, the railways have opened up everybody's lives.'

Rich to poor, the public's appetite for travel had resulted in a massive demand for photographs. Everything from famous landmarks to country scenes, dramatic coastal landscapes to naturalistic studies of people engaged in their everyday jobs — glamorised to the hilt, of course. People don't shell out for misery and hardship.

But as much as portraits, weddings, even *memento mori* were Julia's bread and butter, photography as art was her passion.

'One of the most exciting new developments, pun intended, is the modern camera's ability to capture movement, hence my trip to the cemetery.'

'If you got snaps of spooks and ghouls and dancing dead blokes, I don't wanna see 'em.'

'Birds, my little friend, nothing spookier than birds. A pair of kestrels are nesting in one of the old oaks, and I'm leaning in, poised for the precise moment to catch one in a dive, when, from the corner of my eye, I see a man drop something on the far side of the graveyard.'

He'd been sitting on a stone bench under the big yew. She'd noticed him because he was in shirt sleeves, which was unusual, especially for a man who wasn't an obvious factory worker. Also, because he'd been mopping his face with his handkerchief when it was anything but hot, someone who felt perhaps a little unwell. When he stood up and reached for his jacket, something white fluttered to the ground, which she assumed was the handkerchief. Julia called out, but either her words didn't carry or he was too lost in his own world to hear.

'By the time I'd secured my plate, crossed the graveyard and retrieved the fallen item, he'd disappeared.'

'Where you found a letter addressed to T, not some sweaty snot rag. Bet you was glad about that!'

'Yes and no. There's something rather unpleasant about opening another person's mail, but he left me no choice, if I was to deliver it to the intended recipient.'

'So-o-o-o-o?'

Bug's eyes were bigger than saucers.

'So-o-o-o-o that left me with an even bigger problem.' Her stomach tightened. 'What he'd dropped was a suicide note.'

At which point, the sweats, the shirt sleeves, the preoccupied behaviour fell into place, and also explained why he hadn't realised it had fallen out of his jacket pocket.

'Blimey! D'you think he's topped himself? Coz if he has, it ain't your fault, you know that, don'cha?'

Julia wished she could agree. 'There's nothing in the papers about a suicide, but whether he did or he didn't, Bug, I need to find "T" as soon as possible.'

'Why?'

'Ideally, to trace the letter-writer before he carries out his threat, and put a stop to it. But if I'm too late, whoever this "T" is, she needs to know he loved her with every fibre of his heart, every microscopic atom of his soul, and love was why he took his life.'

Do you, my dearest, know how so very much I miss you? Sleeping, waking, at work or at leisure, the void is excruciating, and if I could spend one night, just one night, in your arms, hope would sustain me. I know, however, and have come to accept, that you will never be mine. That we will never be able to live as a couple, grow old together, die in one another's arms. Oh, but my darling, my dearest, my only true love, if you can't be part of my life — when you are my whole life — then truly life has no meaning. I hope you understand and forgive me, but the void is all I have left.

There were two pages more, but that was the general gist.

'Is that why the rozzer was here?'

'Absolutely. And now you've polished off the last of those sticky buns, I have another commission for Master Bug.'

'Not more diversions?'

'More diversions.'

'Cor!' To celebrate, Bug took another slab of madeira. 'If this ain't the best day of my whole life, EVER.'

Chapter 7

The last thing Collingwood wanted was another unsolved murder on his books, much less some pompous quack telling him what he already knew — that the young man had been beaten, kicked and urinated on, the attack was not post-mortem, and the young man died as a consequence of those injuries.

'It doesn't take a medical degree to know corpses don't bleed.'

'Look on the bright side.' His sergeant winked. 'He could have pronounced it the worst case of suicide he'd ever seen.'

Tall and cadaverous, Charlie Kincaid was forty-seven to Collingwood's forty-one, had seen terrible things, been to terrible places, and lost two fingers and his left ear to prove it. Never once had Collingwood seen him miserable.

'Still no identification?' Collingwood asked.

'Nope.' Years of barking orders as a colour sergeant in the army, combined with an attachment to pipe tobacco and porter, had reduced Kincaid's voice to a gravelly rumble. 'No witnesses, no one matching missing persons, just a lovely, big, fat zero.'

'Time of death?'

'You're asking for the medical examiner's professional conclusion?'

'Please.'

'Last night.'

Collingwood couldn't help himself. He laughed. 'Looks like the good doctor doesn't need a medical degree, either.'

'No chance of this one not making the papers, though. Evening edition's front page is my guess.'

'Hm.' Collingwood leaned back in his chair and put the cap back on his fountain pen. A beautiful tortoiseshell number, with a fourteen carat nib, because, like the care he took with his appearance, small bright spots of elegance went a long way to counteract the ugliness that was his working life. 'That mightn't be a bad thing. Full and frank co-operation with the press should offset their animosity against our clampdown on the other murders.'

'Define full and frank.' Kincaid pulled a face. 'They want photos.'

'I want a million pounds, but I'm not getting it. They can go to hell.'

'I've played the attack down. Hinted at robbery which unfortunately resulted in a young man's death, and that's hard to contradict, considering the kid who found the body's off our patch.' Kincaid flipped through his notes. 'Birmingham, apparently. That's where the barge was headed next.' He snapped the book shut. 'As luck would have it, there was a constable patrolling the bridge, he was on the spot in twenty seconds when the girl who found the body screamed. The problem is, there's bugger all at the scene to help us.'

'Any advances on the three dead women?'

'Give me more men and I might get somewhere,' Kincaid replied, 'but the Super wanted the canal victim to take priority, because of the fuss it would make in the papers, and that's what he got.'

'Excellent. No clues, no witnesses, no leads and no manpower. What more could a DI want?'

'A nice strong cup of tea. I'll fetch you one.'

'Forget it, Charlie. I have four murders and counting without a scent to follow on any of them. I'm tired, I'm grumpy, I'm going home.'

'Confession's good for the soul, sir. By the time you take your morning shave, both killers will have turned themselves in and will be down in the cells, crying like babies.'

'I'll settle for begging for mercy.'

'Either way, they'll hang.' Kincaid's doggedness was one of many qualities that made him a fine copper. 'Sooner or later, we'll catch the bastards. One of them will slip up and make a mistake. Then we'll have him.'

'Fingers crossed it's sooner rather than later, Charlie.'

Later meant another coffin laid to rest in Potter's Field, and it didn't matter what poses those girls struck for the photographer. The things people stooped to, for want of a few bob to pay the rent, would make a stone bleed.

Turning out of Boot Street, Collingwood supposed he ought to count himself lucky. Most murders, while plentiful, were easy to solve. Few killers thought it through, and were either caught red-handed or thanks to basics like blood on their clothes or the murder weapon still being in their possession. In the case of less obvious suspects, new techniques were coming into play all the time. The photographic records Julia talked about, for one thing. The study of criminal behaviour using scientific methods to identify, apprehend and ultimately prosecute looked promising. Detection and analysis of poisons was advancing every day, and using fingerprints as a means to identify villains, first mooted over fifty years ago, was gaining rapid ground in official circles. He imagined it would not be long before that practice was introduced in the force.

Unfortunately, science wasn't moving fast enough for three young women. Or the victim beside the canal.

Collingwood hailed a cab. 'Thorne Road,' he instructed the driver.

He could walk — it was only a mile — but there was something calming about the rocking of the hansom. The rhythmic clop-clop-clop of horseshoe against cobble. The smell of freshly polished leather.

Oakbourne had been a quiet, rural village until the canal was built and the railways arrived, yet for all the industry that had sprung up around it, the steeple of St. Oswald's church still cast a protective shadow over narrow, winding streets, and the stream — the bourne from which the town derived its name — was still resisting planners' moves to divert it underground. Looking at the Common, where boys rolled hoops and magpies chattered in the trees, a stranger could be forgiven for thinking this was a peaceful town. Safe to live, plenty of work to be had, excellent access to seaside resorts for the holidays.

But if that stranger turned his face east, to the choking black smoke belching up to the sky, he would hesitate to apply the same label. Brothels, opium dens and gambling houses contrived to steal what little pay there was from a man's hand, and for those who had no work and no prospects, robbery was the only alternative to starving.

Collingwood didn't believe the canal victim was attacked for his watch-chain and guineas, even though they'd been taken, but the motive was as much a mystery as the victim. Stretched resources or not, his men had done sterling work with house-to-house enquiries. Hardly their fault they came up empty. He was hoping the young man's dandified clothes would identify him, and soon. Because someone, somewhere, was missing a son, a husband, a lover, a brother. They ought to be told he was dead.

He paid the driver sixpence and a tip with his mind still on the case, but the instant he unlatched the gate to his neat new house at the end of the respectable, if not fashionable, terrace, a clamp closed round his stomach. It tightened with every step he took up the stairs and threatened to crush him when he eased open the door to the right.

The curtains were drawn. The curtains were always drawn. But it was never the blackness that struck him the most. It was the smell. Always the smell. The gagging scent of roses and jasmine, that stuck in the back of his throat.

'Hello, Alice.'

The girl in the bed didn't stir. Even in the dark, he could see his daughter's face grey against the pink counterpane, her skin thinner than parchment. The sound of her breathing put rusty bellows to shame.

'This is your fault.'

A woman stepped out from the shadows. In spite of his training, Collingwood jumped.

'Time and time again I've told you, it's your fault my daughter is ill. You still don't listen to me, do you?'

'Emily. Please. Let's not go through this again.'

'My daughter is being punished —'

'*Our* daughter.'

'— because of the work that you do and the evil you bring home, into this house.'

'How many times, Emily?' *For God's sake, how many times?* 'Alice is dying of consumption, not from something that dropped out of my pocket.'

'If you believed in God, she would be cured.' Emily was nothing if not persistent. 'If you believed in God, John, the power of prayer in this house would be doubled, and she would be made well.'

If Collingwood believed in God, his daughter would not be suffering agonies day after day. In fact, if Collingwood believed in God, he would pray for Him to take Alice in His arms right now, right this minute.

'Emily, I know this is hard —'

'It's hard, because you did this to her. You made my daughter like this. *Heavenly Father, come to me at my hour of need. Strengthen me and help me...*'

Collingwood backed out of the room and closed the door. Me. It was always "me" his wife prayed so consistently and so piously for. Never Alice...

He stood on the landing, gripping the banister rail until his knuckles were white. What callous bastard compares the mother of his dying child to a woman he'd just met? Answer: the one looking back at him from the mirror. His wife Emily, so help him, was everything Mrs. Julia McAllister was not. He didn't mean looks — although that, too, his wife being small, barely up to his shoulder, with blonde locks kept rigidly in place — never any wide upsweep of hair for her, perish the thought. The contrast came from their marked personalities. His wife's eyes never flashed, her smile wasn't wicked, the prospect of independence would make her pass out, and she'd die before planting hands on her hips like a fishwife to make her point.

There was no question of Emily's breasts being unrestrained, either. They'd been restrained night and day since they walked down the aisle.

Not to mention restricted.

He ran his hands through his hair. Every time he tried to comfort Emily, she recoiled. As she had every time he'd touched her in their twelve years of marriage.

With a heavy tread, he went back downstairs and picked up his hat.

'John? John, where are you going?'

'What does it matter,' he called up wearily. 'You don't give a damn anyway.'

In some respects, though, his wife was right. Whether he headed to the public house, his latest mistress, or back to Boot Street, there was evil abroad somewhere.

Perhaps it did cling after all?

As Collingwood latched the wooden gate behind him, Evil was staring at a photograph of a young woman bending forward as she stepped out of a bath.

The girl's buttocks were round, her thighs smooth, her breasts full and pendulous. Inviting. That was the word. Inviting…

In the picture, she is reaching for a towel that has — whoops! — fallen on the floor. Except Evil knows the towel didn't fall of its own accord. It has been artfully arranged, just like the girl's leg as she steps out from the bath, her knee hinting — hiding — teasing — at what lay between them. Those curls tumbling over her shoulder? The wide eyes, the parted lips, the tip of her tongue just poking through her lips? Innocence personified, the picture will have you believe.

Young girl, alone and vulnerable.

Unsuspecting that she is being spied on in this most intimate of moments.

Or that someone is standing inches from her ripe, young, naked breasts.

Taking photographs.

Chapter 8

Despite what she said, Julia had no need of diversion tactics. A photographer visiting her photographic supplier? Nothing could be more innocuous. On the other hand, leave Bug to his own devices and you were talking thirty kinds of trouble — and there were thirty kinds of reasons why that was to be avoided. Including added attention from the police.

'This is the address.' Julia wrote it down. 'Your job's to sit on the stairs outside the door and keep watch.' Daisy was a friend of hers, she explained, but a man had been pestering her lately, and although Daisy was pretty sure the man had given up, you just never know. 'If anyone goes in, suspicious or not, you yell blue murder at the top of your lungs, understood?'

'Aye, aye, cap'n.'

Needless to say, she'd had to confiscate two pans from inside Bug's jacket as well as the rolling pin down his trousers, partly because as weapons they were useless, and partly because a small boy was no match for a triple killer. Even then she'd had to frisk him a third time, and make him hand back the bicycle chain.

Still. Two birds with one stone. Bug out of mischief. Daisy and her baby out of harm's way.

Now for a chat with the man who commissioned the photographs, namely Oliver Blackstock.

Sod's law, there was a sign in Oliver's window that said *Back Shortly*, but the Blackstocks lived over the shop, and Julia had, after all, that dish to return.

'Delicious pie, Rosie. Thank you so much.'

'My pleasure, lovey, but there was no need to wash the dish. Plenty of hands in this house, willing to help out. Well.' Rosie pulled a funny face. 'Maybe willing's a bit strong, but they help out. Come on in and make yourself comfy. Olly'll be back any sec, only he had a delivery to make, which he couldn't trust to the nippers.'

Bless her, Rosie wouldn't take no for an answer, which was just as well, really. With Collingwood's bloodhound trotting behind, Julia had no intention of giving her one.

'Budge up, Faith, make room for Mrs. McAllister, that's the ticket.'

Faith, like the rest of the brood, was a pint-sized replica of her parents, a barrel with legs and a quarter as pretty, but what they lost out on in looks, they made up for in nature. There wasn't a time when Julia hadn't seen Rosie the Mother Hen chortling, cracking jokes, rolling her eyes when her chicks made a mess.

'You trap flies quicker with honey than you do running round trying to swat them, isn't that right, Daniel?'

'I like flies,' he said. 'And I like caterpillars and daddy-long-legs and spiders, but I think I like elephants more.'

'I seen an elephant once,' Patience piped up. 'When Dad took me to Regent's Park Zoo.'

'Saw,' Faith corrected, because three years' seniority entitled her to. 'I *saw* an elephant once.'

'You never did, you big fat liar! You never been to the Zoo!' Patience countered.

'Patience, love, fetch that decanter from the sideboard, will you? Be an angel, Faith, pass us a couple of glasses.'

Julia swallowed a smile. Judging by the level of the sherry, she had a fair idea how Rosie kept her strength up!

'I can count to five,' Verity said, splaying her little fat fingers.

60

'Well, aren't you the smartest little smarty in the smartiverse.' Julia gave her button nose a tweak. 'Can you show me your birthday finger? Three? Gosh!'

'I'm six,' said David.

'Me too,' said Daniel.

'I'm nine,' Patience said, 'Hope's fifteen, and Faith's twelve, and the baby, well, the baby's a baby, she don't count.'

Rosie's laugh filled the room. 'That's the Blackstocks, lovey. Pop 'em out every three years, we do, regular as clockwork.'

'I've got a big brother, too, he's in the army —' Patience continued.

'Just made corporal,' Rosie said, her chest swelling with so much pride that Julia feared for the buttons on her blouse. 'He'll be reaching his majority next month, can you believe that? My boy a man! Oh, and talking of men! Olly? Olly, look who's here, love.'

Short, round, with a permanent twinkle in his eye and mutton chop whiskers that somehow contrived to meet under his chin, Oliver Blackstock was hardly the sort you'd associate with the smutty picture industry. Then again, Julia supposed, neither was she.

'I've just heard about Edmund's promotion.' Julia turned to Oliver. 'Congratulations.'

'Seems no time at all since he was knee high, now look at him. Taller than all of us.' Oliver walked over to his wife and planted a smacker of a kiss on her lips. 'Rosie by name, Rosie by nature, that's my Rosie Cheeks, eh?' By way of rounding off his home-coming, he gave her well-padded bottom a slap.

'I tell you, if I had a ha'penny for every time I've heard that, I'd be richer than Queen Victoria, living in a palace and sitting on a throne. Assuming,' Rosie added behind her hand, 'I wasn't too sore to sit down. Join us in a snifter, Mr. B?'

'Depends.' One bushy eyebrow arched at Julia. 'Is it urgent?'

''Fraid so.'

'Then keep that sherry on the table, Mrs. B. I'll be back in a tick. See if we can't empty that decanter.'

That was the thing about the Blackstocks. Laughing, joking, tumbling over one another — you wouldn't think they'd lost their oldest girl to influenza in November. *No mourning clothes for this family, thank you very much.* Rosie was adamant. *No black crêpe ribbon round the door. No stopped clocks, no darkened rooms, no covered mirrors in this house, lovey.*

Their grief was no less, though. Far from it. When Charity died, Rosie howled like a wild beast for days; Oliver could barely stand, the poor sod was that broken. But their dignity and resolve through those bleakest of days was one of the reasons Julia admired them so much. There was nothing they could have done to prevent their daughter's death, so they turned their energies to the living. To Edmund, making a name for himself in the army, to baby Grace, and the five — sorry, six more in between.

You can't change the past, but you can influence the future, JJ.

Dear God, how often had Sam told her that?

Oliver whistled as he led the way down the stairs. It took a discerning ear to recognise *After the Ball is Over.*

'You have some fine equipment here, Oliver Blackstock.'

'That I do, Mizz McAllister, that I do.' He held open the door to an office that would make cats fear for their lives if someone swung them, and motioned her to take a seat. 'Notice the new delivery of Kodaks as you passed? Can't get enough of them, frankly. Flying off the shelves faster than hot cakes.'

'Easy to see why.' Box cameras were simple, light, they used flexible roll film, and for the first time the public could take their own photographs.

'"You press the button, we do the rest", that's their slogan.' He shifted a stack of ledgers and brought out something with considerably more bite than sherry. Rosie would be horrified to see it wasn't in a cut-glass decanter. 'Luckily, the quality of the end result won't put the likes of you and me out of business.'

'That's a relief.'

Oliver's marriage was strong, but his secrets were stronger, hard liquor the mere tip of the iceberg. Hence deliveries like today's, which he couldn't entrust to the nippers. Rosie rarely, if ever, came downstairs — business being a man's role and her having enough on her plate anyway. She was aware her husband traded in postcards. It just "slipped his mind" to mention the content. After all, everyone wants souvenirs of their holidays. Wasn't his fault she made the assumption!

He tossed back the scotch in one swig. 'You look terrible.'

'A word of warning, Oliver Blackstock, flattery will get you nowhere.' Julia should have known people who are ace at hiding their feelings are experts at spotting their own kind. So really, there was no point in beating round the bush. 'I'm being framed for murder.'

'God's body, girl!' The colour drained from Oliver's face. 'Who'd do a thing like that?'

'That's where I'm hoping you can help.'

'Anything, Julia. Anything. You know that.' His hand shook as he topped up his glass. 'Who are you supposed to have killed?'

'Three people, actually. Nellie Stern, Lily Atkins, Birdie O'Leary. You won't know them —' it was the photographer's job to find suitable models, Oliver's to stipulate the poses he wanted — 'but someone in our line of work is setting me up.'

She explained about the photos left at the scene. Her signature purple ink. The missing stamp.

'Why you? You're the last person to make enemies.'

'I'd like to think so, but I'm a woman in business, Oliver, which flies in the face of natural order.'

'Here.' He scribbled names on a piece of paper. 'These are the other photographers I commission. Give this list to the police.'

Only three? That made life easier. 'I'm not giving anything to the police. I'm doing this myself.'

'I've never heard anything more ridiculous in my life. You're not a detective, you have zero training, you don't know what you're up against, which means you'll only bring more trouble on yourself. Hand that list over and step away, girl.'

'Never try to outstubborn a McAllister. You won't win.'

He snorted. 'I'm not happy about this. I think you're wrong. But so help me, if one of my photographers is killing innocent girls and trying to pin the blame on you...' He knocked back the second whisky. Poured another. 'Influenza's a sod of a way to lose a child, but holy Jesus, *murder*?'

The glass froze in Julia's hand. What was she thinking? Blurting on about girls snatched in their prime when his own daughter was barely cold in her grave!

'She'd be celebrating her eighteenth birthday on Thursday.'

'Oliver, I am so sorr—'

'The transition into womanhood, Julia. Imagine that. My baby girl all grown up and ready to marry.'

'I didn't mean —'

'Don't.' His eyes glistened as he held up his hand. 'Don't apologise. For the sake of the nippers, we never talk about it, Rosie and me. The only thing we do is keep Charity's picture at the front on the mantelpiece, and sometimes we'll catch one another looking at it and squeeze each other's hand, but talk about it? Uh-uh.'

'Cross my heart, the last thing I wanted was to cause you pain.'

'You're not. That's what I'm trying to say. She was the apple of my eye, that girl, and there isn't a day that goes by when I don't thank God in His bountiful mercy that she found a decent job in service in a nice, respectable house over in Bentley-on-Thames. At least, if you can say such a thing, she died comfy.' He blew his nose. 'Not to be there, when your child passes, that's a bugger of a burden for a father to carry. And these girls? The three that were murdered? They'd have been around the same age as my girl, am I right?'

Julia didn't dare speak; she simply nodded.

'Well, if my Charity died a natural death and it's eating me alive, imagine how their fathers feel, knowing they weren't on hand to protect their babies from a monster. Whoever's framing you, Julia, this bastard needs to know we're in this together — no, no, hear me out. You take the photographs. Fine. But only because I commission them. So if there's anything you want, anything I can do, and I mean anything at all, you come to me. Day or night, my door's open, you understand? You don't even hesitate.'

'Thank you.' *Good God*, she thought, *now we're both sobbing*. 'You're the best friend anyone could have, you really are. Which is exactly why I have no intention of dragging you into this.'

'Like I said, girl, I'm already in.'

'As far as Oakbourne's concerned, you own a shop selling cameras and photographic equipment, which means people come and go all the time. It's the perfect front, Oliver, and I intend to keep it that way. You have a family, and they don't just need you, they love you.'

'Now who's the best friend anyone could have?' He mopped his eyes. 'Bit heavy with the waterworks, but I can live with that.' He cleared his throat. 'Doesn't have to be a photographer.'

'It's someone in the business, and I'm damn sure it's not you.'

'That's a coincidence, so am I.' It was good to see the smile back. 'I was thinking of this fellow.' He reached across and added another name to the list. 'My distributor.'

'The chap who peddles mucky pictures round respectable gentleman's clubs?'

'Irony is completely lost on the man.'

Julia tucked the slip of paper in her purse. 'I appreciate this.'

'Couldn't help noticing a copper in the doorway over the road. Is he following you?'

'He is, so would you mind if I left through the shop? That way, we can exchange cheery waves, so he knows I haven't added you to my growing list.'

'Bugger that, I'm walking you home, girl. If there's a maniac on the streets, I'll not have *you* added to *his* growing list.'

'I have a police escort, Oliver, life doesn't get much safer. Now, go upstairs to your family and finish that sherry.'

Before Julia reached the door, the twinkle was back, the whiskers were smoothed, and Oliver's jacket was on. Clearly you can't outstubborn a Blackstock, either.

Chapter 9

The new day dawned bright and warm and sunny, bringing different things to different people across the community of Oakbourne.

In the penny shelters round the railway arches, prostitutes, thieves, vagrants and beggars unfurled stiff limbs and tried not to think of the circumstances that reduced them to huddling ten to a room without a bed between them. Men, women, children, sharing the same lice, fleas and sense of helplessness where the proprietors of these squalid establishments condoned, if not encouraged, crime under their roof. Stealing from people who had sod all to start with.

Tailors in the slop-selling business (ready-made garment industry to you) sat cross-legged and shoeless in box-rooms, stitching shooting coats and trousers, shirts, drawers and vests, the floor around them littered with irons, sleeve-boards and sacks stuffed with cuttings.

On the other side of town, the so-called respectable side of town, the beadle at St. Oswald's church tucked into a hearty plate of sausages in readiness for overseeing the workhouse and the orphanage, his chomping accompanied by the rhythmic sound of the sexton digging graves.

For the women who worked in the factories, dawn brought another round of imbalance and injustice that they'd have to grit their teeth through. Wondering why they slogged all hours of the day and night and were still expected to cook and clean, raise children and be tirelessly self-sacrificing, while their husbands drank away or gambled the paltry wages they brought home.

And Julia? Well, every day brings a whole new challenge. In this case, it was slouched against the stonework when she stepped out of her shop.

'Going somewhere, Mrs. McAllister?'

'Your powers of observation put eagles to shame, Inspector, but yes. As a matter of fact, I'm on my way to the Willow Walk Tea Rooms to take, surprise, surprise, a nice hot cup of Darjeeling. Ah, don't tell me. You're intending to join me?'

'I suspect you'll find the atmosphere more congenial than my dingy office in Boot Street, while for my part, nothing would please me more than to escort a handsome young widow to tea.'

'In that case, you can add a slice of fruitcake to your bill.'

The trees that gave the street its name were long gone, but unlike the broad thoroughfares of the modern town, however elegant, Willow Walk retained its medieval charm. Timbered Tudor buildings overhung the cobbles, rickety and narrow, with signs above the shops creaking in the wind. *David Hart & Sons Pharmaceuticals, est. 1823. Js. Simpson, Family Butcher. Thos. Payne, Barber.* You could be forgiven for wondering if women actually existed.

Inside the tea rooms, three steps up from street level, Julia chose her seat carefully. Unlike many establishments — which catered solely for ladies and were all swags and ribbons and overblown roses, or else the tea courts in the more expensive hotels boasting columns, chandeliers and enough gilt to turn you blind in one eye — Willow Walk catered for everyone. Here was a place where women could come without a male escort, and, more importantly, without their reputation in shreds. Equally, couples could enjoy sandwiches and Earl Grey in a convivial atmosphere, as could men, either alone or with friends, without having to toss a coin between the baseness of a public house or the snobbery of a gentleman's club.

'Have you found your canal victim's killer?'

'Ssss,' Collingwood said, sliding behind a table balanced on perilously narrow legs, laid with porcelain that clearly had suicidal inclinations to jump. 'Killers, plural. It's unlikely one person could inflict that level of brutality, but no. Unfortunately, no closer to an arrest.'

'The *Chronicle* says you recorded several different sets of footprints at the scene.'

Collingwood eased himself into a high-backed chair upholstered in grey velvet. The same grey as his eyes. 'The body was found at the edge of the allotments. Assuming one gardener per patch, that's forty boots to start with, but this was right next to the canal, and one of the reasons the barge people are hated and despised is because they steal from allotments.' It might sound petty, a stick of rhubarb here, a few peas there, digging a couple of spuds now and then. But when everyone does it... It would help if we knew the victim's name, but his wallet is gone, and no one matching his description has been reported missing.'

'The paper says the motive was robbery,' she said, taking the menu from the waitress. 'You don't believe that?'

Collingwood waited until the girl left with their order before answering. 'Most thieves snatch and run. They don't hang around to beat, kick and stamp on their victim, and run the risk of being caught. Nor do they ... defile ... him.'

'In what way?'

'You don't want to know, Mrs. McAllister.'

'I am not a nun, Inspector.'

'Then all I will say is that his lower garments had been rearranged, and the state of his clothes hinted at emptying of bladders.'

The picture Collingwood painted sat at odds with the rare feathers, lustrous silks and chinking porcelain and silver around them.

'Contempt,' Julia declared, spreading her napkin on her lap. 'Complete and utter contempt for the victim, which makes this crime personal.'

Either Collingwood hadn't considered the possibility, or he was surprised that Julia had. But one eyebrow arched in a way that might have been surprise, shock or admiration. 'Are you waiting for someone?' he asked.

That was not the question she was expecting. 'On the contrary.'

'Interesting, because the staff didn't seem to recognise you, you chose a seat with a clear view of both the interior and the street, and you glance up — like now — every time the bell above the door tinkles.'

'That's the artist in me, Inspector. Automatically making composition, unconsciously observing.'

'Of course.'

A little more conviction would have been reassuring, but as luck would have it, the waitress arrived with their tea and a cake stand piled with dainty fancies. While the girl set them down, Julia cast another covert glance along Willow Walk.

In his suicide note, the author — *your ever-loving Cyril* — mentioned meetings here with "T", should either of them find the chance to slip away. In the hope today was one of those chances, she'd sat up half the night developing the portrait of the army officer and his wife, and making the extra copies that they wanted. Time poorly spent, it seemed, because apart from a weedy bank clerk in a pin-striped suit, polishing his spectacles over and over, and an elderly gent with a cane, the rest of the tea-sippers were women either old enough to be Cyril's grandmother, or sat with groups of friends.

Re-reading the letter in her mind, she was hardly looking for Romeo and Juliet in the first flush of youth. Yet star-crossed lovers all the same. Committed. Passionate. Doomed.

'Not hungry?'

'Me? Yes. Of course, I am.' Julia forced down the tea. 'Daydreaming again, terrible habit.'

'We all have them.'

'Tell me yours.'

Collingwood's laugh cut through the taffetas and customised fragrances. 'There isn't time.'

'Quite right. Time doesn't exist, Inspector. Only clocks.'

'I heard it was a great teacher. Unfortunately, it kills all its students.'

For a man, Collingwood had surprisingly attractive hands. Square and strong, but without the stubby fingers that tend to go with such features, and neatly manicured without being prissy. The sort of hands, Julia decided, that produced firm, legible writing, as you'd expect of an ambitious detective who crossed every 't', dotted every 'i', and still lifted stones to see what crawled underneath. Those hands would take their time on other tasks too. Police reports. Personal grooming. Under the bedsheets...

But in the end, he was still a policeman, crossing those 't's, dotting those 'i's, and most importantly, lifting those stones. To which end, developing cabinet portraits wasn't the only way Julia had passed her time during the wee small hours.

Waiting for the images to set in the fixing bath, she'd turned the full force of her attention to the names on Oliver's list.

Forget the competition, JJ. You'll either see pictures you wish you had the talent to take, or of such poor quality it makes you wonder why anyone in their right mind would commission this rubbish.

Sam never came up short on wisdom. Marching to the beat of your own drum was the only way forward, meaning she was aware of Tobias Wood and Belmont Photographic, but in name only. Augustus Jones she'd never heard of, and the distributor, Percival Tarrant, didn't enter her orbit at all. Oliver meant well, but he was clutching at straws with that one. A man who peddles pornography doesn't do it for charity, plus it was surely in his own interest that Julia remained in business? A gorilla could take the photos, as far as he was concerned, providing they were saleable.

Ting! A young woman buttoned up in brown bombazine entered the tea rooms, and was promptly shown to a table. Unless Cyril's tastes ran to prunes perched on a cactus while chewing a hornet, this was another candidate to cross out. Besides, his letter gave the impression that the love of his life had a ring on her finger. Julia sighed, wondering how much longer to give this wild goose chase.

And how much longer would it be before Collingwood got to the point?

'You're not from around here, Mrs. McAllister?' he asked.

'I've always maintained that it's never where one's been that matters, Inspector, more where one is headed.'

'And where would that be exactly?'

Not Boot Street jail. 'My ambition is to travel and, through those travels, to educate.' And suddenly it all came tumbling out. How she wanted to compile a book — several — filled with places that lay beyond the spread of the railways, and, by default, the scope of ordinary people. 'Coastal scenes with wild, dramatic rock formations. Arches, bays and beaches. Islands, headlands and coves.'

Not souvenir holiday postcard pictures. She would capture storms, gales, hail, snow. Mother Nature angry and wild, then use superimposing techniques to incorporate living creatures in the pictures.

'Seals, eagles, puffins kind of thing?' Collingwood asked.

'Yes, but also species which have vanished from our landscape. To put them back where they belong, if only in a photograph. The like of wolves and bears, mammoths even, so that people who don't have access to the Natural History Museum — and that's pretty much everyone outside London — can see what they looked like in the flesh.'

'Because they're only available as drawings at the moment.'

'Exactly. Paintings are fine, but I want real life. I've already had a few stabs —' *Was that how Lily died?* Julia flicked her napkin off her lap and bent to retrieve it. Covered the catch in her breath — 'using the layering techniques you saw in my shop.' *Smile. Nothing to hide, show some pretty white teeth.* 'Of course, the subject matter in those attempts came courtesy of the taxidermist.'

'And you want the real thing?'

'I do.' *More teeth, more teeth.* 'I may have a problem finding a mammoth, but I'll settle for puffins and seals. Demonstrate the might of Niagara Falls when it's frozen. Show what it's like to straddle the Continental Divide, knowing every drop of water from rivers to rainfall to snow that lands on my right will flow east, while everything on my left heads to the west. At the same time, I want to push out boundaries. Have people see — no, *feel* the plight of Durham miners, compared to the miners in Tombstone.'

Ting! Two elderly spinsters.

73

Julia watched the spinsters fuss and preen at the table next to the despondent bank clerk, still polishing his spectacles over and over.

'"A man who dares to waste one hour of time has not discovered the value of life",' Julia said firmly. 'Charles Darwin.'

For several seconds, minutes even, Collingwood's grey eyes held hers. She slopped tea in her saucer. It took more than that to throw a wolf off the scent.

'Quite frankly, Mrs. McAllister, you are the most amazing woman I've ever met. I mean that.'

Musky and faint, that was quite a cologne wafting over the table. *Hammam Bouquet*, the staple of many a respectable gentleman, but how many knew its creator's aim was to replicate the atmosphere of a Turkish bath? Think naked sultans, harems, scenes steamy at every level. Collingwood was anything but naïve.

He leaned forward and smiled. 'Your late husband. Buried in the Sudan, you say?'

'Indeed I do.' Julia rummaged in her purse. 'I have a beautiful little daguerreotype of his grave.'

Collingwood examined the photograph and nodded solemnly.

'I would offer my condolences, Mrs. McAllister, I really would. Only —' he handed it back — 'I can find James McAllister's birth certificate, his death certificate, and his quite admirable army record. I know his family lives in Scotland, and his last known address was in Edinburgh. What I can't find, and this is interesting don't you think, is a single shred of evidence to suggest he ever married.'

***

Watching the comings and goings on Boot Street from the first-floor window of his dingy office, Collingwood blocked out the protests of felons who swore blind it was a fix-up, drunks being sick, and the shouts, clangs and clatter in the cells.

He wasn't remotely surprised that his chief suspect in what he called the Purple Ink Murders didn't miss a beat. Right from the outset, Julia McAllister had an answer for everything, which itself was suspicious, given that most people tend to be curious. They want to know how the girls died, where it happened, did they suffer, had they been "outraged" (to use the modern phrase). Jack the Ripper sent shivers far beyond Whitechapel — yet this woman hadn't shown the slighted interest. And who on earth carries a picture of their dead husband's grave around with them, not one of the dead husband himself?

'I'm sorry, Charlie, what was that?'

Slouched against the other side of the window, like a matching bookend, his sergeant's eyes also followed the whiskered old man stepping aside for a dray cart. The butcher hanging a gutted pig by its back trotters from hooks beside geese, rabbits and chickens. The chimney sweep, accompanied by his boy and brushes, kicking a loose cabbage along like a football.

'I was saying, if I hit one more brick wall, so help me, I'm going to invest next week's wage packet, and the sixteen after that, in the London Brick Company.'

'From which I conclude our three female victims didn't have any men sniffing round that connected them?' Collingwood asked.

'Nothing connected the girls. Bugger all.'

'Apart from Whitmore Photographic.'

'Apart from Whitmore Photographic.' Kincaid stuffed his pipe with tobacco and lit it. 'There have to be more pictures.'

'Damned if I can find them.'

'When you do, though, let me know.' Kincaid shot him a broad wink. 'I promise to give them my very, very close attention.'

'Does your wife know you're a degenerate, sergeant?'

'The sole reason she married me, sir.'

Kincaid puffed for a while. Collingwood paced.

French postcards — affectionately known as "Frenchies", the majority being imported from across the Channel — were becoming increasingly popular, and popularity meant pushing out boundaries. No longer did a flash of knee, a glimpse of white thigh above black stocking, or half a saucy nipple cut the mustard. Hell, half the punters won't settle for straightforward nudity any more. The demand — which wasn't growing, it was bloody well exploding — was for salaciousness at every level, and it wasn't a question of smile-for-the-camera-type poses. They wanted stories with their photos. Moments frozen in time. As though the girls were right there with the men — seducing them, seducing someone else, engaged in orgies. Either that, or the buyers wanted to feel they were peering through a window or a keyhole, from behind a curtain, through a half-open door, catching a glimpse of real life.

'Lily Atkins, 17, from the Elephant & Castle, hawked whelks to bargees along the canal.' Kincaid quoted from his notebook. 'Eleanor Stern, also 17, from Clapham, known more commonly as Nellie, also known as Eleanor Crosby, also known as Eleanor Edwards, peddled vegetables round streets by the sugar refinery. Bridget O'Leary, 16, from Waterford, near Dublin, last employed helping out in a Punch & Judy show on Singer Lane.'

'You're telling me these girls posed for pornographic photographs, yet led otherwise spotless, law-abiding lives?'

'What the evidence points to and what I believe are two different matters.' Kincaid tapped his pipe out. 'Nellie Stern was suspected of pick-pocketing, but the only connection between the three is they were all a long, long way from home, they were all young, and all three were pretty much destitute.'

Collingwood watched a cripple — ex-soldier by the looks of him — set up a two-barrel organ across the street, then proceed to put everyone's teeth on edge as he started grinding out *La Marseillaise*.

True, the girls were young, but innocent? Uh-uh. He'd seen that look in Lily's eye too many times for comfort. Even in children. Conditioned to promiscuity from the earliest age by fathers, brothers or uncles, this was why they ran away from home. Ironically, the same reason they fell into prostitution. The only life they'd ever known.

'So the Chief Inspector gave you a bollocking?' Kincaid asked.

'Let's just say he wasn't happy that Boot Street has become a hotbed for unsolved murder.'

'Who is?'

'Not the victims, that's for sure.'

Christ, Collingwood thought, if they could just put a name to the man by the canal, it might point them towards the bastards who cracked his ribs with their fists and kicked his liver to mush, then pissed on the poor sod as he lay dying.

Watching a crowd of children gather round the organ-grinder, every last one fascinated by the monkey in a tiny red uniform on his shoulder, Collingwood was once again struck not only by Julia McAllister's complacent attitude to violent death.

Track the money, trace the villain was the next approach, because someone, somewhere was making money from Frenchies.

'Charlie, have a chat with local photographers. Don't mention the murders, or Whitmore Photographic, spin them a pack of lies, if you must. See if you pick up any undertones.'

'Slightest whiff of fish, you'll be the first to know.'

Men like that weren't hardened criminals. Put them in a damp cell with two burly policemen. Add a truncheon. Surprising how quickly information rises to the surface.

The nails-down-a-blackboard that was *La Marseillaise* ground (literally) to a halt. Collingwood's teeth edges relaxed.

After the discovery of the first girl, one of the first things he'd established was that Julia McAllister's bank account wasn't overflowing with cash. She could obviously afford top-of-the-range equipment, but her clothes, though fine, were far from extravagant. Most telling were the day-to-day purchases he'd watched her stack away. His conclusion was that the books of Whitmore Photographic balanced perfectly.

Contrast that with the financial situation of the three girls. Not to put too fine a point on it, pretty girls don't need to resort to posing for Frenchies — and in Lily's case, plain would be putting it nicely. Nellie's friend mentioned a squint, which you couldn't see in the photograph at her murder scene, but explained why she was so easily identified by her pocket-picked marks. So how come these girls were living in rooms that were merely one step up from hovels?

Was their "modelling" work sporadic? Or were the bastards who ran this operation ripping them off? Did it then follow they were killed to stop them from talking?

Across the street, the barrel organ began screeching out Wagner's *Ride of the Valkyries*, while the monkey held out a tin cup. This time, Collingwood's ear drums barely noticed the assault, because, this time, his mind was elsewhere.

'Oh, and Charlie.'

'Yup?'

'Take a look at Oliver Blackstock's finances, while you're at it.'

Chapter 10

A genteel cup of Darjeeling wasn't how Julia intended to start her day, much less in the company of a wolf in wolf's clothing. On the bright side, it was every bit as urgent to prevent a suicide as it was to keep her models safe, and with none other than the Inspector himself able to vouch for her quiet, respectable, mundane existence, it didn't work out too badly. Now, when she called on her fellow photographers, the police (even Collingwood) would assume they were professional visits.

Which they were. Just not the profession they thought.

'Betcha didn't save me none.'

The sight of a small unkempt oik kicking half a turnip up and down Willow Walk brought no surprises. Twice the waitresses had to shoo him from their dimpled windows, and pity the poor girl who had to scrub that greasy little nose print clean.

'Any,' Julia corrected.

'So did you, then? Did you save me ANY of that sponge cake?'

'No.'

'Fruit cake?'

'No.'

'You kept me a bit of Battenberg, though?'

'I left a comb on your pillow, wasn't that treat enough?'

'Man can't eat a comb.'

'Or run it through his hair, for that matter.'

'There was curly white bits stuck in the prongs.'

'Part of the widow Langley's poodle. She insisted on being photographed with the yappy little thing on her lap, but the comb's perfectly serviceable, you should try it. Here.' Julia handed Bug a couple of cherry almond biscuits and a squashed cream puff. His green eyes bulged like apples.

'See? Knew yer'd never forget me!'

'If only.'

In addition to forcing Bug's acquaintance with soap, Julia had been giving him elocution lessons. Well, trying to. Unfortunately "thrashing a thrush in Thurso on Thursday" still had more f's than was remotely good for it, hedgehog stubbornly remained ejog, while dunno, gonna, wanna might as well be set to music. Worse, if he ate much more, his trousers would burst, and right now it was only the holes that were holding the damn things together.

'They're nice,' Bug said through a mouthful of pastry as he hopped along beside her.

'My heart leaps to hear that keeping starvation at bay isn't a hardship.'

'Not the biccies — mind, they are. I meant Daisy and Minnie. They're what I meant was nice.'

'I told you to sit on the stairs.'

'And she told me to come indoors, so there!'

'Next time you stick your tongue out, could you please swallow first?'

Like some giant leech, only not half as benign, Collingwood had sucked too much time from Julia's schedule for her to fit all three photographers in. Augustus Jones, over in Southolt, would have to wait.

'You ever bin to see this Dickie Lloyd?' Bug jumped up at the hoarding advertising the Cadogan Street Music Hall, ripped off the "understudy" poster, and wrapped it round his head like a bandana. 'Is that who you gets yer jokes from?'

Seen him? Julia hadn't heard of him until now, but perhaps it was time she put that right. 'No, I pick them up at the Welsh Dairy, along with my butter, milk and cream. Blodwen puts half a dozen aside for me every Friday.'

Just when she thought wonders would never cease, Bug surprised her yet again by tossing the last remnants of the cream puff to the pigeons. Now *that*, she decided, would make a lovely flip book. An urchin hopping round the park bench chasing birds, bandana flapping like a spare wing down his back, freckles almost glowing with contentment. Who'd have imagined that having his foot crushed in the bicycle factory might yet turn out to be the best thing that happened to the boy?

'Wait here.' Julia handed Bug a penny. 'Buy a newspaper, check if there are any reconditioned bicycles for sale.' His leg might not ache so badly if he could ride around. 'But under no circumstances, not one, are you to approach Mr. Tobias Wood's shop. Understood?'

'Give us another penny, and I won't budge.'

'Graves are also known to render young boys budgeproof.'

Bug blew a raspberry. 'Wouldn't go near the damn place anyway — ow! What's that for?'

'In the absence of soap to wash your mouth out, a twisted earlobe will have to do.'

'Well, I wouldn't anyhow!' Bug's defiance carried above the crush of taffetas and parasols and wide-rimmed feather hats. 'Shop's boring, and him what runs it looks like he's got a poker up the arse.'

Seriously. Was there enough soap in the universe?

Julia waited for Bug to disappear before entering the shop.

'Good morning, I'm looking for Mr. Tobias Wood.'

'I am he.'

What's one of the most important qualities in a portrait photographer? Making your sitters comfortable. And how do you make them feel comfortable? With warm smiles, a cheery *at-your-service-madam*, perhaps pushing the boat out with an *it's-your-lucky-day*. What doesn't put customers at ease is a bearded middle-aged beanpole with a face set like concrete, a funereal monotone, and the stiffest, starchiest *I-am-he* a man could produce.

Still. Can't rule out Tobias Wood simply for having a face like a badly carved statue.

'My husband asked me to book an appointment for a portrait.' Flutter, flutter went Julia's eyelashes. 'You come highly recommended, by the way.'

'Will it be just the head of the household, Mrs —?'

'Smith. And no, I'll be there, too.'

Not response.

'With our children.' She smiled. 'All four of the little angels.'

Still nothing.

'My mother-in-law, of course.'

That invariably broke the thickest of ice.

'And our two darling terriers.'

Still nothing. Hey ho, one more try —

'We need a dozen copies, at least.'

'Would Saturday at two o'clock in the afternoon suit?'

As candidates for dirty pictures went, Tobias Wood was dropping off the page. But as Julia walked round the shop, examining the welter of weddings and christenings, one thing stood out. Tobias Wood had no bent for art, but he was an extremely adept photographer.

'Your charges seem a little steep,' Julia said timidly.

'Quality comes at a price, Mrs. Smith.'

'Yes. Yes, of course.' A bit of wringing of hands. Biting of nails. She should have been on the stage. 'I wouldn't be above paying for them in kind. For instance, posing for … certain types of photographs.'

Silence. She picked up her gloves. Crossed him off the list —

'You'd be perfect.'

Halle-bloody-lujah.

'I can rely on you not to mention this to my husband?'

'Discretion is guaranteed, my dear.'

'Against the estimate you've given me for the portrait plus copies, I need to know what would be … expected of me.'

'Come with me.'

If ever a man missed his vocation, it was Tobias Wood leading funeral processions. Julia followed Wood to the studio at the back, where he brought out wads of postcards far racier than anything she'd taken, or, for that matter, even considered. Wood sifted out a suitable selection, which basically boiled down to a choice of her posing for a dozen explicit nudes, half a dozen touching herself, or one only, lying on a couch with her knees up by her shoulders, staring into the camera, while a man —

'Is that your hand?' Julia asked innocently.

'*Mrs. Smith!*'

He mightn't be up to much when it came to friendly greetings or smooth customer service, but when it came to outrage, Tobias Wood was without competition. In no uncertain words, he made clear his unblemished fidelity to Mrs. Wood, his loyalty to his children and three grandchildren, as well as his devotion to the Church of St. Michael and All Angels — which, he might add, was exceptionally appreciative of his substantial donations to support the parish poor.

Keep going, Tobias, keep going. The longer the rant, the more time Julia had to flick through the postcards. None of the girls, thank God, had ever modelled for her.

'I take no pleasure from the content, Mrs. Smith, and make no judgment of the ladies in these photographs.' Even though, he added with a cough, half if not two-thirds were on the game. 'I merely gain satisfaction from a job well done.'

'Let's not forget the money, Mr. Wood.'

'Every penny goes to worthy causes, I assure you!'

She felt his lapel. 'Savile Row?' She tapped his shirt. 'Jermyn Street? And as for that half-hunter watch of yours.' She smiled prettily under her hat. 'I'm sure no cause is more worthy. Good day to you, Mr. Wood.'

Oh, the relief of breathing fresh, clean air! A long soak in a deep bath would be better, a good scrub with a brush. But for now, yes, clean air and —

'Told yer. Poker up the arse,' Bug proclaimed loudly, 'and a face like a slapped bum. Sanctimonious twa— mmmmf.'

Julia kept her hand over his mouth until they were round the corner. 'I told you to stay away.'

'If he don't want folk eavesdropping, then he shouldn't 'ave a back door.'

Waste of breath, trying to reason with logic like that. 'How much did you see?'

'Enough to know them girls is being used —' Old. Old before his time, poor kid. '— and as for him playing the organ … well, I'm sayin' nuffin'.'

Inappropriate or not, she burst out laughing.

'Didya get what you wanted?'

'Rarely do any of us get what we want, Bug.'

Or put it another way, no. On the one hand, the girls' murders were cold and calculated, which fitted Tobias Wood's nature to a fault. Men like him are practised at hiding surprise when their quarry rolls up unannounced. And while she believed him when he said he took no pleasure from pornographic postcards, it's not unheard of for repressed men to nurture pent-up passions.

Equally, his motive might not be of a sexual nature, more a fear of competition, especially when it comes to women. At the first challenge to his authority, he crumpled like a paper bag in the rain. Who knows how threatened Tobias Wood might feel about a female muscling in on male territory? What lengths he might go to, to retain balance and order?

Oh, well. One down, three to go. Let's see what the others throw up.

'Mr. Belmont?'

Belmont was everything Tobias Wood was not. Barely five years older than Julia, he was lean, wiry, dapper, blonde, and always — always — on the move. Indeed watching him dart about like a wasp with the runs, he gave the word energetic a whole new dimension.

'Midge, dear. Call me Midge. What can I do for you this lovely sunny morning?'

Different characters require different tactics, and trotting out the false name/family portrait/expensive copies ruse would be a waste of everybody's time. Better to stick to the truth. A semblance of it, anyway. Because although, like Wood, there was no hint of recognition, the business wasn't named after the address on Belmont Street. Oh no. Young Midge had gone to great lengths to find premises fitting his name. A planner, then. A man who thinks ahead. A long, long way ahead…

'Mr. Blackstock gave me your details.'

Julia managed to hand him her card between him turning a chair to face the wall and straightening a picture frame that didn't need straightening.

'Since we both use the same French supplier —'

'Probably not the *same* French supplier.' Belmont's pale eyes danced with amusement. 'But go on.'

What she was hoping, she explained, skipping round the shop after him, was that he could put her in touch with models willing to pose. She added that a couple of her girls had let her down recently — if he *was* the bastard framing her, let him think she had no idea that they were dead.

'Blackie, bless his cotton socks, does enjoy a tipple, and while I've never actual seen him drunk, there's always a first time, I suppose.'

Julia didn't understand. Oliver wrote the name down himself. Midge admitted to being in the French postcard business...

Belmont's work was terrible. All right, not terrible. But those photographs weren't up to standard, not by a long chalk, and honestly, if *this* was the best he could find to display! Half of the women were wearing bustles. How long ago since those were taken?

'You shouldn't use grey,' Julia said.

'You've lost me, dear.'

'The feather duster. You should use black ostrich down, not grey. It's softer, and traps the dirt much better.'

'Does it now?' He peered at the feathers. 'I shall rectify that soonest. Thank you.'

'You're welcome. I apologise for not making myself clear, Midge. When I told you a couple of girls let me down and I'm short of models —' Julia paused — 'I didn't specify which sex.'

'Well, now.' He tapped the side of his nose. 'Maybe we will be using the same supplier after all.' He turned the sign to closed and opened the safe. 'Righty ho, let's see who's likely to be available at short notice.' His eyes might be pale, but by God were they shrewd. 'I'll expect a commission, of course.'

'Of course.'

'Twenty-five percent.'

'Twenty.'

'It's a deal.'

While Belmont's pen scratched down names and addresses, Julia skimmed through the postcards. Nothing compared to the number Tobias Wood held, suggesting Belmont's stock turned over faster, and frankly she could see why. His subjects were exclusively male.

Would a man attracted to men, which Midge obviously was, hate women so much that he needed to kill them? If so, why draw attention to the crimes by dragging a third party into it?

Thanking Midge for his help, Julia left his shop with her head pounding.

Most multiple killers — Jack the Ripper, for instance — revelled in flaunting their superiority over women, the police, the population in general. Each new atrocity was as much a taunt as an obsession, and gave them almost as much pleasure.

The key word was *almost*.

She'd heard how a handful secretly wanted to be caught, and while taunting remained paramount, they left deliberate clues that would lead to their capture and put an end to the slaughter they couldn't control. These clues were never directed at a third party as a distraction, though. That trail of breadcrumbs was their moment of glory, just as Jack the Ripper's cat-and-mouse game was his.

Pointing the finger at Julia fitted neither of those characteristics, and if there was one lesson she'd come away with this morning, it was confirmation that the motive was personal.

Augustus Jones was still on her list, and back on it (you just never know) was the man who peddled the postcards, Percival Tarrant. But however odd Midge and Tobias were, and however unsavoury their business, neither seemed capable of killing young girls and sending an innocent woman to the gallows.

That took a special kind of ruthlessness.

Daisy and the others were closer to danger than ever.

Chapter 11

'Come along, Davey, wash your face. Just because you've got a sniffle's no excuse for being dirty. Verity, take those bloomers off the table, please, they're your sister's anyway. Be a love, Faith, hold Baby Gracie while I pluck this chicken.'

'Why me? Why does it always, always have to be me?' Verity whined.

'Because, lovey, Hope and Patience are at school, which is exactly where young David would be, if he wasn't sneezing nineteen to the dozen.'

Julia had dropped by with a bottle of amontillado to make up for commandeering Rosie's husband. She also relished the break from violence, suspicion and murder, with the distraction of a clutter of children alongside towels drying on a pole in front of the oven while feathers flew every which way through the air.

'Either I'm getting fatter or this room's getting smaller,' Rosie chuckled, disentangling her cap from the grater hanging on the rack, alongside the ladles, spoons and strainers.

'For the fourth time, are you sure I can't help?' Julia asked.

'For the fourth time, certainly not. You've done your bit with this sherry!'

'Dad says you should get a maid.'

'I'm well aware what Dad says, thank you very much, Faith.'

'Dad says we can well afford a maid.'

'Then perhaps Dad can show me the money tree that's going to pay for her. Besides, who needs help when we have you, eh? You're worth a dozen maids-of-all-work any day.'

Faith wasn't the kind of girl to be won over by an affectionate pinch on the cheek. 'Charity was a whole *year* younger than me when she left home, how come *she* didn't get lumbered with rolling pastry and washing sick off baby clothes?'

'Mummmmmmy,' a little voice piped up. 'That thing there's making a noise.'

'Thank you, Verity, I'm not deaf. Here, I'll take the baby, Faith, you go answer the telephone. Ask who's calling, then say you'll see if anyone's home.' She shot Julia an exasperated look. 'Whatever possessed Oliver Blackstock to install one of those new-fangled contraptions up here, I have no idea! Doesn't he think I've got enough new appliances to wrestle with? First there was that electric sewing machine, which I have absolutely *no* intention of using. A woman could kill herself with a monster like that. Then that carpet cleaning wotnot, which blows up fifty times more dust than is in the bloomin' room to start with. And as for —'

'It's some Mr. Tarrant, wanting to speak to Dad,' Faith called.

'I tell you,' Rosie said behind her hand, 'if that telephone thinks Rosie Blackstock has nothing better to do with her time than talk to stuck-up types with noses like a woodsaw and voices that could pass for water down a drain, it's got another think coming!' To Faith, she said, 'Be a love and take a message. Gracie needs her nappy changed.' She leaned towards Julia with a giggle. 'That was naughty of me. Dunno how many times Olly's said how important that man is, how our entire wealth and comfort's down to him. *What bloomin' wealth?* I ask, to which he says, *One day, Rosie Cheeks, and in the not-too-distant future, we'll be living in a swanky mansion, wearing fine brocades and silks, with flush toilets on the landing, caviar in the larder, peacocks on the lawn.* Poppycocks, more like!'

Julia laughed, then planted a kiss on Grace's downy head and tweaked her little toes. 'I must go.'

'Well, don't you be a stranger, love, and thanks again for the sherry.' The respite might be over, but Rosie's voice still carried down the stairs. 'Davey, really! *Must* you wear that chicken on your head?'

'Spiders,' Bug said decisively.

'Spiders?' Julia repeated.

'Y'know. Them big black hairy things with lots of legs.'

He was still encased in the Dickie Lloyd understudy sticker from the music hall poster, wafting it around like a feather boa, even though in his mind he was Sir Francis Drake and this was his cape. The captain's garb was stained with gravy from the hot beef and oyster pies they'd devoured on the Common like a pair of tramps, but Julia supposed that's the risk a man runs, when he's driving off Spaniards.

'Only, I had a thought,' Bug continued.

'Actually, you had a penny, which I asked you to buy a newspaper with to check the second-hand bicycle section.'

'Didn't need to. Some bloke left his on the park bench when he'd finished.'

What he really meant was: an unsuspecting gentleman placed his newspaper beside him while he lit a cigarette, and when he went to continue reading, it had gone.

'In that case, I'll have my penny back.'

'Can't.'

'The word you're looking for, I believe, is won't.'

'Uh-uh. Can't. Bought this, see?' Bug blew hard on the contraption. If you shut a cat's tail in a door, twisted it in a knot then set fire to it, the sound would be sweeter. Mother of God, ungreased axles grinding uphill would sound sweeter. Chinese water torture would be a positive blessing. 'S'why they call 'em penny whistles. Coz they cost a penny.'

'Here's what's going to happen. You are going to put that away until you can play it, and then you are going to tell me where spiders come into it.'

'Cow,' Bug mouthed cheerfully.

'Spiders,' Julia prompted.

'That's what I'm trying to tell yer, except you keep interruptin'. You said you wanted another diversion, like them pots and pans in the street, and I got it.'

Which is how Julia came to be twirling her parasol with becoming nonchalance as she perused the shops of North Street, any smugness hidden by a hat piled with enough turquoise blue feathers to leave an ostrich bald, the exact same shade as her gored skirt and exquisitely slashed leg o'mutton sleeves. As she approached the milliner's, a piercing scream rang out.

'Ugh! Spider! Flew right in my face!'

Julia just about caught — 'Look! There it is! A monster, can you see it?' — before slipping into Rowan Lane, turning left down the alleyway, right on Leman Street, then right again to Marden Terrace.

More fool her, she'd nearly asked where Bug found the wretched thing, but discretion triumphed over valour. Suppose he'd said, 'in your darkroom'. Or worse still, 'in your bedroom'.

Striding down Marden Terrace, nodding polite *good afternoons* left, right and centre, Julia would have preferred to forego the insect charade in favour of a visit to the third photographer, Augustus Jones. Unfortunately, when she tried telephoning, the phone rang off the hook. She might as well fill the time usefully until he returned.

'Mitchell Street,' Oliver had said, when she asked his advice about where best to set up her secret studio. 'Far enough from the factories not to be robbed, close enough to suburbia for ladies of quality to come and go without attracting attention, but equally an area where girls with less means won't stand out.'

More importantly, Mitchell Street wasn't far from the canal, so there would always be people milling about, he had stressed, making it safe for her and her models to be walking alone without risking ribald comments, or worse.

'There's warehouses at the far end,' Oliver had said, 'which might serve your purpose. Respectable neighbourhood, too.'

He was right on that score: it epitomised what Julia thought of as Clerk Class. Neither working-class nor middle-class, the area catered for the explosion of office workers that had arisen as a result of industrialisation. She dug out her key. After much consideration, she'd opted to rent two rooms in a lodging house, with Oliver, of course, signing the paperwork, women being too weak and too stupid to manage such matters themselves. For single ladies, coming and going at unusual hours, a private residence was less suspicious than a shed — but still suspicious enough for any policeman on her tail to want to take a peek. It was her job to make sure those wolf eyes weren't prowling here.

Once inside, she opened the curtains and sunshine flooded the floor. Or what little was left, after she'd turned the room into a studio.

'It's like that theatre on the poster, innit? All these sceneries and props.'

Give me strength. 'I'm not going ask how you found me, because you've already proved you're as slippery as an eel and twice as crafty —'

'Cor!' Bug interrupted.

'That wasn't a compliment.'

'Says you. This bed's comfy, how often d'you sleep here?'

'Never, and you aren't Goldilocks. Out!'

Julia regretted grabbing Bug's collar — the wool stuck to her fingers — but it was the only piece she could find under Francis Drake's cape.

'You don't need to worry, the rozzer ain't here. I sorted him good and proper, coz you tell me what copper don't rush to help a little old duck when she screams?'

'I'm grateful to you, Bug, and your logic's commendable, but right now I have work to do, which, strangely, doesn't involve you bouncing up and down on the bed, much less in those filthy boots.'

'Is that what the sea looks like?'

Julia stopped. Swallowed. Wondered why irritation popped and its place taken by a pain under the ribcage, all in less than a second.

'Sometimes,' she said steadily. 'Sometimes, when it's stormy, the waves are this high, and sometimes it's so calm, you'd think it was a lake.'

Bug's eyes were bigger than saucers as he traced the painted waterline.

'Sand's REALLY this yellow?'

'Not always. It can be brown, it can be white. On some beaches it's soft, like walking on sugar, on others it's shingle, and sometimes there's no sand at all, just waves crashing against the rocks.'

'Whassit sound like, the sea?'

'Again, it depends. I'll tell you later, only Daisy's due any minute — you did deliver the message?'

'Course.'

'Well, then, you'll know I promised to take her photo.'

'And Minnie's?'

'Not today. Now go off and slaughter some Spaniards, there's a good Bug.'

'I could stay and —'

'Hop it.'

Julia counted to twenty. Bug didn't bounce back. She got down to work.

One of the advantages of renting lodgings, as opposed to a warehouse, was that she was able to leave her equipment rigged up in one room, and turn the second into a dark room. Another was much-needed anonymity. The disadvantage, of course, was that unlike Midge or Tobias Wood, she had to shell out for two lots of rent, as well as invest in two sets of everything from cameras to lenses to chemical baths.

Still. It was a damn sight cheaper than jail.

She counted out the thirty or so glass plates that would make up the folio scope for the flip book she'd told Daisy about. No two ways about it, this was going to be a challenge for both of them. Julia having to work quickly, the model doing the exact opposite. Holding her pose then varying it imperceptibly for the next shot, so that when the pages were flicked through at speed, the girl appeared to be moving.

'Got to tell you, Mrs. Mack, I'm dead excited about this *What the Butler Saw*,' Daisy said when she arrived.

Daisy, Daisy. Please don't use words like dead. 'I was worried you might have second thoughts.'

'Are you barmy?' Daisy nestled her sleeping baby among the white, lacy pillows on the bed. 'I didn't nod off counting sheep last night. I was counting guineas. The Swedish Princess is off for a bracing dip in the briny, eh?' Daisy flashed her wide, wholesome smile at Julia's set laid out with starfish, beach balls and the bright red bathing suit the princess was supposedly stripping off for. 'I've only been to the seaside once and that was Brighton, but my oh my, that pavilion thingy, have you seen it? Like a sultan's palace!'

'Before we start, Daisy, you do understand we'll be stretching the boundaries further than we have in the past?'

'Not a problem, Mrs. Mack, but like I said yesterday, I wouldn't do this in front of a man. And as long as none of the perverts who buy these flop books know who I am, I'll keep doing it for as long as the money runs and my looks last.'

'Flip books, Daisy, flip books.' Julia laughed. 'I doubt anything will be flopping by the time they reach the end of your striptease.'

Tease being the word. Daisy was a natural. She'd practised in front of the mirror, she said, until she'd found the exact thirty poses for her routine. (No mean feat, given the size of her mirror). Now, thanks to her enthusiasm, the shoot went like clockwork.

Having changed into the royal evening gown — which Swedish princesses always wore to the beach — she then proceeded to inch her way out of it, one salacious step at a time, while Julia put her camera through its paces. Insert plate. Slide cover from holder. Expose lens, fraction of a second, that's all, replace cover. Remove plate for processing. Repeat. And repeat. And repeat with rapid efficiency.

'Aaaah. Minnie, bless her. Slept right the way through.' Daisy removed the tiara, rings and pearls — which no Swedish princess would be without on the beach — and wriggled back into her blue cotton frock and flowery bonnet. 'She's an angel, this girl of mine. A proper little angel.'

Julia couldn't argue with that, but as she locked the door behind them, Lily's voice filled the room. *I was standing at the station yesterday, overheard two men talking about their wives. One of them said, mine's an angel. The other said, you're lucky, mate, mine's still alive.'*

Oh, Lily. You'd have been a natural, too. No inhibitions, none at all — you'd have taken to flip books like a duck to water. Remember the last time you were here? Peeling off your stocking with one hand, the other taking the word provocative to a different plane, while telling me, 'The bloke over the road got robbed last night. The police are looking for a man with a wooden leg called Bert. So I said to the copper, what's his good leg called, then?'

Julia had to take that picture of Lily twice — the first negative came out blurred, because she was laughing so hard. And now, thanks to some monster with a selfish, vile agenda, Lily's colossal breasts would never jiggle like milk puddings again.

Or feed the babies she so desperately wanted.

Opposite the lodging house, unnoticed among the swarm of flower sellers, dray carts, hansom cabs and delivery boys pushing barrows, that monster with the selfish, vile agenda watched a young girl with a wide smile and blue bonnet set off down Mitchell Street, singing softly to her baby.

Chapter 12

Lugging the first batch of negatives into her secret dark room, the only thing on Julia's mind after Daisy left was their fragility and weight, and the happy prospect of the income the flip books would bring. An income which would secure escape from Collingwood's probings, her independence, her freedom and a comfortable future, as well as funding round-the-world travels.

You don't take a photograph, JJ. You make it.

Damn right. The Taj Mahal, Victoria Falls, the Pyramids. Those were the images lined up in front of her imaginary lens when she'd entered her secret dark room. And even if she'd stopped to consider that three days had passed since she was last in there, the penny probably wouldn't have dropped.

Until she saw them. Nellie. Birdie. Lily, laid out on her table like pieces of a risqué jigsaw puzzle. It was all she could do not to drop the glass plates, but the sight of the girls in the photos — so vibrant, so alive — made her burst into loud howls of grief.

How could they? How could anyone in their right mind snuff out their lives and vitality without conscience?

Julia's grief switched to anger. How DARE they? How dare some evil bastard steal these girls? Their hopes. Their dreams. Their comfy old age surrounded by grandchildren, knitting and dogs. What kind of sick coward is too scared to own their crime? Happy to let someone else take the fall?

'So help me, I will find you. I will find you no matter what, and if the police fail to lock you up, I will kill you myself. But know this. Die you will.'

One by one, she'd kissed the girls goodbye. Bridget O'Leary, saviour of insects everywhere, whose springy dark curls would no longer be the curse of her hairbrush. Lily Atkins, bursting out of her corsets and stockings. *We're not fat because it runs in the family, luv. We're fat cause no one in the family runs.* And Nellie, aka Eleanor Stern, aka Crosby, aka Edwards, aka heaven-knows-what. As busy and as bustling as the names she went by. And just as perennially good-natured.

Julia had taken one long last look at the photos, drinking them in through her tears.

'Rest in peace, girls.'

Scooping them up, she then burned every single one in the grate. There was no way could she sell these pictures now. Not in a hundred, million, years, not for a hundred, million, pounds. Let their dignity die with them. It was the only thing the girls had left.

'Make no mistake,' Julia promised their killer. 'You will die with fear in your eyes, and I will dance on your unmarked grave.'

All the same, the emotion was too overwhelming to stay in the dark room. The flip book would just have to wait.

As, it would seem, would Augustus Jones. There was still no answer from his photographic studio. Perhaps he just didn't trust telephones?

'That was mean of you,' a voice piped up. Of *course* Bug would have been sitting on the stairs in the lodging house. 'Telling me to hop it. You only said that, coz of my foot.' He performed an exaggerated limp as she locked up behind her. 'You bin crying?'

'Chemicals in the dark room. Make my eyes water. What are you doing here?'

'Came to report, milady, Daisy got back safe. I walked 'em home, her and Minnie.' He made two bony fists. 'In case that bloke wot was bothering her came back, see.'

Dammit, Julia had no intention of bursting into tears a second time.

'Cor! Another penny!'

'Treat yourself to anything you fancy, providing it isn't musical. I'll meet you back home in an hour.'

Damn. She said *home*. Had he noti—

'Home, eh? Fair nuff, reckon it'll do for now.'

Julia could swear that Bug's cheeks had filled out in two days. She tugged at his increasingly ragged cloak. At this rate, the bloody thing would need surgical removal. 'Does Sir Francis know what an understudy is?'

'The bloke what steps in when the real bloke drops dead?'

'Close enough, but guess what, Captain. I have boys your age lined up by the dozen, out there in the wings.'

'Yer telling me to hop it again, ain't yer? Well, seeing as how I been paid off,' he waved the penny, 'maybe I don't wanna walk you HOME anyway.'

Off he scampered, exaggerating the limp, chortling like an elf.

Julia was still rolling her eyes when she reached Willow Lane. Seeing the inside of the Willow Walk tea rooms twice in one day hadn't figured in her plans. But if Cyril meant business, the pendulum was ticking.

Over and over, she saw a shadowy figure standing on the bridge that spanned the railway line, waiting for the milk train to pass. The *Chronicle* hadn't reported any sensational deaths — or mentioned suicides at all, come to that. Some might construe this as encouraging. Cyril might have changed his mind. Others might be tempted to wonder if he'd, say, hanged himself in Southolt Woods, which was out of the reporters' jurisdiction...

This morning's table was taken, but she'd managed to find one with a good view round the shop.

'Nothing to eat, thank you.' Julia held up her hand to the waitress. 'Just tea.'

Hold tight. Hold tight just a little bit longer. Please, Cyril, please. If I can only find T, I know she'll talk you out of it.

Cyril was an educated man, that was obvious from his writing, his grammar, the smooth use of language. Instinctive, at even the lowest of ebbs. But love has no boundaries; why should it follow that it didn't cross class?

Julia was clutching at straws, admittedly. Especially when he wrote of meeting here when they had chance — but suppose by "we" he meant just him? Here was a man literally at his wit's end. Julia owed it to "T" and to him not to rule anything out, certainly not for snobbery's sake. It took mere seconds, though, to establish there were Pearls, Abigails and Marthas by the score. There were Lucys, there were Kittys, Louisas and an Eve. But no one at Willow Walk boasted initials beginning with T. Not even a nickname.

Julia thanked the waitress setting down her tea. (Winifred, spelled, of course, with a big fat W).

'I found this on the floor.' Julia held up a Flemish lace hankie embroidered with T in one corner. 'Belongs to one of your patrons, I think.'

Before she'd taken two sips, the girl was back, smoothing her apron and shaking her head. 'Sorry, madam. None of the ladies recognised it. Perhaps she dropped it on her way out.'

'I'll level with you, Winifred. I didn't find this here at all.' Julia leaned forward and slipped the waitress a sixpence. 'The thing is, my husband is seeing another woman … and one of the places he meets her is here.'

'Oh, madam, that's … that's *terrible!*'

Terrible or not, that sixpence disappeared faster than you could say knife.

'That's her handkerchief?'

Julia nodded.

'Oh good Lord alive! Not in your … your own home?'

Julia added a desolate pout to the nod.

'Thought you'd been crying, madam, if you don't mind my saying, and as it happens, I do pick up the odd snippet of gossip here and there. Can't avoid it in this line of work.'

Needless to say, Winifred didn't recall any Teresas, Thomasinas, Tabathas or Tillys, especially taking tea with a man. Neither did any of her fellow waitresses, when she questioned them. Not a Tina, Tanya or Tara in sight.

Julia watched scones being scoffed, toast being buttered, boiled eggs being cracked.

Now what?

Her heart sank as she rose to leave a scene barely changed from this morning. Widows, spinsters, the old duffer with the cane, the prune perched on a cactus chewing a hornet, the doleful bank clerk, polishing his spectacles, over and over.

A man who dares to waste one hour of time has not discovered the value of life.

Ah, but these people aren't wasting their time, Mr. Darwin, these people are lonely. Deeply, desperately, achingly lonely. How lonely is T without Cyril?

103

Chapter 13

Sauntering back along the towpath, Collingwood touched his brim at two ladies in characteristic barge people garb, one polishing the brass rails, the other pegging out aprons and smocks. Those bonnets must weigh a ton. Wide brims at the front, row upon row of stiff, starched frills on top. Hotter than Hades inside, he wouldn't mind betting, and hardly what you'd call fetching. The women returned his smile, and as he continued to dodge horses and tow ropes, bidding good day to the men leading the barges, he knew their eyes were following his progress. And not out of curiosity, either.

Days like this, he wished he'd taken up a different profession. Inn-keeper. Barrister. Cheesemonger. Cow hand. Doctor. Dancing master, for God's sake. Anything except the bloody police force.

He'd gained nothing, a hundred percent bugger all, from recreating the victim's last moments. Not surprising. He still didn't know where the poor bastard came from. Had he arranged to meet someone? Why this side of the canal, not the other? Had he come from the east, passing under the bridge? Or was he headed west at the time, away from the lock? Despite manpower stretched thinner than a thief's alibi, his men didn't appear to have missed any clues.

Appear being the operative word.

Around his feet, butterflies danced from thistle to thistle, donkeys brayed in the field, ducks quacked round a small girl feeding them bread. It would be an idyllic rural scene, were it not for the factories rising from the opposite bank, the sun's rays blocked by their soupy, brown smoke, their reflections an affront to the gentle, still waters of the canal.

Would his findings be different, had a photographer been able to preserve the murder scene? (A female photographer, for instance, more in tune with nuances?) Hard to say. By the time Boot Street was alerted, who knows how much evidence had been destroyed? A ten-year-old girl screaming blue murder brought the canal people running, as well as passers-by, two old men digging their allotments, and a constable whose patrol was fortuitously taking him over the bridge at the time.

There was a rush to cover the body. Pull up his trousers. Check his pockets, to see who he was. It had been well-meaning, without doubt, but in preserving the man's decency, these good Samaritans were unwittingly helping his killers.

Had there been a photographic record, Collingwood might have been able to give it to the papers as a means to identify the victim. As it stood, the sketch on the front page could be anyone. Himself. That fellow painting distinctive folk art on the barge. The lock-keeper's son. Anyone.

'That frown tells me the Chief Inspector still wants your balls for breakfast,' his sergeant had said earlier.

Collingwood was coming out of the station, Kincaid going in.

'Lightly curried on toast,' he'd admitted. 'Apparently Inspector Collingwood is failing in his duties as the officer in charge of Boot Street by allowing violent crime to triumph. Either he does what he's paid to do, namely solve these effing murders or —'

'They appoint someone who will. Nice.'

'*Or* … Charlie. They will close the station altogether.'

'He's bluffing. The Chief Inspector'll never be able to run his own nick on top of everything we do here.'

'The top brass are mooting the idea of knocking down Boot Street in favour of a new station, a bigger station, and appointing a more senior officer to run the whole organisation.'

One which had no place for Collingwoods of any description.

'Guess we'd best take our thumbs out of our arses and start pulling rabbits out of our hats. Sir.' Kincaid's laugh could pass for the creak of a gallows chain. 'Then we can see what humble pie tastes like. Lightly curried on toast.'

Nice idea, as dreams go.

In addition to the usual list of petty larcenies, house-breakings, embezzlements, arson, extortion, blackmail, tax offences and frauds, they still had one unknown victim of unknown assailants, dead end. Three girls killed by the same hand, dead end, dead end, dead end.

There was bound to be a vacancy for a dancing master somewhere. Until then, though — call it coincidence — but Collingwood's route back from the canal happened to take him past Whitmore Photographic. Seemed a waste not to drop in.

'I know why yer here.' The urchin munching his way through an Eccles cake the same size as himself didn't *look* like he was robbing the place of its equipment. 'It's about tea, innit?'

Collingwood might be failing at solving murders, but he was an expert when it came to non-committal grunts.

'Milady'll be HOME any minute, if you wanna wait. She said an hour, and that was fifty eight minutes —'

'Home from where, exactly?'

'How'd I know? I'm only the hired help.'

'Goodness, Inspector!' another voice interrupted. 'How refreshing to find you inside my premises, instead of dusting my doorway with your well-tailored shoulder.'

'Mrs. McAllister.'

'Case not going well, then?'

'What makes you say that?'

'I've photographed better looking corpses.'

'That's a grave accusation to level against the police.'

'Then stop working graveyard shifts.'

'You know the man who coined cemetery jokes was sentenced to death?'

At some point between Julia putting down the parcel and unpinning her hat, the urchin and the Eccles cake had vanished without trace. Quite honestly, the way Collingwood was feeling, he wouldn't be surprised if he'd imagined the whole bloody incident.

'This better?' he asked, stretching his mouth into a humourless grin.

'Only if I was a dentist.' Julia picked up the pile of afternoon mail and perused it in a way that fooled no one. 'I was rather referring to your hollow eyes and sallow skin, both of which suggest more than one sleepless night.'

There was nothing wrong with his skin tone or his eyes. The lovely Mrs. McAllister was fishing.

'I'd rest a whole lot easier, if you weren't hell bent on giving my officers the slip.' Collingwood picked up his derby. 'Makes me think you might have something to hide.'

He was still grinning when he closed the shop door behind him — not quite so much when his shin collided with a bicycle wheel, because he'd forgotten to look where he was going.

The girl at the telephone exchange insisted she was connecting the call to the right number. Augustus Jones simply wasn't answering. *Damn.* Julia might be tempted to think Oliver had written the number down wrong were exactitude not a prerequisite in the photographic trade.

'Who's this bloke we're going to see?' Bug asked.

Once this nightmare was over, and before she left Oakbourne with a new name and no forwarding address, there was one other man Julia intended to track down. Bug's father. Whether it was to reunite him with his missing son or break both the bastard's legs was yet to be decided.

'The one I'd get my jokes from, if I wasn't picking them up from Blodwen at the dairy.'

'Dickie Lloyd?' A whoop of delight rang over the Common. Even the squirrels' eyebrows shot up. 'The music hall! Hooray, hooray!' Bug paused. 'A real one?'

'Is there another kind?'

He chewed that one over for a couple of steps. 'Which hall?'

'Cadogan Bridge.'

'That story about me Pa and the priest. Didn't give you no ideas, did it? I mean, you not gonna leave me behind there?'

'No, but screech that penny whistle one more time, and I'm selling you to the factory that turns knackered horses into glue. What are you doing?'

'Scratchin'.'

'That wasn't a question, more a polite request to stop, and please take your hand out of your trousers while you do it.'

'Me clothes itch.'

'New clothes don't itch, at least they won't if you can stop wriggling about in them for thirty seconds.'

'Can't help it. S'uncomfortable, this pansy clobber.'

The shirt, jacket and trousers were second-hand, cheap. The way Bug was eating, he'd grow out of them by the end of the week. The boots, though, the boots were new. The kid deserved that much.

'Then go home, take it off and get comfortable.'

'S'all right, this pansy clobber.'

Finally — finally — glory Hallelujah — there was a way to render the boy speechless. Even the smallest bugs can't jabber with their jaws on their knees at the sight of the atrium, all arches, sweeping staircases, wrought iron and glass skylights. Shame she hadn't thought of this before. His silence was worth the admission price twenty times over.

'Must be a hundred foot up, that ceiling.'

Closer to half, but Julia understood Bug's reaction to the vast open floor set with tables catering for hundreds, not dozens, and galleries running the length of both sides. Four giant chandeliers lit the floor from each gallery (French, what else?), two more flanked the stage, but without doubt the *pièce de resistance* was the ornate gilt ceiling adorned with two of the biggest chandeliers Julia had ever seen in her life. Amazingly, the ceiling stayed up, and the combination of pillars and panelling gave the building a cathedral-like feel.

'He's dead funny, him.'

Bug pointed at the leprechaun bouncing round the stage in a bright green suit and orange whiskers, singing, 'The banshee, the banshee, bejabbers, don't you hear? Its groaning and its moaning, begob it's moighty queer.'

'Pity Dickie Lloyd's still off. He's gotta be better than the understudy bloke,' Bug said.

'You didn't find him funny?'

'Reckon I'm the only one.' Bug's little nose wrinkled. 'All these swells in here, laughing like they're fit to bust over that song about taking a picture with, how d'it go? *One little flaw, coz thro' a window just behind, was a sweet domestic picture, 'cept they forgot to draw the blind.* What's funny about that?'

'No idea.'

'Or girls sticking stuff in their drawers with their knick-knacks?'

'Search me.'

Ten acts later, Julia's sides aching as they pushed towards the exit, she had almost forgotten Collingwood's warning. It didn't matter. Another few weeks and several flip books behind her, she'd be moving on to a place where no one would ever unravel her past. To that end, she'd drawn up a list of things to take when she left.

'Why isn't it moony?' Bug asked.

What had she missed this time?

'Yer can have skies what are sunny, or cloudy, or rainy, or misty, or like tonight, skies what are starry. So why can't you have moony?'

Bug turned his freckles at a moon that would be full in three days. Three days, after which the weather would break. And possibly other things, too.

'From now on, Bug, you can. Moony skies it will be.'

'*Champagne Charlie is my name —*'

'Let's sing something else.'

'Why? Makes me laugh, that. Swimming in champagne.' Bug made paddling motions with his arms. 'What's PFRG stand for anyway? Poxy foreign rot gut?'

'PRFGs,' she corrected. 'Private Rooms For Gentlemen that are linked to various supper rooms, where patrons can retire with a companion and enjoy a quiet meal, just the two of them.'

'*Champagne Charlie is my name —*'

'I thought we'd agreed you weren't singing that.'

'You agreed. Me, I'll be singing it through to this time next Saturday, unless you tell me why you don't like it.'

Julia ran her finger under her collar. She was aware of a trickle of sweat down her back. Ruffles, especially silk ones, bear little resemblance to a noose. Still. Who wants to take that chance?

'It was sung at the last public execution in Britain.'

'Yer kidding! They used to string 'em up outside for everyone to watch?'

'Your eyes aren't supposed to light up at the prospect.'

'Cor!' Bug made a series of gargling sounds. 'What'd he hang for?'

'Setting light to a barrow filled with gunpowder.'

'Blimey. What d'he do that for?'

The condemned man's name (if she remembered correctly, this was over twenty years ago) was Michael Barrett. He was an Irish republican, and the bomb was intended to effect a prison break from Clerkenwell. 'The Fenians only meant to blow out the wall, but the explosion was so great, it rocked the tenements over the road, killing several people and injuring a good many more.'

'Don't sound right that he should swing for it, though. Weren't like he meant to hurt no one.'

'Maybe not, but the slaughter of innocent women and children destroyed any sympathy the British had for the republican cause, and unleashed a tide of hostility against the Irish in general.'

What the public wanted was a scapegoat. And right now, that was too close to home for Julia's liking.

Every girl dreads the thought of being doomed to spinsterhood, and walking that lonely, godforsaken road to childlessness. Fat or ugly, dull or disfigured, they don't deserve that fate. No one does.

Respectable girls, though, put up with bending their spines twelve hours a day at the knitting machines in the hosiery factory. They don't complain at the unremitting clack of the machinery in the shoe factory, or baulk at carrying heavy pots of boiling jam, or at the gagging stench of oil, or the bitching and backbiting from the women they're stuck with, day in day out, on those backless benches, turning wooden spindles.

They know it's a decent day's pay for a decent day's work, and modelling — if that's what you can call it, when you're touching yourself with one hand and sucking your thumb with the other — might buy them pretty clothes, and it might even earn an admiring glance from a gentleman in the street, or envious stares from other women. But it will never buy them decency. Not in a month of Sundays with a blue moon every night.

A finger traced the almond eyes, high cheekbones and jet black hair of the exotic creature in the photograph. "Rose of Shangai?" Not even Rose of bloody Chingford, the little phoney. Like a player on the stage, or one of those female impersonators at the music hall, it was nothing but an act.

Live it long enough, though, and they probably believe it.

Especially if someone, a photographer for instance, is feeding them the lies.

Chapter 14

Stroking his dying daughter's hand, Collingwood's failure to clap the Purple Ink Killer in irons and his fruitless efforts to identify the canal victim, and therefore the attackers, paled into insignificance.

A father's role is to protect his daughter. What happens when he can't? What happens when the only thing he can do is watch her suffer?

'If I could take this from you, Chicken, give my life for yours, I would,' he whispered.

For just one year — one month — of happy normal childhood, he'd willingly swap his healthy lungs for bellows eroding like acid from the inside out. What father wouldn't take her parchment skin, or give his strong teeth for her transparent ones, to watch her dance and skip once more?

'Hug me, Daddy.'

Her voice was so hoarse, he could barely make out the words.

'Anything, Alice.'

'Like you used to, before I was sick.'

There was nothing to scoop up. Just nightdress, bone and laudanum.

'Harder, Daddy. I won't break.'

He brushed the hair from her eyes, remembering when it used to be shiny and silky, and bounced when she ran.

'When I held you for the very first time, you were no bigger than a kitten, and I was scared, so scared, that I would hurt you. But you know, Alice, that's exactly what the midwife said. "She won't break, Mr. Collingwood".'

So he squeezed his daughter hard, just like he used to before she was sick, and felt tears scald his cheeks as he rocked her in his arms.

'When you're better, Chicken, you and I are going to strip this wallpaper off the walls. No more dark red roses, no heavy tassels on the lampshades; you'll have light bright walls and light bright paint, and you can choose whatever counterpane you want for your bedroom — lace, silk, satin — and fill your wardrobe with whatever pretty frocks take your fancy.'

For Christ's sake, this was a death chamber. An old woman's room, not a child's. A room where cloying scents of roses and jasmine had no place, any more, for that matter, than the piano in the living room, which neither he or Emily could play, or knew anybody who could.

'Ba-ba.'

'What's that, darling?'

A bloodless hand flapped. In the blackness, he could barely make out the direction, then he remembered. Ba-ba was the name she'd given her favourite toy, at an age when she was too tiny to pronounce the word "bear".

'There you go.'

He tucked the moth-eaten toy in her arm and kissed the two red patches that stood out on her sunken, ghostly cheeks and which proclaimed her disease for all the world to see.

'I know! Why don't we count the stars tonight?'

'Mother says the curtains must stay shut to keep the evil out.'

Collingwood pulled back the drapes, opened the window and gave her an exaggerated wink. 'Then this'll be our secret, Alice. I won't tell, if you won't.'

Her giggle induced a coughing fit. A desperate, hacking gargle that wracked her frame from head to foot and brought up thick, white phlegm.

'Enough.' The door flung open, framing his wife in an incongruous warm glow from the wall light on the landing. 'Now look what you've done!'

She pushed him aside and fed Alice ten drops of laudanum. The liquid was bitter and vile, and Collingwood's jaw clenched at her little face puckering as she swallowed. She was so weak, the effects were almost instantaneous.

'I told you what would happen, if you opened that window.'

He grabbed his wife's arm and dragged her out of the room. 'How dare you blame me for that child's suffering.'

'If you believed in God, John, she would be cured. Instead you bring blasphemy and evil into this house —'

'Me? What about your long, trailing skirts that physicians claimed were, and I quote, "responsible for sweeping up germs on the street and bringing disease into the home"?'

'That's nonsense, and you know it.'

'Exactly. It's all bullshit —'

'John!'

'Skirts can't collect germs, any more than consumption is hereditary, or the result of corsets restricting the lungs and impeding circulation of the blood. It's passed through the air, and frankly we should count ourselves lucky that we haven't caught this hideously contagious disease.' *Yet.*

'A lady's undergarments should not be discussed, and to do so is boorish.'

'Is it now?' His anger flared and he did nothing to stop it. 'And what would you call it when your husband, the father of your child, wants to look at those "undergarments"?'

'John, please —'

She clawed at the blouse he was ripping open. He heard buttons ping on the floor.

'What would you call it, when your husband, the father of your child, wants to look at your breasts? Remind himself what they actually feel like?'

'Now you're being vulgar.'

Years of Collingwood's pent-up fury exploded. 'There's nothing vulgar about a man claiming his marital rights. Will you stop me?'

For a moment, he thought she was about to deny him. Dear God, he actually wished it —

'No. No, of course not. If that's what you want.'

What he *wanted* was a woman with dark restless curls. What he *wanted* was a woman with a sparkle in her eye, who put her fishwife hands on her hips, and jabbed her finger to make her point. And dear God, if Julia McAllister's breasts heaved when she talked about travel and art, what the hell would they heave like in bed?

Once again, though, life proved that what you want and what you get are two very different things. Because what Collingwood got was a passive doll with tears coursing down her cheeks in accusing silence.

'Where are you going? I thought you wanted to, you know…'

He closed his eyes. Twelve years of marriage, she still couldn't bring herself to say the words. 'You'll be relieved to know, Emily, I have changed my mind.'

'What will you do now, then?'

The same as any other decent, self-respecting Englishman whose daughter is reaching the end of her life and whose wife is a bitter, delusional nun.

Get drunk.

Chapter 15

Today would have been Charity Blackstock's eighteenth birthday, and despite a mountain of pressing calls on time and energy, Julia was determined to drop in on the Blackstocks. No flowers, though. After Charity died, she'd taken round a massive hot-house camellia, with stunning froths of pale pink petals set against dark, waxy leaves. For the Chinese, camellias symbolised young sons and daughters — what better memorial for Charity Blackstock? But when Oliver opened the door, he had wagged his finger.

'Lovely gesture,' he'd whispered, eyes red and swollen with tears, 'really appreciate this. But right now, flowers, any flowers, remind Rosie of the funeral — it'd be like a stab to the heart. Do you mind?'

Mind? How could he even think such a thing? A photographer, of all people, should have understood that for some (Flora's parents), a photograph of their dead child was a comfort. For others (Rosie), physical reminders were simply too painful. Her thoughtlessness made Julia sick to her stomach.

On the other hand, Oliver wasn't his wife. Every time he called at Julia's shop, he'd kiss his fingertips and lay them on the leaves of the potted camellia she'd set by the door. And every time, Julia's heart thought it would break.

'Not in? Either of them?'

'Sorry, Missus McAllister.' Oliver's assistant, a ruddy-faced Scot, pulled a face. 'Mrs. B's taken the bairns to the park; Mr. B nipped out to order another wee batch of glass plates.'

Julia should have guessed. Busy-busy-busy was how the Blackstocks had coped with the pain of bereavement. It stood to reason that busy-busy-busy was how they'd get through Charity's birthday.

'Glass plates?' Julia smiled. 'Is that the best you can come up with, when two days ago your boss swore blind the stock room had shrunk overnight, because he had nowhere to store anything anymore?'

'Aye. Ye caught me. But that's what he told me ta tell anybody who asked, so between you, me and the gatepost, he might have gone ta the book binder's.' The ruddy assistant checked the shop to make sure they were alone. 'Ta have the latest photies made into flip books.'

'That'll be Mr. Curtis on Southolt Street?'

'Who? No. Never heard o' him.' Probably not. She'd just made it up. 'Mr. B only deals with Edwards in Sloane Row.'

'Ah. Mr. Edwards. Lovely, lovely fellow. I've only ever heard good things about his work.'

She'd never heard of him at all. But with Tobias Wood and Midge Belmont looking unlikely suspects, Augustus Jones not answering his telephone, and any motive for the distributor, Percival Tarrant, too tenuous for Julia's liking, she wasn't in a position to rule book-binders out. There were proving more trades in the dirty picture business than she'd originally imagined, so could she be wrong? Suppose the photos at the murder scene bearing Julia's stamp *weren't* personal? Merely aniseed to throw the bloodhounds off the scent?

If so, it was working a treat.

'Is he here, Angus? Olly? *Olly?*' Rosie's face was flushed with excitement. 'You out the back there, Mr B? Oh, hello, lovey! Didn't see you, hiding behind that display stand.'

'He's a' the book binder's,' Angus said.

'His loss, because now *you'll* have to come and have a sherry with me to celebrate.'

The Scot's eyes lit up, but Rosie wasn't talking to him. She'd already taken Julia's arm and was practically pushing her up the stairs.

'You'll never guess what the postman delivered. Today of all days — now isn't that the very treat that we need?' Rosie threw her hat on the chair. 'Sit down, sit down — no Daniel, not you, and not on my hat, please. I was talking to Mrs. McAllister. Davey, fetch — no, no, you'd best do it, Hope. The decanter and glasses from the sideboard, if you please.'

'Come on, Rosie, what is it? I'm biting my nails to the quick here.'

Rosie's ample bosom looked fit to bust. 'You won't believe it. A letter from my son —'

'He's just made a purple for the Army!' Patience interrupted excitedly.

'Corporal, Patience. Edmund just made corporal.'

Like most nine-year-olds, the child was undeterred by detail. 'Edmund's my brother,' she announced proudly.

'Mine, too,' Davey said, wondering why everybody laughed.

Everybody bar one, that is. Julia couldn't quite put her finger on it, but somehow the oldest girl, Faith, looked different today. As though she had a secret, with every intention of keeping it safe.

'That's a pretty boater, Faith. Have you done something different to your hair?'

'Like what, Mrs. M?'

'*Faith!* Few things rattled Rosie Blackstock, but bad manners was one of them. 'It's "Mrs. McAllister" to you, and don't you forget it!' She leaned across the table, this time her face red with shame. 'Fifteen,' she whispered. 'Between you and me,

119

that girl is growing up far too fast for comfort. Now then!' The mother hen bounced back. 'Who wants the honour of opening Edmund's letter?'

Julia glanced at Faith. The word that kept going round in her head was smug, but where did a fifteen-year-old get the money to buy boaters that had only just come into fashion? Or buy the expensive magazines that advertised this new look? American magazines at that. *Vogue, Harper's Bazaar.*

Oliver strode in, kissing Julia on the cheek, ruffling the twins' heads, and slapping his wife's bottom so hard that it wobbled.

'What-ho, sherry for breakfast.' He picked up the baby and swung her round over his head. 'Gracie girl, if there isn't a law to say every day should start off with Amontillado, there should be.'

While Rosie fussed for another glass, he leaned over and whispered so only Julia could hear. 'Any luck clearing your name?'

'I'd have better luck clearing the Augean Stables.' She gave him a brief summary of her visits with Tobias and Midge, how Jones wasn't answering his phone, and how she'd pretty much ruled out Percival Tarrant.

'My advice? Pay the man a call anyway.' Oliver glanced at his wife, busy pouring him a veritable goldfish bowl of sherry. 'Never know. Might be something in it for you. Ah, Rosie, Rosie, Rosie, now that's what I call a drink. Bottoms up, me hearties!'

Was Oliver slipping his daughter pocket-money on the quiet? By his own admission, Charity was the apple of his eye; he'd denied her nothing. Even though they didn't need the money she sent home — and he could easily have afforded to keep her here — once Charity started begging him to let her go into service to 'have an adventure, be independent, have a life of my own', he only pretended to hold out.

'Why don't you sell your investments?' Julia asked him at the time. 'Move to that mansion you keep promising Rosie? Give the children — all your children, Charity included — the comfort you keep teasing them about?'

Oliver wasn't a miser, hoarding for its own sake, so keeping his savings secret made no sense. Until he pointed out that he was itching harder than a Scot with fleas in his sporran to spring his wife with the biggest and happiest surprise of her life. The trouble was, Rosie wasn't good with secrets and he didn't want the cat out of the bag yet.

'Move too soon and you're talking servants, gardeners, the whole shebang, Mizz McAllister, and overnight you have kids grown up spoilt with an unearned sense of privilege, and this family's name is Blackstock, not Bratstock. I won't have my brood turning into wastrels.'

Another six months, a year at the most, he said, then he'd drop his bombshell and watch his family's eyes light up like fireworks at the Crystal Palace on Bonfire Night.

'That's the time the boys will need serious schooling.'

Until then, Rosie would have to stay in the dark, because that way, the children would continue to take nothing for granted, and it wasn't as though the girls were old enough to be married. Apart from Charity, of course, who had no intention of becoming a spinster, but at the same time, every intention of spreading her wings.

'Too many suffrage meetings, I reckon.' Julia remembered how his eyes had twinkled. 'She wants to spread her wings? Go ahead, I say. Let's see how long those wings flutter, cleaning up after idle rich folk day after day.'

He'd expected her to be gone for a couple of months.

It turned out to be for ever.

'I'll let you read Edmund's letter in peace,' Julia said, rising. 'Stay put, Oliver. I can let myself out.'

But as she turned to close the door, she couldn't resist framing the scene through an imaginary lens. Family gathered round the table, like Christmas morning. Father stroking his mutton chop whiskers, stringing out the suspense. Mother, biting her lip in happy anticipation. Baby chortling. Children from three to fifteen hanging on every word.

What a perfect, perfect picture that would make. Especially when, from this angle, she could incorporate Charity's photo propped up on the mantelpiece.

Chapter 16

Some lucky stiffs sail through life with barely a ripple on the sea of happiness. Collingwood veered more towards tropical typhoon, one in which his ship was taking in water, the crew constantly mutinied, and most of the topsails were shredded.

Admittedly, much of it was of his own making. He chose the police force, immersing himself in crimes of the worst kind, committed by criminals of the worst kind. It was hardly the most uplifting career. Right from the outset, though, he was determined to work his way up, no matter what, with the aim of retiring at the top of his profession. Log jams? Setbacks? Brick walls? Dead ends? Inevitable as night follows day, and with the primary role of the police being to prevent crime, you don't sign up for the job if you don't think you can make an appreciable difference.

Promotion, however, puts a man under pressure to marry, and ambitious as he was, after a wild sowing of oats, he'd been pretty much ready to settle down anyway. Emily — slender, blonde, shy little Emily — had been the perfect antidote to the liars and cheats, killers and thieves he confronted day in and day out. She was serenity amid chaos. Purity among filth. A beacon of light at which to aim his rudderless ship.

Hard to credit, but back then Collingwood found restraint captivating, detachment endearing, and then, despite signs emblazoned in fire, compounded the felony by not stopping to question his judgment. Still, a man believes what he wants to believe. The raging storm that was his marriage was his own bloody fault; he had no one to blame but himself, no choice but to ride it the best that he could.

But Alice? Oh, Alice was a different matter. Born nine months after he returned from a honeymoon in which he did, too late, question his judgment, she proved to be a bright-eyed, dancing spirit, calming the waters and lifting his heart.

How could he know it was the eye of the storm? That the White Plague would crush more than her body? That it would strangle that beautiful spirit?

As with many victims of consumption, she'd improve — one might almost say blossom — before the sweats, the coughs, the vomiting sank their teeth back in, leaving her weaker than ever. Watching blue veins pushing up through paper-thin skin, listening to the wheeze that, dammit, meant her heart was still beating, there were times when he longed to place a pillow over her face — end her torment and the hell with the consequences. So what if he hanged, providing Alice found peace? Then she'd open her eyes. Twist her little face in a smile. Hold out shaky arms for a hug.

Harder, Daddy. I won't break.

As long as Alice retained one spark, just one spark, of her true self, he was damned if he'd extinguish the flame. In any case, the doctor said it wouldn't be long. A little more laudanum nearer the end, and his daughter would not feel it coming.

'You been in the office all night?' Charlie Kincaid's lip curled when he asked the question.

'Paperwork.' Collingwood patted the heap of reports that had sobered him up. 'Not having the top brass accuse us of not pulling our weight.'

'Or airing the place.' Kincaid opened the window, letting in smoke from the factories, the smell of stale bloaters, and yelps of pain from the poor sod having his tooth pulled by the barber next door. 'Stinks like a bleedin' distillery in here.'

Collingwood closed the window. 'The Crown & Anchor had run out of ginger beer.'

Kincaid opened it again. 'Like you said. Not giving the top brass any excuse.'

'Excellent. No need to resign, I'll have choked to death.' Collingwood began pacing. Anything to block out the torture next door. 'Now what's so urgent, you need to drag me away from the delights of filling in forms?'

'Thought you'd prefer a verbal report, than a written one.'

'Especially when the written ones resemble two dozen millipedes drowning in ink.'

Kincaid shot him a ha-ha-very-funny smile. 'Anyway. Tobias Wood would be *delighted* to take my portrait. Assuming I could afford his services, without robbing a bank.'

'Kindly make sure it's not mine.'

'Do I look daft enough to come away empty-handed?' Kincaid stuffed tobacco in his pipe and lit it. 'High quality, high prices our Mr. Wood, but despite my expressing an interest in nudies and putting out feelers subtle and not, our man didn't bite.'

'Nothing, then.'

'Did I say that? Because arithmetic mightn't be my strong point, but it strikes me that our Mr. Wood needs to take an awful lot of portraits to sustain the generous donations to his church, while remaining tailored to within an inch of his life.'

'Hm.'

Collingwood intended to mull that over for a bit. Instead, he mulled over how a war-weary colour sergeant, who'd seen things no man should see, and done things no man should be ordered to do, still counted himself among those lucky stiffs sailing the sea of contentment. His secret, of course, was a fiery redhead he'd married before Noah built the Ark, and who remained as devoted to him as he was to her, the way it had been from the day they tied the knot.

'Wood the only photographer in the area, apart from Whitmore's?' he asked eventually.

'Nope. Belmont by name, Belmont by location, but apart from being more inclined to take my hand than my photo, there's nothing untoward about call-me-Midge that I could tell. Photographically speaking, that is.'

'Do we have cause for arrest? Take the opportunity to search his premises?'

'A mince here, a flick of the hair there? Hardly the most compelling of grounds, and besides, if we nicked every shirt lifter in Oakbourne, the cells would be overflowing in half an hour.' Kincaid jabbed his pipe in mock accusation. 'Imagine what the top brass would say about *that*.'

Good night, Boot Street. 'At the risk of repeating myself, nothing, then?'

Kincaid let out a low, throaty chuckle. 'And at the risk of repeating myself...'

'There's yet another happy snapper on our patch?'

'Not exactly.' Kincaid leaned against the desk and crossed his legs at the ankles, while Collingwood paced. 'Oliver Blackstock. You asked me to check his financial position. Well, guess who runs a low-scale photographic supplies shop, yet owns three houses — not palaces, admittedly, but not fleapits either — over Mitchell Street way, and rents two rooms in a fourth?'

'Good work, Charlie. In fact, bloody excellent work.'

'Save your superlatives, Inspector, the Kincaid isn't finished.' He shot his famous broad wink. 'Ask me what these three upright citizens have in common. Or rather, who they all have in common.'

Collingwood stopped pacing.

'Bull's eye,' Kincaid said. 'Choose yourself a coconut, Johnny C, because yep. The fragrant Mrs. McAllister paid a visit to each of these establishments over the course of the past twenty-four hours.'

Collingwood couldn't quite decide whether he'd chosen the wrong profession — his sergeant making miles better progress than him — or whether that cell at Bedlam was looming closer than ever. What did doctors say was the definition of insanity? Repeating the same actions over and over, and expecting the results to be different?

Over and over, he'd tried ruling Julia out. Over and over, the results were the same.

'You know what I think, Charlie?' Collingwood reached for his jacket. 'I think I need a Brownie box camera. Don't suppose you happen to know any shops that sell such things around here?'

Which is how he came to be crossing the street to Blackstock Photographic Supplies when a certain chief suspect came swanning out. Coincidence? Possibly. If ducks wore braces.

'Why, Inspector Collingwood, if I didn't know better, I'd say you were following me.'

'Then you'd be wrong, Mrs. McAllister.' Collingwood saluted the constable trying unsuccessfully to blend into the doorway of a haberdashery shop. 'He's the one following you, not me. Are you all right? Only you seemed to miss your step when you saw me.'

She was wearing duck egg blue this time. From the froth of feathers on top of her head, to the dainty kid shoes with fashionably elongated toes. He'd seen whiter faces on ghosts.

'Thought I heard a bicycle behind me. Tripped getting out of the way.'

'Please. Allow me.' He knelt to retrieve the contents of the reticule she'd dropped when she stumbled.

'I can manage perfectly well, thank you.' Her smile was as false as Charlie Kincaid's mother-in-law's teeth. 'You know what we women are like —' giggle, giggle — 'stashing silly trifles we'd rather gentlemen didn't see.'

'Luckily for you, Mrs. McAllister, policemen aren't gentlemen.'

He picked up a perfume bottle. He told himself he was passing a purely professional eye over it before sniffing its citrus scent and handing it back. As for the rest of the "trifles" spilling over the pavement, they were pretty much what one would expect. A small beaded coin purse with kiss clasp. Keys. Two handkerchiefs, one embroidered with T in the corner. (T?) An embossed silver calling card case. Small revolver…

This woman never ceased to amaze him.

'Most women carry powder puffs.'

'I'm not most women.'

'I'd noticed.'

He weighed the revolver in his hand. Sniffed the barrel. British Bulldog, fifteen-yard firing range.

'Interesting that you feel the need to carry a revolver, Mrs. McAllister.'

'Really? And why is that, Inspector?'

He dangled it from his little finger. 'Because Lily Atkins, Bridget O'Leary and Nellie Stern were all killed with such a weapon.'

Chapter 17

How do you define fear? The punch in the stomach? Lungs that stop working? Knees that buckle?

He knows. Then almost immediately, even before Julia's bag hit the ground, she adjusted the assertion. *He knows, but cannot prove it.*

'…all were killed with such a weapon.'

Was this a joke? Only Julia knew about the revolver. THE revolver. The bastard framing her couldn't possibly know that.

But the wolf's eyes were cold, his voice colder still.

The girls had been shot, and suddenly fear turned to terror. To chest pain, to dizziness, and nausea so bad that she nearly threw up on the cobbles.

'Not this weapon,' she somehow managed to croak.

'Worryingly, I'm inclined to agree with you. Now if you'll excuse me —' Collingwood helped her to her feet, and tipped his hat — 'I need to see about buying a Brownie box camera.'

Brownie box camera her bustle. He'd made the connection between Oliver, the girls, French postcards and her. Just not strong enough to secure a conviction.

It was too late to warn Oliver. By the time she found a telephone, Collingwood would be there. Thank God she'd confided in him the other night! Oliver was smart. He'd bluff his way through; he could talk his way out of Armageddon, that man.

Once round the corner, Julia slumped against the wall, amazed her legs had kept her upright that long.

'Are you all right, dear? You look terribly pale.'

'I … had a bit of a shock.' Her eyes filled with tears as she thanked the old lady who'd rushed forward to help, and whose kindness caught her off guard. 'I'm over it now. Honestly.'

She'd had close calls before, admittedly none as close as this, but it was only in the past couple of years that she'd grown complacent, and complacent means vulnerable. Julia would not make that mistake in the future.

It was easy to pretend that life runs as normal. An art she'd practised her entire life. But tonight she would put into practice the plans she made after Sam died. The plans she'd honed since Collingwood first set foot in her shop —

No, it can't be!

She wasn't halfway across Oakbourne Common before her heart stopped. Literally.

Psychiatrists talk about fight or flight. What they don't mention is the third reaction to terror. The total, uncompromising immobility that stops you from running, stops you from fighting, what, in the Army, is called cowardice but everywhere else is called freezing.

Paralyzed, Julia could only watch that familiar strutting walk, that military build, the distinctive tip of the head on one side.

The sun shall be turned into darkness — Quotes tumbled into one another. — *and the moon into blood* — Only this time, they reverberated in the same monotone he used to spit them out. Timed with the same vicious rhythm when fists collided with flesh. *They that wait upon the Lord* (thud) *shall renew their strength* (thud), *and shall mount up with wings like eagles* (thud, thud, thud). New Testament, Old. Memories hurtled back, brutal, relentless, and that's when Julia knew. *The Devil cannot die.*

She wanted to reach for the revolver. Put it to her head. Why not? There was no place to hide. But her hands had become stone; she couldn't move if she tried.

Then the Devil bent down. A small child ran into his arms. And Julia's knees finally betrayed her.

It was not the Devil. This was a man. A father. A loving husband home from the wars.

Sinking on to a park bench, she waiting for the shaking to subside. The Devil was dead, and that's how he'd stay.

Shot, and buried in an unmarked grave.

Chapter 18

'Welcome, Mrs. McAllister, welcome indeed.'

Despite Rosie's depiction of a man with a nose like a woodsaw and a voice like a train in a tunnel, Percival Tarrant turned out to be a very handsome, very wealthy man, living in a very handsome, very wealthy neighbourhood. And when it came to modern mansions, none was more elegant, more spacious, or indeed more impressive than Bay Tree Villa. Rising four storeys from a wide, sweeping drive, from its narrow arched windows to its symmetrical turrets, this house had gothic revival written all over it. Right down to the orangery on the right of the house, as you faced it.

'I appreciate you meeting me at short notice, Mr. Tarrant.'

Was there time to save another girl's life before Julia's moonlight flit? Probably not, but Collingwood hadn't arrested Julia yet, and until the moment she stopped flying McAllister colours, by God, she'd keep trying.

'My pleasure entirely.' Tarrant's voice might well betray a genetic fault, but his delivery was smoother than fifty-year-old cognac, and it was easy to picture this lean, angular man with his lean, angular moustache gliding round military clubs, charming his audience into conversations about naked girls, fantasies, and solutions to marital frustrations. 'Oliver said you might be paying a professional visit. Not using that thing, I hope?'

Julia placed the box camera on the table. Behind her, the butler closed the door without sound. 'No, but one never knows what scenes one might capture on one's travels. I would be lost without this little treasure.'

In truth, she'd grabbed it at the last moment, knowing Constable Bloodhound would have no trouble convincing himself that photographer plus camera equalled professional assignment. What he wouldn't know, of course — at least she bloody well hoped so — was that no portrait taken by "this thing" would be anywhere near up to scratch.

'Enterprising, as well as beautiful. I'm impressed.'

Tarrant motioned for her to take a seat on his embroidered ivory silk sofa. On the way over, she'd imagined his home life to reflect the environment he trawled. Dark brown leather wing chairs, busy wallpaper, low ceilings to muffle the noise. The contrast couldn't be greater. Here, mahogany panelled walls, which could have been overpowering, were offset with floor-to-ceiling bookcases, floor-to-ceiling windows, floor-to-ceiling drapes … and it had to be said, the distance between floor and ceiling was considerable. Mr. Tarrant, it seemed, revelled in light and space. There was nothing fashionably cluttered in here. Julia's pretty beaded brocade shoes almost disappeared in his red, patterned carpet.

'Coffee?' Tarrant asked.

'Lovely.'

Of course, the monster might well turn out to be Tobias Wood, threatened by a woman operating in a strictly male preserve and desperate to retain balance and order. Or Midge the planner, who thinks a long, *long* way ahead, concealing his hatred of women with smoothness and charm — but at the same time, like Jack the Ripper, finding justification for his twisted emotions. Julia wasn't prepared to take that chance, but the short timescale meant she had to work quickly, and be selective in who she approached. That ruled out the elusive Augustus Jones, but what could she lose, talking to the man who bought Frenchies and flip books from Oliver Blackstock, and touted them round gentlemen's clubs?

'You must see my latest acquisition.' Monet. You don't see many of those in the average parlour. 'One of his early Dutch landscapes, and utterly delightful, don't you agree?'

The first skill a photographer masters is patience. Taking a tour of rooms that gave the National Gallery a run for its money, Percival Tarrant proved to be a smooth-talking ladies-man (despite a wife somewhere in Surrey, who Oliver maintained he never bothered with): intelligent, cultured, in fact exceptionally good company. But when the sand is slipping through the timer at alarming speed, fifteen minutes can feel like fifty. Julia feared he would never get down to business.

'Oliver vouched for you, which is good enough for me,' Tarrant said at last. 'Tells me you're looking to extend your portfolio, and I can certainly help with that. The demand for postcards and flip books is still commercially strong,' he added. 'Insatiable, in fact, some might say.'

'Good news is always welcome.'

'When it comes to the tastes of the discerning gentleman, slide shows are becoming increasingly popular. Might this be of interest to you?'

Slide shows? What were they? 'Absolutely.'

'Good, because images of young men mother-naked sell for blissfully rewarding rates. Greek love being forced to hide itself, and all that. If you find the concept offensive — and frankly I wouldn't blame you — let me stress there's no shortage of bankers, civil servants, indeed, Members of Parliament, who pay handsomely to watch nubile young women frolicking about in the flesh. And that's merely the start, Mrs. McAllister. I have high hopes for the latest innovation. Projections on a screen, which are animated at such speed that the person, or persons, appear to be moving.'

'I'd be very interested in compiling slide slows of ladies, Mr. Tarrant, and if this also involves getting in on the ground floor of the moving-picture industry, then consider me very, *very* interested.' It's said you can't lose what you never had. An hour earlier, Julia knew nothing about these amazing developments, involving skills she'd loved to have mastered. So why did it ache that she missed her chance to make spectacular slide shows of Victoria Falls? Or produce moving pictures of rain forest tribes and stampeding zebra?

'Talking of short notice, you would be doing me a huge favour, Mrs. McAllister, if you could accommodate a certain client of mine. A High Court judge — no names, of course — has been pestering me for more and more saucy French postcards, and with demand outstripping supply at the present, I haven't been able to meet his requirements.'

What could she say? 'Then let's not keep M'Lud waiting.'

'I could arrange for the models to call at your studio tomorrow, if that is convenient?'

'This afternoon would suit better.' It would take her mind off the packing, as well as her last chance to help two young women boost their meagre income, and besides, who knows when a girl might need to keep on the right side of a High Court judge?

'I won't forget this.' Tarrant reached for paper and ink on the antique inlaid writing bureau. 'What address shall I send the models to?' Was he genuinely in the dark, or was Tarrant bluffing? Because from the moment she walked up the drive, it struck Julia that a 15mm British Bulldog revolver was the perfect choice for an articulate upper class murderer.

***

'I thought it was a bloke, that soldier in the grey uniform and red cuffs at the Music Hall last night.' Bug poked her in the ribs. ''Ere. You ain't listening to me, are yer? I said I thought it was a bloke, right up the end, when she threw her cap in the air and her hair fell past her shoulders.'

'Mmm.'

Buoyed up by the prospect of freedom, Julia rehearsed her escape route for the fiftieth time. Flag down a hansom to Victoria Station, the gondolas of London according to Mr. Disraeli, which a constable can't follow. Make sure to switch cabs two or three times —

'Not alive, are they?' Bug peered suspiciously at contents of the jar standing on the counter of the shop.

'Mmm.'

Get the boat train to Dover. France. Europe. Anywhere in the world. She would be free! A spider on the wind, photographing anything and everything that took her fancy, anywhere she liked.

'Do you eat 'em, play with 'em, or feed 'em to the polie bears at the zoo?'

'Mmm.'

She mustn't, absolutely mustn't, allow herself to be distracted by the thought that another girl might die, if she left. That was the job of the police. It was definitely, DEFINITELY not her responsibility, so stop fixating on guilt, start concentrating on ways not to stand before the gallows.

'Bet they bite, though.'

Julia forced herself to focus. 'Pickled herrings are only dangerous when you get between the mothers and their young. I've seen terrible injuries sustained by small boys brined to death.'

She'd left Bug five pounds in cash, nothing to worry about there. He'd get by, would Bug. He was smart, he was sharp, he was tougher than nails. Julia returned to her plans. The important thing was to leave the place looking as though she'd return any moment.

'You're doing it again,' Bug said.

'Huh?' Two days. That's how long she calculated it would be before Collingwood grew suspicious at not seeing her. Dotting all those 'i's takes time, when you're an ambitious inspector with other cases to solve —

'Not listening to me.'

— and in two days, she'd be in Paris.

'Technically, then, I am *not* doing it again.'

The trick was to make sure Bug didn't come after her.

'Them little sisters was good, too.'

For pity's sake, it wasn't like his Pa, leaving him with the priests. She'd only taken the kid in for the night. (All right, three). Made sure he had a few square meals. (All right, one continuous feed). And bought him a new pair of boots. It was not the same thing at all.

'The three girls with hair and skirts and bright green stockings like Alice in Wonderland, playing the mandarin.'

'Mandolin.'

'They weren't much older than me, and I can't even play a lousy penny whistle.'

'If it helps, you can't sing, either.' Actually, the sisters on the stage were much, much older than him. From a distance, yes, they could pass for fourteen. Keen eyesight put them closer to forty. The blessing and curse of a photographer's eye. 'Suppose,' she said, 'I was to say pots and pans. Or spiders.'

He jumped up and down. 'Code! Like French spies! You want another commotion.'

'Distraction would be more accurate.'

The constable was already on high alert. Too much drama, and he wouldn't take the bait.

'I can do zat.' Bug stretched his arms wide and twirled. 'I am a Fwench spy, I can do anyzing.'

'You knock those china dogs over, and it'll be the last zing you do.'

'Oops.' Bug waited until the cocker spaniel stopped rocking. 'Ven do you vant me to start?'

'First, you have to make up your mind. Are you a French spy, or Prussian?'

'Frussian. And since you got your hat on, I'm guessing I start now.'

'You guess right.' Julia glanced across the street. 'Nothing to frighten the horses, please. A minor distraction to let me slip out unnoticed.'

'Who's in charge of the shop while you're gone?'

'You are, and these pickled herrings are for your tea.'

'Cor!' Faster than lightning, a small hand unscrewed the jar and shoved one of the contents into his mouth whole.

'I said tea.'

'You said I'm in charge, and on my watch, the manager eats when he likes. All right, all right, I'm goin'.'

And so much for don't frighten the horses. Before she could blink, the handsome grey pulling the delivery cart owned by Stamford & Sons, Bakers and Confectioners on James Street, was rearing and kicking, whinnying and snorting, trying to buck free of its traces. Apparently, something had stung it on its soft underbelly, poor thing, and in a particularly delicate part of its anatomy, too.

Julia was gone before the first loaf hit the cobbles.

***

'Hello, Miss. I'm Beryl.'

'I'm Dora.'

'No one calls her that, though. We call her Cocoa.'

'On account of how much I drink.'

'She means cocoa, not booze.'

The first thing that struck Julia about Percival Tarrant's models was how short they were. Barely up to her armpit. The second thing was how nervous they were. (For pity's sake, what kind of dragon had he painted her?) And the third thing, and there was no way to wrap this up nicely, was just how incredibly unattractive the girls were. Or how repulsive the smell of mothballs.

Lily, bless her, was never what you'd call a beauty, Nellie sported a squint, and the exotic beauty of Anna Chen, "the Rose of Shanghai", was disfigured by burns on the left side of her face. Those were challenges Julia could work with, though, especially given Lily's larger-than-life personality. But to say a photographer had their work cut out with this pair was an understatement. Moles and warts all over the place, and that's with them both fully clothed.

'Can we take our cordial now, Miss?'

Muffled by the heavy camera cloth as much to deaden the stink of mothballs as prepare for work, Julia assumed she'd misheard, but no. Upside down through her lens, she watched both girls swig from a little brown bottle until it was drained.

'There's no question of a photo shoot, if you two are unwell,' Julia said firmly. Sod how desperate Tarrant was to please his Lordship, or how badly the girls needed the money. She wasn't taking advantage of ill health. 'Mr. Tarrant can jolly well rearrange the appointment —'

'No, no, it's not that, Miss.'

'Just that me and Cocoa is cousins —'

'— and neither of us likes women,not in this photo sense —'

'— then Pandora showed us how drinking this cordial makes it easier to … y'know … put up with.'

'She was right, too —'

Wait, wait, wait. They swallowed drugs to calm their nerves? Percival Tarrant, how dare you.

'There's a first time for everything,' Julia said softly, 'but the important thing to remember is this. Don't do anything you don't want to. Either of you. There's no shame in saying no.'

'It's not new. We done it loads of times, haven't we, Beryl?'

'Loads.'

'But like I said. Kissing, rubbing, all that other stuff? It's not natural.'

'Especially us being cousins.'

Julia's chest tightened. 'Slow down. Are you saying you've done more than pose nude?'

Beryl nudged her cousin in the ribs. 'You forgot, didn't you?'

'Ooooh, sorry, sorry, Miss!' Red-faced and flustered, Cocoa fished into her pocket and came out with an envelope containing a set of postcards. 'Mr. Tarrant said to give you these, asks if you can make tons more like 'em.'

Mother of God. These weren't saucy postcards or What-The-Butler-Saw. This was explicit Sapphic love.

'How often do you pose for photographs like these?' Julia asked.

The girls exchanged glances. 'Once a fortnight maybe?'

'We do the other stuff more often. Once a week at least.'

Silence filled the room. 'What other stuff?' Julia said eventually.

'It's not so bad.'

'I mean, it's not like the men touch us or nothing.'

'They just watch.'

No shortage of bankers, civil servants, indeed, Members of Parliament, who pay handsomely to watch nubile young women frolicking about in the flesh.

'Rich gentlemen, what buys us pretty things. Look!'

With a flurry of mothballs, Beryl pulled down the collar of her cheap lawn blouse to reveal a cross of low quality gold. Julia's stomach dropped to the floor.

'If lie back and think of England's what married wives do —' Cocoa giggled, as the drug kicked in. 'I'll take guineas over the Union Jack any day.'

'And it's Mr. Tarrant who arranges these … assignments?' Julia clarified.

'Pandora,' Beryl corrected. 'Pandora sorts it out.'

'Pandora's nice. She looks after us.'

'Oh, dear,' Julia said, 'my lens has broken. Looks like we can't do the shoot, after all.'

Pushing the girls out the door with a promise that they'd still be paid, she'd blame the negatives failing, she tasted bile in her throat. Risqué postcards were one thing. The models pose, they're in control, they decide how far they're prepared to go. Girls drugged into prostituting themselves for the sake of a few gewgaws was something else entirely.

Someone, somewhere had to stop it.

It might as well be her.

Chapter 19

The despondent young clerk in the pinstripe suit, he of the nervous condition that made him polish his spectacles over and over, held open the door of the tea rooms. Julia thanked him, but was pretty sure he didn't hear. Hardly surprising. Half of Willow Walk's regulars came here out of loneliness, the other half to submerse themselves in muted chatter and sponge cake, poached eggs and bone china, to cushion themselves from the pain of reality.

That afternoon, she understood why. She, too, needed to lose herself. To think. To plan. To kick herself for not asking who this Pandora was and where she could find her, then kick herself harder for not leaving tonight.

'The full tea, please.'

You'd think a mix of anger, revulsion and nerves would leave a girl queasy. Julia was nothing short of ravenous, which only a mountain of savoury puffs and dainty sandwiches was going to cure. Especially when they were followed by rock cakes and scones piled with jam and rich, clotted cream.

'With extra shortbread.'

Frussian spies were notoriously unreliable when starved.

She turned her chair for a better view of the door, because if you're going to draw up a strategy, you might as well do it watching for 'T'. Unfortunately, the only thing in Julia's line of vision was the clerk dragging his black patent shoes through the revolving doors of the bank, to a job he obviously hated. Small wonder he'd developed a nervous condition. The poor sod fell into both categories of Willow Walk's patrons.

Right then. Down to business. Tomorrow night — no ifs, no buts, no matter how strong the pull — she would flag down that hansom, and come what may, the woman who called herself Julia McAllister would vanish. The big decision was how to best spend her one remaining day. Trying to prove her innocence? Or work to closing down Tarrant's operation?

Pimping didn't evolve with the Industrial Revolution, and Julia wasn't naïve enough to imagine shutting off his oxygen would be the end of it, or that another wouldn't spring up to take its place. But it broke her heart to see vulnerable sixteen-year-olds duped into believing they were doing well out of engaging in incestual sex, simply to satisfy High Court judges, who should — and did — know better.

Ting! Two elderly widows in black bombazine.

Julia's eyes wandered over the same old crowd taking the same old tea and eating the same old Madeira cake at the same time every day. The spinsters, the old men, the widows, the close friends who sat talking about one another behind each other's backs, wearing smiles as wide as the ocean.

Why is it dogs always race to the front door when somebody knocks? Lily's giggle echoed in her memory. *I mean, it's never for them, is it?*

Such vibrancy, such vitality, such youth, those girls. But what they'd give now, eh, to take boring tea and tasteless Madeira, moving from one empty day to the next.

Julia's throat tightened at the injustice of it all. Was there a way to find their killer, clear her name, and put Tarrant and his accomplice out of business in the one day she had left? Of course not. But as long as Collingwood was in charge, the monster who'd robbed them of their futures would at least be hunted without mercy.

Or would he?

Collingwood was conscientious, relentless and clever, but he was also ambitious. Cracking this case would be enormous kudos for him. Did it matter he didn't arrest the right person? Proving guilt was the job of the Prosecutor, not him, and as things stood, the Prosecution had enough circumstantial evidence to convict Julia seven times over. The worry was, with three murdered girls and a suspect vs. a young man beaten to death and no suspects, would he take the easy option to clear his casebook and thus be assured of another step up the ladder?

No shortage of bankers, civil servants, indeed, Members of Parliament, who pay handsomely to watch nubile young women frolicking about in the flesh.

Damn. Just when she had everything planned. New life, new name, new freedom, the kaleidoscope that was India, the wild that was the West… Julia ran her hand over the passport in her bag. Please don't be a waste of 13/6d.

'The tea's that good here, Mrs. McAllister?' *Speak of the devil.*

'The jam roll is irresistible.'

'You don't know how relieved I am you don't fancy the tarts,' Collingwood replied with a wry smile.

Common sense told Julia that senior officers don't shield their eyes with their hands and squint through the dimpled glass windows of genteel establishments if they intend to arrest a suspect. And they'll certainly wait outside, rather than pick their way through a forest of feathered hats and Darjeeling to take a seat that left the suspect's escape route wide open.

Unfortunately, common sense and churning stomachs don't always communicate.

'My, my, what a witty re-torte.'

'Not as witty as the lady photographer who likes to have her cake and eat it. Preferably while giving my constable the slip.'

If there's one advantage of Society's insistence that women wear gloves outside the house, it's that cotton does at least absorb sweat.

'He's not here?' Julia peered up and down the street, as though completely mystified. Or as mystified as a girl can look, when her heart's threatening to crack through her ribcage and her mouth's so dry she can only croak. 'Seems I'm so accustomed to my uniformed shadow, that I don't even notice him now.'

'Not surprising.' Collingwood helped himself to a cucumber sandwich off the tiered silver rack. 'Since you're so accustomed to giving him the slip. Oh, these are delicious. Mind if I have another?'

'Take them all, I've finished.' Strange how fast ravenous appetites fade. Julia studied him over the rim of her teacup. 'Do I assume you're now the proud owner of a Brownie box camera?'

'Sadly, no. I'd like to have discussed the concept in detail with the proprietor himself, but Mr. Blackstock was out. Apparently stocking up on glass plates.'

Well done, Angus! Still got your employer's back. 'Oliver was telling me only yesterday how his stock room was so bare, he was thinking of renting half out as lodgings.'

'A home for the mentally weak, I presume,' Collingwood replied. 'As I was leaving, I was accosted by a small child shaped like a cricket ball, who told me her brother had just made a purple for the Army.'

'Patience.'

'I'm doing my best.' Collingwood polished off the last tiny triangular sandwich, then proceeded to work his way through the rock cakes. 'My officer reports that you own one of these new Brownie cameras. Took it to one Bay Tree Villa this morning, in fact.'

Julia munched through a scone as an excuse not to answer.

'Property of one Percival Tarrant,' he added. 'Bay Tree Villa, of course. Not the camera.'

She gave him a mouth-filled *mmmff* and a nod.

'Perhaps you'd do me the honour of showing me how these contraptions work?'

'Any time, Inspector.'

He laid down his napkin. 'No time like the present.'

Damn. 'Excellent.' Julia squeezed out a smile, and wondered what she, too, would give to take tea at the same time every day, with the same old Madeira cake and the same old venomous friends. And was it stepping out of this cosy cocoon that propelled Oakbourne into focus? The disgust at young girls being duped? The poignancy of grief? The fact that this was the last time Julia would ever look at this view? This street? This town?

Who knows, but like fitting a new lens to her camera, every sound, every scent, every detail became sharp. A rolling spectrum of colour and mood, peppered with the chimes of St. Oswald's, the rustle of silks, the song (can you believe) of a goldfinch singing its heart out from its prison as it was carried in its cage through the streets. Door knockers gleamed like gold nuggets in the afternoon sun — but what of that other gold? The golden age of industrialisation? At the end of the street, looking eastwards, not west, the spectrum changed out of all recognition. Smoke belched from the breweries, factories, refineries and mills, clogging the lungs of the workers and sending them to paupers' graves ahead of their time. Over there, clangs from the tinker's cart replaced the clop of gentlemen's broughams, children in dirty shawls played in the gutters, and babies wailed with the croup, while their fractious mothers calmed themselves down with gin.

Two worlds. One jewel-bright with respectability, at least on the surface. The other gloomier than the Black Forest in winter, spreading all the hope and joy of a tumbrel.

'I have a theory about your canal victim,' Julia said, wishing she hadn't brought tumbrels into the picture. 'I think I might know who he is.'

Admittedly it was a long shot, but wasn't it strange that Dickie Lloyd's understudy was still standing in at the Cadogan Street Music Hall after all this time?

'The comedian?' Collingwood's eyebrows shot up.

'Of course, he could have done a runner.'

'Not an uncommon occurrence in the entertainment industry, but after four days and no clues, I freely admit I passed desperate a long, long way back.'

Julia was wrong. There was, in fact, a third world in Oakbourne. A watery ribbon with a fluctuating population, that united and divided both halves of the town, and was responsible for its prosperity every bit as much as its misery...

Maybe it was Disraeli's description of cabs, the gondolas of London, that brought it to mind, but another of his quotes sprang into her head. *Action may not always bring happiness; but there is no happiness without action.* If, using the illusionist's age-old trick of distraction, Julia could set Collingwood on the canal killers' tracks, she would buy herself more time. Frankly, actions don't come much happier than that.

'Thank you.' He jotted *Lloyd, CSMH* in his notebook. 'I shall follow that up.'

Starting now — excellent! — by marching up to the constable outside Whitmore Photographic and laying into him in no uncertain terms. For the officer's part, it would have been comic, had his job not been on the line. His bulging eyes and dropped jaw showed he didn't understand how the object of surveillance could be in two places at once. He would swear on a whole stack of Bibles that Julia hadn't left the shop, and while feeling guilty for putting the poor man through Hell, disciplinary action was good for Julia. It confirmed the breathing space she so desperately wanted.

'You. Out.'

A jerk of the thumb was enough to show Bug that Collingwood meant business. The instant the boy left, Collingwood locked the door, turned the Open sign to Closed, and pulled down the blinds.

'Dear me, I don't know if I'm about to be robbed. Or molested.' *Keep it light, keep it light.* 'Should I call the police?'

But Collingwood's eyes were cold steel. All trace of urbanity vanished. Dipping into his inside pocket, he held out a photograph, reverse side facing her. The setting sun, slanting through the skylight, showed too clearly *Whitmore Photographic* stamped in purple ink. Julia put her hand over her mouth to keep the scones from returning.

'Do you recognise this woman?'

No, no, no, please no — Not Anna Chen, the gentle "Rose of Shanghai". Not Mollie Becks, "Scheherazade". Oh God, oh God, not Daisy!

Snatching it disguised any shaking. Don't be silly, she told herself, you're over-reacting. Did you recognise even *one* of Tobias Wood's models? Of course not. There are scores of girls in this business. She turned it over. Another racy pose. Girl putting on her pearls, head back, elbows out, and whoops, guess whose breasts burst out of her stays? Julia counted to three, then to five, before daring to look at the face —

'Elizabeth Mansell.'

There was no point in trying to hide it. Her only hope was to convince Collingwood that they were acquainted through other means, and this pose was part of the shock.

'Mother of God!' Julia shoved the photograph back in disgust. 'And her a schoolteacher, too!'

'Now a dead schoolteacher. At least we assume the body on the bed was Miss Mansell's.' Collingwood paused for effect. 'Hard to tell with her face shot to pieces.'

This wasn't real. Just a nightmare. Any moment, Julia would wake up, call at the Blackstocks to celebrate what would have been Charity's birthday. She would give them her love, flag down a hansom, leave Oakbourne, and never look back.

'W-when?'

'Yesterday morning, judging from the fact that she was found in her nightwear, and the sheets suggested the bed had been slept in. Alone, I might add.'

Julia's skin pebbled. She could actually feel her blood thicken. A girl who only posed three or four times, her last session months ago, is now dead? Simply for associating with Julia McAllister? 'I am truly sorry to hear that.'

'Which brings me to my problem, because, more fool me, I genuinely believe that you are. What can you tell me about Elizabeth Mansell?' The caged tiger returned to his pacing. 'Her headmaster paints a picture of a young lady who was well-respected and popular with staff and pupils alike. When she failed to turn up for school, he claimed he wasn't unduly worried. But the second morning? Without so much as a note? Despite asserting that his only concern was his employee's wellbeing, I suspect the headmaster went round to give her a piece of his mind. It was only when the neighbour said she was worried, having knocked several times and received no reply, that he, too, became alarmed and called for the landlord. Who promptly kicked the door in and made the grisly discovery.'

'I didn't know her well,' Julia replied. 'Our paths crossed in the post office from time to time, we'd engage in small talk —'

'Small talk? You?'

In a way, it was true. She hadn't gelled with Elizabeth the way she gelled with, say, Lily Atkins or Daisy. Agreed, the sessions were few and the relationship between them coolly professional, but Julia could honestly say she knew no more about Elizabeth Mansell after the last photo shoot than the first. Or had any deeper insight into her personality.

'Julia, look, I know you have something to hide, and I know it's connected to your past.'

'I don't have a "past".'

'Enough.' Collingwood stopped pacing and leaned in. 'I don't give a damn why you fabricated your marriage. I don't care how you somehow run a business when women have no legal rights. I don't care how — God help me, I don't even care why — you're hell bent on giving my constables the slip.' Grey eyes bored into hers. 'Whatever you tell me, I give you my word, it stays within these four walls. What I *do* care about is doing what I'm paid to do. Keeping Oakbourne safe. And the only way to ensure that happens is to catch the Purple Ink Killer, and enjoy watching him hang.'

Silence filled the room. Heavy. Thick. Like the fall of fresh snow. And as the sun dipped, twilight enveloped the shop, and all Julia could smell was *Hammam Bouquet*, radiating Eastern harems, steam baths and sex.

'I need a drink,' she said, reaching under the counter. Eighteen years old, the Glenlivet was rich, amber and peaty. You could almost smell the lochs and the heather and braes.

Crystal lips chinked.

'To Miss Mansell,' she said thickly.

They drank in silence. He poured another.

'To you, Mrs. McAllister.'

'To you, Inspector.'

'To us.'

'Too soon.'

'Too bad.'

He leaned closer. So close, she could smell the starch of his collar, felt his warm, fresh breath on her face, and suddenly her hands were shaking again, which had nothing to do with another girl's death, and now it was she who was leaning in —

His lips were soft. A butterfly touch. Hands cupped her face. The same strong, square hands she'd watched in the tea rooms. Hands that took their time compiling reports. Hands that took their time under the bed sheets…

The kiss deepened. In the last vestige of light, she saw two reflections entwined in the glass display cabinet. Saw he had green flecks in the grey of his eyes.

'I must go,' he rasped, minutes — weeks — hours — later, because suddenly time had no meaning. It had become fluid, artificial, unnatural even. Another dream. Another nightmare. Yet another illusion, because he made no effort to pull away.

The kiss was infinity. Another universe. Delicious, beguiling, a world without end. A world she could stay in, be safe, and forget.

Except she wasn't safe. Not with him.

He was the wolf, she was the quarry.

It was Julia who pulled away.

She couldn't forget, either. A fourth girl, viciously robbed of her future, with Julia's trade stamp left next to her body. That doesn't fade with a kiss. A kiss that was probably a trap. A means to get her to lower her guard.

Lighting the lamp in the corner, she was tempted to ask, 'Why aren't you arresting me?' except Collingwood wouldn't give a straight answer.

The shocking part was, she barely knew Elizabeth Mansell. Their paths might not have crossed in the post office, but their meetings were few, and to her shame, she'd actually forgotten about her. *Think. Think. Where did it start?* Julia hadn't approached her, suggesting she pose for the money. For once, it was the other way round. So which of her models recommended Elizabeth? If she could trace the link, she might trace the killer. But their last contact was months ago, and so much had happened since then: photoshoots, portraits, distressing *memento mori* like Flora. The sad truth was, business was business, and like it or not, memory faded like dust on the wind. She didn't even remember taking that picture.

'You called him the Purple Ink Killer,' Julia said.

'Don't, whatever you do, let the press hear you say that. I'm not giving this bast— this *brute* the satisfaction of notoriety, like Jack the Ripper.'

Hear, hear. 'You also said watching *him* hang.'

'In twenty-two years on the force, I've seen enough premeditated killers to last me a lifetime. Men mostly, though yes, sadly, women, who plot and plan and scheme and conspire. Without exception, they take satisfaction in their sport, and some even believe themselves so clever, they leave calling cards like this to taunt the police.' He slipped Elizabeth's picture back in his pocket, and picked up his hat.

'Mrs. McAllister is not such a person, and in any case, this isn't a woman's crime. But.' He unlocked the shop door.

'But?'

'Mrs. McAllister *is* hiding something.' Collingwood touched his hat brim. 'By the way, you should know I found your demonstration of the box Brownie extremely enlightening.'

'Only enlightening, Inspector? I was under the impression that you found the whole experience stirring.'

His chuckle carried down the street into the night.

Chapter 20

In a change from sensationalising of the incompetence of the police in their inability to identify the robbery victim by the canal, the evening headline of the *Oakbourne Chronicle* ran with the finding of the remains of one Cyril Strauss, found floating in the canal near Bridge Street.

Mr. Strauss, aged 26, of Cadogan Street, and employee of the Snowdon Lane branch of the West London Bank, apparently tied a heavy weight around his chest before jumping off the bridge. Whether the knot unravelled or the rope became frayed wasn't yet clear, but either way the unfortunate Mr. Strauss had broken loose from his moorings. 'At this stage, the police are unable to confirm whether this was suicide or murder, but sources close to the *Chronicle* say there were no signs of a struggle.'

Mr. Strauss appeared to have been in the water for several days.

Two in one day?

The Chief Inspector's fury was still rattling in Collingwood's head an hour after he'd left his superior's office.

What the *blank* was he trying to do, put him in the *blank-blank* hospital? For *blank's* sake, he was only one *blank-blank-blank* step away from *blank-blank* apoplexy. At this rate, his wife would be a widow by the end of the *blank* week.

Vaguely, Collingwood imagined the woman would shake his hand warmly and thank him.

'Are you listening to me, man?' He had half a mind to sack him, he'd bellowed. Relieve him of his post on the spot, he was clearly *blank-blank-blank-blank* incompetent. 'You can't prevent crime, you can't halt crime, you can't even solve crime, for God's sake. What *can* you *blank-blank-blank* do, eh?'

'Stand here and take a bollocking. Sir.'

'Christ, I'm *this close* from going to the gallows for striking you dead with this paperweight. You know what's stopping me?'

'A third corpse on the books in one day?'

'The time it would take for a newcomer to pick up on these investigations. Time we don't *blank-blank* have.'

Interesting that he mentioned bringing in an outsider, rather than taking over himself. For all his bully and bluster, though, he knew what Boot Street was up against. How the Purple Ink Killer could well turn out to mirror the nightmare that had become Jack the Ripper. Insatiable, unsolvable, spreading suspicion and fear. How the suicide's motive would, in all likelihood, remain a mystery, since few of these helpless, lost souls left a note. And how the canal victim's killers would probably get away with it. Random murder being well-nigh impossible to solve.

Not all Chief Inspectors were concerned purely with statistics, reports, and how well they reflected on them. But this one was. There was not one hope in Hell that he'd risk shit sticking to him.

The bells of St. Oswald's were chiming eight by the time his boss ran out of expletives, and Collingwood was starving. A handful of paper-thin triangles filled with see-through slices of cucumber don't stand by a chap for long. He bought a hot rabbit pie from a vendor on the corner, then too late discovered that gravy and enthusiasm made for a lethal combination. So much for his brand new suit jacket.

There was, of course, no question of going home to change it, much less sign-off from his shift. Murder, he'd found out to his cost, never sleeps. Which means police officers don't have that luxury, either.

Add on the usual drunkards, vagrants, street walkers, pickpockets and thieves, by the time he returned to Boot Street, the place was already a riot. Another hour, and even the rats would start plugging their ears.

'Whoa!' Collingwood put his arm out to help a staggering constable, whose uniform was covered in blood. 'What happened to you?'

'Three Irishmen, that's what happened to me. Felt the landlord of the *Greene Man* short-changed them and decided to wreck the pub in retaliation, to hell with everyone in it.' He snorted. 'My dad always told me, never go and break up a fight, the buggers'll turn on you instead, so what do I do? I join the police.'

He tried to wave away the inspector's assistance, but Collingwood wasn't taking no for an answer. With every officer stretched to his limit, he was far better placed to help the poor sod upstairs.

'Where did they get you?'

'Right hook to the nose —' The cause of his need to change before returning to shift — 'one attempt to dislocate my shoulder. The third landed a penalty kick in the goolies.'

Collingwood winced. 'At least you have the satisfaction of knowing your heroic intervention saved numerous civilians from injury.'

'Tell that to my balls.'

The accommodation for single policemen, regardless of rank, was on the top floor above the station. Constables slept four to a room: one iron bedstead per man, a chair and a locker each, and a table and dresser that they had to share. Needless to say — being an old building — there was no sanitation, and if Collingwood had been Catholic, he'd have crossed himself and offered up a prayer of thanks.

These depressing living conditions once served as married quarters, and indeed would have been his, had he not inherited his house after his parents died. And as much as he wanted to save the bleak, solid building that was Boot Street, if the station was demolished and a new one built, the men would be assured of better lodgings. Lighter and brighter for one thing. Hopefully more spacious. Decidedly more sanitary. In short, rooms that didn't make them envy the men downstairs in the cells, whose lodgings were at least temporary.

'I'm signing you off for the rest of this shift.'

'I'm fine —'

'That's an order.'

He was sending for a doctor, as well. The man's nose wasn't broken, but it needed stitching, and Collingwood wasn't convinced the shoulder was completely in place.

'Can't wait till we move to eight-hour shifts like the Met.' The constable groaned as he pulled off his boots. 'Don't suppose there's any news on when that's likely to happen, is there, sir?'

Try when unicorns grow wings. 'I've made the case to the Chief Constable more than once.'

In tune with Oakbourne's rapid expansion came the inevitable escalation in crime — and while twenty-eight shillings was an amply attractive enough salary, it wasn't proving attractive enough to balance long hours and poor living conditions, and just four Sundays off every year. Men simply weren't joining up. Unfortunately, Chief Constable and his Deputy felt that if it was good enough for them, while they were rising through the ranks, then it was more than good enough for police officers today.

'No one denies times are changing, Inspector —'

'— and for the better, we might add —'

'— but once we start going soft, it's a slippery road —'

Not for the first time, Collingwood felt there was a sign on the Chief Constable's door reading *Square One*. And underneath, *Welcome Back*.

'Sir?'

Charlie Kincaid closed the door to Collingwood's office in a bid to muffle the din. Nothing if not optimistic, that man.

'Tell me you have something, Charlie.'

'Do you want the good news or the bad news?'

'Let's get it over with.'

'Nothing on the schoolmistress's murder.' As usual, sergeant leaned, inspector paced. 'Three wise monkeys at every bleedin' turn. Nobody heard anything, nobody saw anything, despite — and this is what I find strange about this particular killing — it taking place in the morning.'

That worried Collingwood, too. It was an unusual — very unusual — time of day to commit murder, and he could tell himself until he was blue in the face that that little British Bulldog didn't smell like it had been fired recently. But the cold fact was, he'd caught his chief suspect coming out of premises that were already under suspicion, just two streets away from Elizabeth's lodgings, and very shortly after the murder took place. Did he mention, having taken great pains to give her tail the slip...

'What's the good news?'

'Who said I'd finished with the bad stuff?' Kincaid lit his pipe to the orchestral backdrop of foul-mouthed drunks, shrieking whores and police whistles. Back when he walked the beat, the police carried rattles. What a difference one little pea makes, eh? 'Cyril Strauss,' he said. 'By the way, did I thank you for allowing me to escort his mother to the mortuary?'

'You can make it up to me later.'

'Poor woman.' Kincaid ran his hand over his face, as though that would somehow erase the memory. 'Not just a case of having to identify her only child; I tell you, no one should be forced to look at a loved one who's spent three days underwater.'

That was another odd thing. Canals, by their very nature, are shallow. 'How come none of the barge people noticed a body in the water?'

It was the same question Kincaid had asked when they were fishing him out, but apparently it was all to do with shadows from the bridge meeting shadows from the tunnel. 'Seems our Cyril chose a spot three times darker than Hades, and of course the Southolt arm's part of the new network.' Not like the old days, before barges were fitted with engines and men "walked" the boats through the tunnels by lying on their backs and propelling the barge through with their feet. 'They'd have noticed him then. But not now. Not under steam.'

Collingwood sighed. 'Mr. Strauss didn't want to be found.'

That was hardly unusual. By the time it came to taking his own life, a man's thoughts were long past rational. At some point, he must have stopped to consider the impact on his mother, not having a grave to weep over, or even knowing what happened. But in his desperate, tangled mind, family and friends were better off without him, and if he disappeared — simply vanished off the face of the earth — they'd forget about him that much quicker, and be able to carry on with their lives that much easier. No expensive funerals to organise. No taking flowers to the cemetery out of duty on a Sunday. Better for everyone this way.

'The mother's too distraught to think straight. Won't leave the body, and is in too much shock to believe her son killed himself, poor cow.' Kincaid rocked on his heels. 'I'll go round first thing in the morning, see if her vigil's helped shed light on Cyril's motive, but at this stage, my advice is don't hold your breath.'

He puffed on his pipe while his inspector paced. 'Shut yer coal hole,' he said at length.

'If you think insulting me will get you fired, sergeant, you're way out of luck. I'm two men short as it is; the best I can offer you is demotion.'

'I'll take it, but before I cut the stripes off my uniform, you should know that that was my good news.' Kincaid shot his signature wink. *'Shut yer coal hole* was Dickie Lloyd's catchphrase, making your informant bang on the nail.'

Despite the mountain of tragedies, dead ends, threats and brick walls, Collingwood felt a spike of excitement. Boot Street was only a small District, with one inspector, one sergeant and eighteen men at full complement, which, of course, it currently wasn't, still being two short. But small means intimate. It means the patrolling officers knew every inch of their beat, and while some parts were rough — and getting rougher — and the station itself left much to be desired, the system worked well. Once you start absorbing Boot Street into a much larger district, Collingwood saw nothing but trouble.

'No kidding? A positive identification on our canal victim? Charlie, I could kiss you!'

'If it's all the same with you, sir, I'll delegate that particular pleasure to Mrs. Kincaid. She's always had a soft spot for you.'

'I was under the impression she hated me for the hours I make you work.'

'And if that's her soft spot, imagine what the rest of her's like.' There it was again. Laugh like the creak of a gallows chain. 'Your informant. Didn't happen say where they got the idea from, did they? About it being the comic from the Music Hall?'

'Sir Francis Drake, apparently.'

'Wish I hadn't asked.' Kincaid tapped his pipe out. 'Anyway, in between escorting Mrs. Strauss to the mortuary and getting nowhere with Elizabeth Mansell, I traipsed over to Dickie Lloyd's lodgings, and sure enough, everything's in its place: clothes brush, razor, cufflinks, comb, scissors, shaving brush, laid out like a surgeon's operating table. The neatest wardrobe I have *ever* poked around in; even the moths wore bow ties. I tell you, you've never seen so many snazzy outfits in your life. Shine on his shoes that'd put the military to shame, not a single sock was darned, and something else I've never seen in men's quarters before. Bottle upon bottle — and I'm talking fifteen, twenty — of frankly overpowering cologne.' He pulled a face. 'Funny bunch, theatre folk.'

'Hardly a moonlight flit, then.'

'Money in a clip under the mattress backs that theory, but the clincher? Newspaper clippings pasted floor to ceiling, along with posters, photographs, you name it. The young man on the walls was the young man beside the canal. No question of it. Dickie Lloyd.'

'Good work, Charlie.' *And good work, Julia McAllister.*

Outside Collingwood's office, the cussing, spitting and shouting ramped up to screaming pitch. When did it change, he wondered? When did the police stop being Robert Peel's lofty "civilians, members of the public, paid to give full-time attention to duties which are incumbent upon every citizen in the interests of community welfare and existence." Did change roll in with the factories and mills, the poverty and the shame, the dirt, the disease and the dust? Or was this lack of respect a consequence of progress? That the more overcrowded cities become, and the further their inhabitants removed from open environments in tune with nature, the more bestial and feral they become?

Whatever the answer, the protests and yelps, scuffles and yells had become such a common occurrence that Collingwood failed to notice them anymore. What did that say about him?

He glanced at the sword mounted on the wall below a portrait of Queen Victoria. Purely ceremonial, it was only worn with uniform on special occasions, a mark of his rank. But there were times, he remembered them well, when hangers — similar to a naval cutlass, with curved blades — were issued to constables during riots or serious public disturbances. An effective deterrent, if ever there was one.

He leaned his hands on the windowsill and stared down a street punctuated by gas lamps, standing stiff-backed like soldiers guarding the night. You'd think lighting would make Oakbourne safer, yet more and more frequently Collingwood found himself seeking authorisation from two Justices of the Peace to have his men issued with hangers for personal protection at night. Cutlass training took place on an increasingly regular basis. He himself often carried a firearm after dark.

He couldn't, obviously, pinpoint the moment Her Majesty's police force lost the admiration of the people they signed on to protect. But was he really peering into a future in which foot patrols were armed with more than a truncheon and whistle?

Fortunately, he didn't have a crystal ball. He left that for the psychics. More accurately, the growing number of con artists peddling sketchy scenarios and dangerously false hopes to vulnerable folk in need of comfort and faith. The point being, he couldn't put this bloody report off any longer. Collingwood uncapped his pen and pulled out a clean sheet of quarto.

Writing was cathartic. Reports forced him to summarise a day's work in one or two pages, and when matters are condensed, they become that much easier to deal with. In this, he was aided by the exquisite beauty of his tortoiseshell pen, its fourteen carat nib glinting like a harlot's smile in the lamplight. Beauty was also therapeutic.

He began by outlining the successful identification of both the canal victim and the suicide. Progress which would stave off the Chief Inspector's apoplexy enough for him to acknowledge it was a leap towards finding out who kicked a young man's organs to pulp, and accept that a multiple killer along the lines of Jack the Ripper was hardly going to turn himself in. Some wanted to be found. This one didn't. If these types weren't collared within one or two days, they were in for the long haul.

All of which ought to give Collingwood pleasure as he wrote. Another weight off his back. Instead, all he could think of, as St. Oswald's struck ten, was *THAT* kiss.

And the prospect of Julia McAllister on his front.

Chapter 21

Around the time the contents of a juicy rabbit pie were acquainting themselves with the fine woollen blend of Collingwood's jacket, Julia was taking a telephone call from Oliver Blackstock.

'If you want to save yourself four pence and a trek out to Southolt,' he whispered, 'our good friend, Augustus Jones, is in the shop at the moment, stocking up on supplies.'

Two hours ago, she'd have thanked him warmly, and pleaded a prior appointment. Then again, two hours ago, she didn't know Elizabeth Mansell was dead.

As it happened, she hadn't saved four pence. The instant Collingwood left the shop, she'd grabbed Bug, shoved eight pennies in his hand — the standard fare, penny a mile — pushed him on the bus to Southolt, with strict instructions to find out anything, everything, he could about Jones Photographic.

'Cor! An adventure!'

'I don't expect you —'

'Never bin on a bus!'

'— to pick much up infor—'

'Or to Southolt.'

'Are you listening to me?'

'That's rich, coming from you! Course I'm listening, look at me. Ears flappin' like bloomers on the line in the breeze — *ow*.'

'Less about bloomers, please. More about gossip, and you picking up as much of it as you can, as quickly as you can.'

'Hey, I'm a world expert, when it comes to picking up dirt.' Bug twisted his head on one side. 'See the back of me neck?'

'Are those carrots growing under your hairline?'

Time was certainly of the essence, if Julia was to thwart Tarrant's sordid career before she left, but even so. Who could have predicted errand boys would be so fast, much less so efficient?

'Them buses is tremendous!' Bug's cheeks were flushed with excitement, green eyes glistening when he got back. 'Went upstairs both rides, and sat right at the front like I was driving the horses. Felt a right toff, I did.' Coppers well spent in every sense. 'First off.' He saluted. 'This bloke's photies ain't got *nothing* on yours. Clear enough, mind, but when it comes to compervision —'

'Composition.'

'That's what I said. When it comes to compervision, you're *streets* ahead of this Jones bloke.'

'Is the shop open?'

'Not sure. Blinds is up, sign says closed, but kids begging on the corner says it's often like that. Thing is, your bloke's up to his noseholes in debt. Gambler.' Bug tapped the side of his nose. 'Big time.' *Interesting.* 'Dog tracks is just round the corner, see. That's where he spends most afternoons and evenings, but they says he bets on the gee-gees as well.' He sniffed. 'Mug's game, that. Oh, and your bloke was married until a year or two back, when his wife and kids drowned after some ferry or other cops— cups—'

'Capsized.'

Poor man. No wonder he took risks. How else could he forget?

'That's all I got, though, coz you said to be quick.'

Julia passed him the shortbread she'd sneaked out of Willow Walk in her hankie.

'You didn't catch the bus home, did you? You gave the return fare to the kids on the street.'

'Only threepence,' Bug said. Crumbs sprayed like a geyser. 'Would of given 'em the extra penny, only you said be quick.' Bony shoulders shrugged. 'Would have bin quicker, except the conductor give me a clip round the ear when he saw I'd ridden two stops past me ticket. Threw me off, the rotten bas— Lemme go, that hurts!'

'Isn't it past your bedtime?'

'Fwench spies don't sleep. Here, that's what I'll do! I'll stand in the street with a sign round me neck. *Fwench spy. Will work for shortbwead.* Can we go to the music hall next week?'

Next week, Julia would be in Paris. 'Of course.'

'Whoo-hoo. *Prussian spy. Vill vork for singink and jokink.*' Bug threw his cap in the air. 'Can't wait to see that lepercorn again.'

'Leprechaun.'

'Peppercorn, lepercorn, don't care if he's a unicorn, he's funny. *The banshee, the banshee, bejabbers, don't you hear? Its groaning and its moaning, begob it's moighty queer...*'

Oh yes. He'd definitely manage without her, would Bug. Born survivor, that kid.

And now, thanks to him (and some perfect dovetailed timing), Julia was being introduced to the third photographer on Oliver's list.

'Thank goodness, dear lady. Another customer keeping unsociable hours.' Short — Augustus Jones had to raise his eyes to meet hers — thin, dapper, and with a shining bald pate, there was no trace of tragedy behind those ingenuous blue eyes. 'I feared it was just me.'

The men were in the back room, whisky on the table, smoke in the air, jackets draped over their chairs.

'Look at me, Gus.' Oliver stood up. 'Trouble is, once I start yakking, I can't seem to stop. I'd best go fill your order, before Rosie starts serving breakfast.'

He excused himself with a gesture that only Julia could see, indicating that he'd drag it out to ten minutes.

'I've been away these past few days, visiting my sick mother in London,' Augustus Jones said. 'Pneumonia, I'm told, but she's on the mend now. That's my excuse for this out of hours call, what's yours?'

'My models.' Julia sat down beside him, and found it wasn't too difficult to produce a fraught expression. 'Takes me so long to relax them enough to lose their inhibitions, I'm constantly running late. If only there was a way to speed things up, and not waste so much time.'

'Try spinning the young ladies a story,' Jones said, leaning back. Quite a feat, given the size of the room. 'Much depends on who I'm dealing with, but my family-lost-at-sea tale works a treat, sometimes my kitten died, you get the drift.'

'Bit like the poor-sick-mother tale, then?'

'You saw through that?' His eyes shone as he slicked his hand over his little bald head. 'I must be slipping.'

If he'd been more specific — said Chelsea, or Wandsworth, or the Elephant & Castle, instead of London — she might not have picked up on it. Then again, it did seem odd that he needed to explain his absence to a complete stranger. Unless, of course, he was laying an alibi to the woman he was trying to frame…

'I'll certainly give the hard-luck stories a whirl,' she said, thanking him with puppy dog eyes. 'Anything that helps me fit in extra photo shoots will be wonderful, because, oh please don't tell anyone —' She leaned closer and lowered her voice — 'I'm in a terrible pickle.'

'Financial?'

Julia dredged up a desolate nod.

'Tch, nothing to be ashamed of, dear lady. I am a member of that club myself, and my solution to keeping the snapping jaws of the moneylenders at bay? Quality over quantity every time.'

'That has an appeal, I must say.' Glance to the left, glance to the right, another over her shoulder, then lean closer still. 'There is one gentleman, in particular, an Irishman, to whom I owe money, and whose patience is growing decidedly thin.'

'Think I know the fellow,' Jones said, wincing at a memory in which kneecaps were the prime topic of conversation. 'In which case, I urgently recommend you switch to — how can I put this delicately? Fetishes. Whips, spanking, these images, oh and let's not forget folio scopes, command top prices.'

'Surely the conundrum there Mr. Jones —'

'Gus.'

'Gus. Is that the girls will be even less willing to … um … perform.'

'Sangaree.'

'I beg your pardon?'

'The name derives from the Spanish word for blood.' He flexed his surprisingly long, mobile fingers. 'Mix Madeira wine, port if you prefer, with sugar, nutmeg and an opiate blend. When the flibbertigibbets knock on your door, you feign surprise — *my, my, that time already?* — coyly own up that you were in the middle of this refreshing Sangaree Cocktail, would they care to join you?'

'So a sob story and laudanum gets them to lower their guard —'

'Not laudanum. Too bitter. Trust me, dear lady, follow my instructions and I assure you, the subjects won't suspect a thing. They'll blame the wine, going straight to their heads, but more importantly, it means they'll happily engage in activities that would make a brothel madam blush.'

Repulsive, calculating and devious, but was Augustus Jones a cold-blooded killer? A man "up to his noseholes in debt" might well eliminate a rival in order to grab their share of the business for himself. But shooting girls at close range, then callously framing a third party had an element of nastiness that did not seem to fit even his repellent standards.

On the other hand, who knew what went on the minds of serial killers?

'Can you believe, he actually *bragged* about his tactics,' she told Oliver after Gus Jones left. 'Sat here — *here!* — and gave me advice on how to dupe vulnerable women!'

'Believe it or not — here, can you give me a hand with this collar? Digging in like a bloody garrotte, it is, ooooh, that's better. Anyway, what I was saying is, he meant well, did Gus. Does that read 16 or 16½?'

She peered at the collar he'd handed across. '16½.'

'Darnation. I've only just gone up half an inch, too.' Oliver ran his hand round his neck, exposing the red mark where it had been digging in. 'Rosie's feeding me too much, that's the trouble.'

'You could always eat less...'

'Don't be daft. You've tasted her cooking, I'd be mad to leave that.' He chortled. '17 inch collar coming up.'

'Oliver Blackstock, you are incorrigible.'

'Encourageable, I believe, is the word you are looking for.'

All things come to an end, good or bad, and Julia had always known her tenure at Whitmore Photographic had a limited future. For pity's sake, this was why she went into the mucky picture trade in the first place. To put money aside for when she eventually left, although to be fair, she'd rather hoped her savings would have grown faster. A consequence of running two properties, of course, but she was not unhappy with the growth in investments. She had more than enough to fund her next venture.

Human connections were a different kettle of fish. After Sam died, she swore she wouldn't grow close to anyone again, but try telling that to the Blackstocks. They'd welcomed her in to their hearts, made her part of the family, the only true friends she had. Leaving these people, whose laughter and daftness bounced off the rafters, was going to hurt for the rest of her life.

'I think the police might be on to you. The Inspector at Boot Street.' She described Collingwood to Oliver. 'He missed you this morning, but he'll be back, that I promise, and don't be fooled by his homely pretence of wanting a Brownie box camera. He's looking for proof.'

Oliver stroked his mutton chop whiskers. 'Perhaps I'll move a few bits and pieces out later tonight,' he said. 'Better for Angus, that I stop keeping Frenchies on the premises. I won't have his kids in the workhouse, because he's banged up in prison.'

'Or your own!'

'Don't worry about me, Mizz McAllister. I'm covered in foot-thick armour plating; it'd be sticking a pin in a crocodile.' He puffed away on his cigar for a while, eyes fixed on the ceiling. 'I'm thinking of bringing forward my announcement.'

'The mansion?'

'I'd intended, as you know, waiting until the boys were older. Learned a few core values along the way before they went to "proper" school, but —'

Julia waited.

'It's not so much the twins,' he said, more to himself than to her. 'Edmund I'm not worried about, either. Toyed with the idea of buying him a commission, although between you and me, I don't know that's even possible for people like me. The point is, one day Edmund will be taking over from me, and it's important that boy understands what it is to fight your way through life.'

'You're worried about the girls.'

'Tell me if I'm making mountains out of molehills, today being Charity's birthday and perspective going bonkers, but Patience, for instance. The focus at school is on laundry, sewing, and all things domestic; consequently, she's lagging behind on other things and still getting her words wrong.'

'Like Edmund making a purple for the Army?'

'Like playing charades in the parlour, when she pipes up "is it animal, vegetable or miserable?" Well, of course we roared, who bloody wouldn't? But she's nine, Julia, going on ten, and I want her to have a proper education. Hope, too. Times are changing. We're edging towards a new century, one in which science and technology is moving faster than light, where women work in typing pools and telegraph offices, and I don't want my girls left behind. I want them to take up Charity's baton, be independent, make something of themselves, have adventures before they settle down. Or leastways have the choice.'

'What does Rosie say?'

'My Rosie Cheeks,' he said slowly, 'was born before female education was compulsory. She sees things different. Staunchly believes a woman's role is mother, wife and home-maker, and in all conscience, I can't argue with that.'

'She doesn't see me in that light.'

''Cause you're different. You're a widow, and don't take this the wrong way, she feels sorry for you. She respects that you take portraits and sell china dogs to support yourself. But in her mind, you're just treading water until you find another husband and have babies.'

Julia smiled. 'Thus restoring the natural balance of life.'

'Knew you wouldn't take offence.' The chuckle faded, and he rolled the cigar round in his mouth. 'What's precipitating the advancement of my bombshell on the Blackstock Clan is Faith. Have you noticed anything different about her lately?'

Did he mean the smug expression? Expensive magazines? New boater, that really didn't suit her small, round face? 'Such as?'

'Sulking, lying, sneaking out, bad-mouthing her mother, possibly even stealing — because that girl's getting money from someplace, and it's not me.'

'How is that behaviour different from any other fifteen-year-old who doesn't have to work the factories?'

'Well now, that's where you've hit the nail on the head. My feelings exactly! Faith doesn't have a job, she doesn't have interests, and now she's left school, my girl's bored. Well, I'm buggered if I'm letting her go into service. Not that she'd want to, mind. But she's coming up to the same age Charity was, when she first started getting itchy feet. Here, give me a hand with this collar, will you? I've been stretching it and stretching it, but still can't get the damn thing back.'

'Keep still, man! How am I supposed to fasten the studs, when you're wriggling around like an oiled pig?'

The next few minutes were taken up with various moans and groans and ow's and chuckles, as Julia fought to fit a collar at least one size too small in a room that was also at least one size too small. Ledgers, lamps, cabinets, waste bins, inkwells, blotters quickly became casualty to the Thirty-Year Collar War. Collateral damage, in both their opinions.

'Wait, wait, wait, I need to fix your cravat.'

It didn't help that he was compacted into a mahogany swivel chair that needed a carpenter to free him. Clearly, his neck wasn't the only thing that had expanded with Rosie's cooking.

'It looks like it's been chewed by a donkey.'

They were both out of breath by the time she finished, mostly from laughing — *oiled pig, indeed! I'll remember that, missie, next time you want your order filling!* — but it didn't detract from the fact her friend was worried.

'So you're going to fix Faith up with a job?'

'Job?' His eyes nearly bulged out of their sockets. 'JOB? Hell no, pardon my French. I let one daughter spread her wings, and look how that ended. This —' He tapped the whisky bottle on the table — 'this is the only thing that lets me sleep at night. I should never have let Charity go.'

'It was her decision, Oliver.'

'Girls don't know their own minds at seventeen. Fathers do.'

'She might still have contracted influenza. Some people are more susceptible than others.'

'Don't think Glenmorangie and I haven't had this discussion many times. She might have contracted it, I fully agree. And she might well still have died. I'll never know, and that's the point. I'll never know, because I wasn't around to protect her. Faith, on the other hand…'

'Let me guess. It's a toss-up between women's suffrage and the Temperance Society?'

'Wash your mouth out, Mizz McAllister. No, I have in mind a Swiss finishing school. What do you think of that proposal?'

Disaster. That's what Julia thought of that proposal. Absolute crushing disaster. Imagine the bullying, coming from such a wildly different social class. (Assuming any school would take her in the first place, money and breeding being very different animals.) And Faith? How happy would she be, walking round with books on her head to improve her deportment? These academies were designed to school girls in the art of hooking husbands. Husbands from the nobility, no less. Julia couldn't see how a fish out of water, friendless and alone in a foreign country, was going to solve Faith's underlying problem.

Or his.

'It's not what I think, Oliver. It's how Rosie would think about another child leaving, when she's still in mourning for her daughter.'

'Ach. You're right, dammit.' Tears filled his eyes. 'Didn't think of it from that angle.' He pulled out his handkerchief. Blew into it with a honk any gander would be proud of. 'Back to the drawing board as bloody usual, eh? I ask you, who'd be a father!'

Julia clenched her fists until her nails bit the palms of her hands. You will not, repeat NOT, cry when you walk out of this office. You will smile. You will wave. Your back will be straight, your step firm.

And you will not — *will not* — look back.

'Going back to Gus Jones,' Julia said, helping tidy the blotters and files. 'It troubles me that he talks so flippantly about fetish postcards.'

'You're the only one who's not involved in — let's say, the next level, or didn't you know that?' Oliver stopped mid-tidy. 'Ah. Obviously not. But there's a reason I didn't put that line forward to you —'

'I know, I know, you're protecting your girls.'

'Bloody right.' He leaned forward, and his eyes were the most serious she'd ever seen them. 'So when I tell you, you don't want to get involved in that lark, you trust me.'

'I do trust you, Oliver.'

'I know it pays well —'

'You're saying mansions don't come cheap.'

'Too true they don't, girl, and before you ask, no. I'm *not* proud of what I do, and I'd burn my own eyes out before I let Rosie or the nippers catch once glance of this filth. But.' He returned to straightening his ledger. 'If masochism, sadism, or whatever hoists their Jolly Roger is the price for educating my boys and seeing my daughters taken care of, then I can look God straight in the eye and tell him, man to man, that I'm not sorry.'

'He drugs them, Oliver!'

'Don't be too hard on him, Julia. Gus is a good man.'

'Good men don't dupe young girls into doing things they'd be otherwise ashamed of.'

'So he slips the girls something to calm them down? Believe me, they know exactly what they're in for when they turn up at the studio, and what Gus does is nothing on the scale of Midge Belmont — oh, come on, don't look at me like that.'

How was she supposed to look at him, when the ground she was standing on — this happy, hallowed, laughter-filled ground, the rock on which she'd built her life these past four years — was collapsing underfoot?

'Your standards are different, and rightly so,' he said evenly. 'But not to put too fine a point on it, your material, this What-the-Butler-Saw stuff, is pretty bloody tame. Midge's subjects, on the other hand, are exclusively male, no holds barred, and every aspect of that business, every bloody aspect, risks a prison sentence. The boys are bound to need some kind of chemical assistance.'

Something had ripped out Julia's heart and was crushing it to pieces.

'How could you?' Glass, books, papers, pens crashed to the floor as she smashed them off his desk. The stench of ink mingled with whisky and dust. 'Jesus Christ, Oliver. I don't even know who you are any more.'

'Calm down —'

'Calm down? When I find you, of all people, condone drugging, coercion, what is effectively prostitution!'

'Turning a blind eye is how I see myself,' he said levelly, 'but before you topple off that high horse of yours, just remember we're all in the same business, and we're all in it for the money. It's simply a question of levels.'

How could she EVER have found mutton-chop whiskers meeting under the chin comical? Linked arms and sang silly songs on the Common? Giggled like a schoolgirl when wrestling his collar?

'Tobias outshines us all when it comes to banking guineas, photographing explicit sexual acts —'

'Another man who can look God in the eye and say he isn't sorry, because he contributes to the Church, rather than mansions for his family?'

Julia couldn't stomach any more. She spun out of the room where, sod's law, she cannoned straight into Rosie, Verity and one of the twins coming up the path, and everyone went flying.

'What on earth will people think,' Rosie chuckled, stumbling to her feet. 'Us three throwing ourselves in the rose bushes like lunatics, and not a full moon either. Make that four. Didn't see you under your sister, Davey, love.'

'Rosie, I am so, so sorry.' *Could the evening get any worse?*

'Don't be daft. All my life I've wondered what soil tasted like.' Rosie straightened Verity's skirts, then spat on her hankie and wiped it over the little one's face. 'Well, I'll be blowed if it isn't Daniel Blackstock underneath that muck.' She shot Julia a look that said *Whoops!* 'Verity, see if you can find the teapot, will you, sweetheart?'

Triumphant, the little one grabbed the receptacle whose leaves they'd been emptying to help fertilise the flowers. In the light of the swelling moon, Julia could see that it was pewter. That it was embossed. That it even had a little cameo on either side. She could also see it wouldn't be pouring tea again. Not unless you poured it sideways.

'Dear oh dear, my poor old damask rose! Oh, well. The smell was overpowering anyway — hey, hey, hey.'

It wasn't meant to end like this. The lifetime of hurt was supposed to come from the whole family laughing, happy, pulling the standard Blackstock magic trick of bouncing back no matter what the world threw at them.

'It's only a rose bush, lovey, please don't cry.'

Everyone lets you down eventually, JJ. Everyone except you, Sam. Everyone except you…

'You come up and have a cuppa. I do have other teapots, y'know!'

'Thanks, but I should go.'

'Not in that state you don't, and I'm not taking no for an answer and that's final. Come along.' Rosie scrubbed Julia's eyes the same way she scrubbed the children's. With the same hankie that wiped the soil off Daniel's face. 'That's the stuff. Now, you plonk yourself down and take Baby Grace while I sort out a teapot. Verity, will you please take your brother's sock out of your mouth, and Davey, if I've told you once, I've told you a hundred times, you are not to lick the walls.'

Soon they were sipping tea laced with whisky.

'Don't tell Olly I keep this stashed away, only I've always made it at night when the babes are teething. Never fed it to *them*, of course, but I tell you, love, I slept right through like a log, every night till dawn-break.'

Julia's heart lurched.

This was how it was supposed to be. A cocoon of silliness, warmth and love, and as she walked home, the steady plod of police boots echoing through the night, her thoughts flew to Sam. His portrait was one of the few treasures packed away in her valise in Mitchell Street, along with her passport, cash and papers. With his Buffalo Bill looks, right down to the long hair and goatee beard, Sam Whitmore was the father she never had, and when he died, she was lost. Vulnerable and bereft, maybe she'd been hasty in her assumptions. As any photographer knows, the eye sees what it wants to believe. Hearts are no different, and with hindsight, she realised that her need to be needed heaped unrealistic qualities on this roly-poly surrogate father-figure. In the end, nobody forced Julia McAllister to wear rose-coloured spectacles. She'd put them on herself.

Now, as the moon turned the pond on the Common to molten silver, the spectacles fell off.

Oliver was right. She was every bit as bad as the men. She didn't drug her models, or force them in any way, but Mother of God, she was no less guilty.

Like the shiny gewgaws that Mr. Tarrant's "discerning gentlemen" plied Cocoa and Beryl with, Julia used cash as the bait, reeling in models to pose for postcards with the express purpose of funding her escape. Telling them — telling herself — that, this way, everyone was winning. That the only people being exploited were the sad, little men who jerk off with the photos.

With all her stupid heart, she'd believed no one was getting hurt. The hell they weren't. It's just that the bruises didn't show.

Humble pie sticks in the throat, but first thing tomorrow morning she would telephone Oliver and apologise. He was her friend, he'd always been her friend, and since Sam died, all he'd ever done was try to help her. Throwing that back in his face on his dead daughter's birthday was inexcusable.

Families fight all the time, girl, he would say. *Forget it. I already have.*

Least-said-soonest-mended worked for Julia, as well. But not when it's the last time you will ever see someone.

It was only when she was crossing the street to her shop that she remembered Faith, and pulled up short. Holy Mother of God. Whose father was in the photographic trade? Whose father deals with people engaged in taking dirty pictures? *And who suddenly has extra shillings in her purse?*

Chapter 22

Maybe it was the power of suggestion, maybe there really were magic properties in drinking tea laced with whisky before bed, maybe, just maybe, she was exhausted both mentally and physically. Either way, Julia (to quote Rosie) slept right through like a log till dawn-break, waking with more energy than she'd had for days.

Dear God, was she going to need it.

She made another quick tour of the house, checking cupboards, checking drawers, making sure there was nothing left behind that she was ashamed of anybody seeing. Silly as it sounded, she didn't want Collingwood, or indeed anybody else, sneering at faded tea towels or blouses stained from dark room chemicals, or turning their noses up because the bread in the bin had gone mouldy. Julia McAllister might have disappeared, but her reputation for cleanliness, efficiency and precision would remain intact.

The clock on the wall of the shop chimed the half hour, and for a moment, she faltered. Sam picked that up on his travels, and she'd always meant to ask what he was doing in France, and why he should want to lug home a walnut clock complete with barometer and thermometer, when time and weather had little meaning for the man. Then suddenly he was gone. Taken too young and too quickly. That clock was simply one more unanswered question. One more regret on the list...

Clearing her throat, Julia opened the shop blinds and unlocked the door. Rosie respected her for taking portraits and selling china dogs to support herself, did she? What would she think if she knew Whitmore Photographic had only had two commissions this week (excluding Flora's, where Julia had made a thumping great loss), and had sold only one china spaniel? Which in turn was marked down, on account of a slight chip out of its tail.

Let's face it, without the income from French postcards, she'd never have been able to keep this place going, much less follow her dreams. But did that make it right?

And if Faith *was* picking up a shilling here, a shilling there, by posing, how was Julia supposed to break the news to Oliver? The best she had was a hunch, and a hunch is a long way from proof. Suppose she was wrong? It's one thing kicking a hornet's nest while you're still on the spot. Quite another to start stirring then just bugger off —

Which reminded her. Where was Bug this morning? Not like him, not to be stuffing his freckles with devilled kidneys or Yarmouth bloaters, washed down with a pint of tea, while simultaneously hacking off a quarter of a farmhouse loaf and slathering it with butter.

The five guineas that she'd set aside would see him through, if he was sensible. But boys his age weren't sensible — how could they be? And here was the problem. Five guineas. Ten. Twenty. However much she left him, it wouldn't compensate for tossing him aside. Equally, though, she couldn't take him with her.

If she'd had the luxury of time — one more week would do it — she could have come up with a plan to fake her death. That way, there would be no more Collingwoods trying to track her down. She could start afresh, any place she wanted — stay in England, even — without having to look over her shoulder ever again. With Oliver as his appointed guardian, Bug would inherit the entire contents of the house. The equipment in the studio alone was worth a fortune. Then the kid could rest easy, knowing Julia hadn't abandoned him —

She wiped her eyes, and pulled herself together. Tough times made for tough decisions. *Get on with it.*

One day left. Four girls dead. God knows how many others being drugged and duped, no doubt blackmailed into doing more work or their family/friends/the police/the public would be shown the photographs. She had to put this right.

And dammit, she still hadn't found that wretched boy a bicycle! Lucky she hadn't thrown out last night's *Chronicle*, then. Not that she ever intended to read it. Where would Julia find that kind of time? But any ruse to keep Bug out of trouble, or more accurately away from that bloody penny whistle —

Mother of God, how could she have missed that headline?

She read, then re-read the front page.

Mr. Strauss, aged 26… Twenty-six. Same age as herself.

All this time, I was hoping, praying, that somehow "T" had found you, she thought. *And if not sorted out your problems, between the two of you, you were working towards some kind of solution. All this time, you were lying face down in the water. Inches from where Bug and I were laughing until our sides split.*

Cyril, Cyril, Cyril. I am so very sorry.

'Oliver!'

'Here you go, Mizz McAllister.' He pushed a little potted plant in her hand. 'Not sure if it's a peace offering, a thank-you for the heads-up about the rozzers, or an apology for the things I said last night. Anyway, Mrs. Corbett from the florist's told me it's an African violet, quite delicate apparently.' He gave a mock shudder. 'Mind, why I ever imagined you and delicate flowers went together is beyond me.'

'It's me who should be apologising.' Julia warmed the teapot, swirling it round while the water boiled on the range. 'I'm in no position to judge anyone, especially you.'

'Quite right, girl. Friends don't judge one another. They meet up, have a drink, and judge everybody else.'

The relief — the RELIEF — to be parting from Oliver on good terms.

'I asked Mrs. Corbett, "are these things like conch shells?"' He held the pot against the left side of his head. '"That if you put it to your ear, you can hear Africa?" "Africa!" Mrs. Corbett snorts. "What sort of sounds would you expect to hear from Africa!" So I shrug. "I dunno. Elephants rampaging, lions roaring, camels hissing" — only, and I swear it was an accident, the "h" came out more of a "p".' He clutched his side. 'You should have seen her face.'

Julia could only imagine her expression, honest mistake or not.

'Tried to throw a bucket of slimy flower water over me, she did, but we Blackstocks are dab hands at dodging bullets — oh, hey, before I forget. Your payment for the Swedish Princess on the beach. Nice sea shells, by the way,' he added with a wink. Then promptly proved his ducking skills were no idle boast when Julia threw a rock cake at him.

That missed, too.

'Tell me Dickie Lloyd owed money to the wrong people, who sent a bunch of heavies round to duff him up and things got out of hand,' Collingwood said to his sergeant.

'I can tell you the Pied Piper's leading rats and children down the street right now.' Kincaid shut the door on another morning of penitent drunkards, irate victims of vandalism, distraught victims of theft, protesting prostitutes and hysterical mothers seeking news of offspring missing for yet another long night. 'It would be every bit as accurate.'

'Hmm.'

Lucre, lust and loathing. The three L's that topped Collingwood's list of motives, usually in that order, and at first glance, this murder was no exception. Any man who kept a dandified wardrobe while simultaneously juggling several bottles of cologne proved that he enjoyed the good things in life. Compare that with music hall owners paying their performers twenty shillings a week, and there was clearly a shortfall in the equation. Unless it transpired that the owner of the aforementioned dandified wardrobe was exceptionally adept at juggling his finances.

'Very well, Charlie, I'll settle for lust. Dickie Lloyd was a personable young man. Tell me there was a jealous husband seething away in the background.'

Kincaid lifted the sash on the window. 'Yup. Herr Hamelin's still piping.'

'And naturally Dickie was the most popular artist both on stage and off.'

'You know what it's like with theatre folk. As fluid as the canal people, equally flamboyant, and although it's hard to judge, probably every bit as hardworking. In their way.' Kincaid closed the window and took the weight off his aching feet in Collingwood's chair, while his inspector was busy wearing out the floorboards. 'Obviously, there's a bit of rivalry and backbiting going on somewhere,' he continued. 'But the acts are so varied, there's rarely competition; consequently Mr. Shut Yer Cakehole seems to have been well liked by pretty much everyone. Universally cheerful, universally pleasant. Went out of his way to avoid trouble.'

Excellent. All three L's down the drain. So much for wrapping that up quickly. Still. This wasn't the only hot potato on Collingwood's desk. 'Cyril Strauss,' he said. 'You're just about to report that when Mrs. Strauss was going through her son's belongings after her overnight vigil, she discovered a note outlining the reasons he chose to attach a boulder to his ribcage and end his life.'

Kincaid cocked his head. 'Listen. Must be a hundred rats by now.'

Cyril rented a room on Dell Street, and that's where his mother spent the night. Sobbing, praying, laying out the body according to tradition, but still too distraught to even contemplate going through his belongings.

'He lived alone, paid his rent on time, his landlady couldn't ask for a tidier, quieter tenant.' Kincaid read from his notes. 'Right little bookworm, she said.'

Collingwood let that sink in. 'Twenty-six years old, lives alone, no hobbies, no friends, works in a bank. Christ, Charlie, if that was the sum total of my life, I'd top myself, too.'

'No, no, don't do that!' Kincaid rushed across the office and put a comforting arm round his inspector's shoulder. 'Let me do it for you.'

'Ha bloody ha. Now before I issue an official reprimand for trying to cheer me up, spit it out. What's the good news?'

'Ah. Well. The good news is that we haven't found another body. Mind you,' he added as an afterthought. 'It's only ten past nine.'

Chapter 23

Julia dodged two boys running barefoot up the street with jugs of ale apiece — spilling more than they were carrying — and gave a wide berth to the chimney sweep, whose rods and brushes cast off clouds of sooty snowflakes while his boy assistant hopped behind, black as a witch's cat and twice as lithe.

Perspective. That's what she'd lost. The heat of emotion last night, coming on top of Elizabeth's murder, had robbed her of normal perspective. What she had to remind herself was this: it was the men poring over the Frenchies and flip books who objectified the girls. Not the models themselves.

The income from standing in front of Julia's camera was their lifeline. Let's not lose sight of that fact. Ask any of them, and they'll tell you that one day they'll fall in love, marry and have children — but until that happened, the few shillings they earned from posing didn't simply tide them over. It was the difference between prostitution and the workhouse, and frankly, unless you've looked poverty in the eye — smelled its corrosive breath and felt its iron grip around your soul — you've no idea what that means to young kids struggling to survive.

Unfortunately, there was a gaping difference between the likes of, say, Lily, and the likes of Beryl and Cocoa.

The gusto with which Miss Atkins embraced modelling proved she found it far from demeaning. She had no sense of shame. On the contrary. Lily was empowered. Like Daisy, like Nellie, like little Birdie, she decided how far she would go. The choice was hers, and hers alone — and yes, they were young, but runaways trying to keep their heads above water grow up fast and make decisions wise beyond their years. Survival of the fittest, Mr. Darwin.

Contrast that with naïve young creatures cowed into performing acts that revolted them — who were then drugged and almost certainly blackmailed to keep them pliant — and you were looking at evil personified.

At the corner by the taxidermist, Julia paused. Was it really only three days ago that she'd stopped here and let her handkerchief flutter to the ground, the signal for Bug to collapse a trestle piled with pots and pans to make a clatter they could hear in the Colonies? The parrot with the exotic blue and yellow plumage had gone, she noticed. Its place was taken by a rather sleepy looking barn owl, perched on a rock and encapsulated inside a glass dome for eternity.

'Are them curly horns real?' Bug had asked, when she'd returned from Daisy's that first morning to find him leaning against the wall, chewing on a straw.

'African antelope,' she'd replied, following the line of his grubby finger. 'They're real.'

'What's them things with the mask, then?'

'Racoons.'

'How about that?'

'An armadillo. It eats little boys.'

The V-sign he flashed wasn't for victory. 'I know that snarly one in the corner: it's a stoat. D'you know the difference between weasels and stoats?' He didn't give her a chance to answer. 'A weasel's weasily recognised, and a stoat's stotally different.'

Three days. Three days in which life had spun her round, punched her breathless and thrown her off a cliff. Was it any wonder perspective had gone flying out the window?

The bell of the muffin man, distinctively flat thanks to its wonky clapper, reminded her that she didn't have time to waste staring at stuffed carp and rabbits.

'Muffins, lovely muffins, still hot from the oven!'

Tempted as she was by the yeasty smell wafting from the tray balanced on his head, not to mention the treat it would make for growing urchins, Julia pressed on.

She was under no illusions. If his Chief Inspector turned the screw much tighter, Collingwood would strike faster than a cobra, and for her sins, she wouldn't see it coming. Which meant tonight. Tonight, and no exceptions, no excuses, Julia must also play the snake. Shed her skin and disappear forever.

But that transformation was still twelve hours away, and, as she turned into Belmont Street, she reviewed the situation as it stood.

Firstly, some animal was butchering girls and trying to frame Julia for their murder. Was it Midge? Tobias? Tarrant, Jones, some unknown book binder on Sloane Street called Edwards? Hell's teeth, why not throw Uncle Tom Cobbly 'n' all; it made no difference to pinpointing their killer.

Secondly, despite hopes for a happier outcome, Cyril had followed through with his intentions, and his obituary in this morning's *Chronicle* made it pitifully clear that there was no one in his life. If there was a bright spot in that, it was that he hadn't taken his secret to the grave. At least, not yet. Julia still had the note addressed to "T". Would the poor girl ever learn how deeply he had loved her?

Meanwhile, some bitch by the name of Pandora was pretending to befriend vulnerable girls, then persuading them to turn tricks by feeding them opiates. If ever anyone deserved to rot in jail with the key thrown away, it was her. Ditto Percival Tarrant.

The question was, what could Julia do about any of it in the time available?

Well, for a start she could hold on to her temper when she confronted Midge about the drugs.

The bell above his door tinkled, as she deftly turned the open sign to closed and flipped the latch.

Was it possible? Find "T", trap a killer, stop Pandora, thwart Tarrant, and wrap it all up nicely in a big, fat, yellow bow in twelve short hours without Collingwood either arresting her or digging deeper into her past? One thing was sure: she'd have a damn good go. Of course, she'd have to suddenly acquire superhuman strength and magical powers, but when it came to working miracles, why not?

Given that she'd already gotten away with murder.

'If you're expecting me to fall on my knees, wring my hands and swear I'll never be a naughty boy again, you're looking at the wrong man, dear.'

The meeting had started off well enough. Midge calling out a breezy, 'My, aren't you the early bird?' followed by, 'Did any of those names pan out?' and neatly rounded off with 'Thanks for the tip about the duster, by the way. Black feathers are ten times more efficient — who'd have thought!'

Sadly, superhuman miracle workers poised to do a moonlight flit don't have the luxury of small talk. Hoping to shock him into spilling every tiny little bean, Julia cut straight to the chase. Only to find contrition wasn't in Midge's vocabulary.

'I'm a businessman, Mrs. McAllister. Same as you, same as Blackie, same as every other person in this trade, and we all share the same incentive.' He rubbed his fingers and thumb together in the age-old money gesture. 'Agreed, we have different motivations for the extra financial cushion. Our

189

mutual friend, bless him, thinks a posh house will lift him and his tubby brood above their social station — isn't he in for a shock? You, I'm guessing, couldn't hang on to your independence without it — oh, really? You didn't think I knew Whitmore's been feeding the worms in Southolt Cemetery these few years?' So much for secrecy, burying Sam out of the local jurisdiction. 'As for me.' He flitted about, straightening a picture here, a picture there, smoothing out the blinds, and basically living up to his nickname. 'Do you have any idea how much it costs to keep my affiliations secret?' He rolled his eyes. 'For an organisation that's supposed to be resistant to bribery and corruption, the judiciary doesn't come cheap.'

'And that makes drugging models perfectly acceptable?'

'Chemical reinforcement is not illegal. For all these wretched Quakers trying to pressure Parliament into outlawing the opium trade, one can freely purchase all manner of potions, drugs and poisons from any dispenser in the country. Physicians dish them out like barley sugar sweeties.'

'Physicians only prescribe opiates to their own patients, and no pharmacist worth his licence will sell drugs, unless they personally know the purchaser or their intermediary.'

Legislation saw infant mortality rates plummet after "mothers' little calmers" ceased to be readily available, putting an instant stop to lethal overdoses.

'Well, don't *you* know your law.'

'What I know, Mr. Belmont, is that the quantities being peddled far exceed personal use.'

'Is that so?' His pale eyes narrowed. 'And who's to say what the different thresholds for pain are, when it comes to female troubles? Or how much relief a lady might need to alleviate her fainting fits and mood swings? Her, dare I say, hysteria?'

'Don't you mean induce them?'

'Please, Mrs. McAllister — may I call you Julia?'

'You bloody well may not.'

'Can't we just agree to differ? You have strong views, and I respect you for them. Equally, I hope you respect mine when I confess that I am partial to a smidgen of cocaine myself, whenever the fancy takes me. Indeed, my own father, God rest his gentle soul, never took a tankard of ale without first dropping a stick of opium in it.' He flicked his tailcoat, presumably having run out of anything else to meddle with. 'All I'm saying is, one way or another, everyone involved in the Frenchie industry is meeting a demand — and believe me, some of the gentlemen who enjoy Greek love are demanding in the extreme.'

Julia didn't hold cocaine use against him. We each combat the stresses of modern life in our own way, and while his wouldn't be the path she'd choose to walk, Midge was free to unwind in any way he chose in the privacy of his own home.

She turned to the window, and a street bristling with florid matrons straining corsets to the limit; housewives whose baskets brimmed with cauliflowers, pigs' heads, rhubarb and fruit buns; wasp-waisted ladies walking their silly dogs; boys playing marbles; girls skipping with ropes; babies sleeping like angels in rocking perambulators.

What percentage of these upstanding citizens had husbands, fathers, brothers, sons who had never so much as peeked at a smutty photo at least once in their lives? Exactly. And what percentage went on to collect postcards for their (very) personal pleasure?

Experiencing first-hand the advances in flip books and slide shows, and with moving pictures being the next big step forward, Julia didn't doubt Tarrant when he predicted that current demand would soar through the roof. There was no way to stop the avalanche, and in fairness, she didn't want to. What had to be stopped was the pernicious manner in which the material was being acquired.

She turned back to Midge, dusting his tripod, testing the leather bellows, polishing the lens of his camera. Rosie was convinced honey worked every time, when it came to getting results. Mrs. McAllister was not Mrs. Blackstock.

'How many sticks of opium do you drop in their ale? Two? Three?'

'Enough to get them hooked, dear, enough to get them hooked.'

Don't. Don't lose your temper. Not at this stage — Julia took a deep breath. Then another. Maybe Rosie was right. Maybe Julia should take a leaf out of her book, try that for size? Maybe hell would freeze over first.

'Scum like you give despicable a good name.'

'Scum like me get results, dear.' He stopped flitting, and once again she was struck by just how shrewd those pale eyes were. 'This,' he said. 'This delivers everything I need and more besides.' He took a syringe from his safe and set a small cobalt blue bottle beside it. 'Together, these little beauties ensure my subjects will do anything, and I do mean anything, for their next dose of heaven.'

'How can you even sleep at night.' It wasn't a question.

'They choose to take the drugs.'

'Silly me. I should have realised it was their fault all along.' But the pendulum was swinging. Time to set disgust aside and get her hands on what she'd come for. 'Do you know a woman named Pandora?'

Belmont seemed to find the question amusing. 'I would say that everyone in this business, apart from you obviously, knows Pandora.' She was the lynchpin holding it together, he explained. 'Quite frankly, without her unique blend of chemical compliance, how else could we procure so many subjects, then have them acting in the manner that they do?'

And there was Julia, thinking it couldn't get any worse. 'Give me her address.'

'If, for one second, I thought your intentions were honourable — all right, all right, wrong word. Sound. Is that better? If I thought your intentions were *sound*, I'd pass on the lady's details in a flash. But you strike me as more passionate about this anti-opiate campaign than the Quakers lobbying Westminster. Consequently, my lips, on this score, are sealed.'

'Would you prefer I call the police?'

'You've already proved your knowledge of the law, dear, which means you're well aware that posing for lewd photographs isn't illegal, neither's taking them, nor is the administration of drugs for personal consumption.'

'I am aware. You're right. It's the distribution and possession of pornography that constitutes a criminal offence.'

'The reason certain judicial pockets are lined so very handsomely.'

'The question is, are you prepared to risk it?' She tapped the pile of photos in the safe. 'I can think of many circumstances under which they might well look the other way. Unfortunately, material of a homosexual nature isn't one of them.'

They couldn't hush a police raid, which made a jail term inescapable. Midge was cornered and he knew it.

'You so much as telephone Pandora,' Julia said, waving the address Midge had scribbled down, 'or warn her in any way that I am coming, I will have this shop of yours closed within the hour, and you in prison.'

To make absolutely sure there was no misunderstanding, she snatched a batch of his "Greek boy" Frenchies as insurance, and stuffed them in her bag.

My, oh my. Midge Belmont speechless and contrite at last.

Didn't that feel good.

Chapter 24

'This come for yer in Mitchell Street.' Bug dug into his pocket and fished out something that might, once, have been an envelope.

'What were you doing at Mitchell Street?' Julia asked.

'Looking for you, what d'yer think? Only when I saw the place all locked up and you wasn't there, I didn't think I should leave that letter sticking half under your door.'

'Where were you at breakfast?' *Dear God, she was starting to sound like his mother.*

'Took some ham and eggs and black pudden round to Daisy's. Would have given her the cheese, 'cept I ate it. You're out of digestive biscuits, by the way.'

Julia whisked open the larder. 'And everything else, by the looks of it.'

A scrawny shoulder shrugged. 'It ain't easy, being an unmarried mum. Men don't wanna know, and women are right bitches — mmmf.' His nose wrinkled in defiance when she took her hand away. 'Well, they are.'

'You need to mind your language.'

'You need to read that letter.'

Give me strength. Julia slit the envelope with the letter opener.

'Well? What's it say?'

'What it says, not that it's any of your business, is that a friend of mine is very sorry, but she's unable to attend this afternoon's photoshoot.' Just as well. With everything else going on, it had completely slipped Julia's mind. 'It would appear that she has found herself a beau.' *Good for you, my little Rose of Shanghai, good for you!* 'He lives in the building opposite, she writes, so their paths cross frequently, but the night before last he finally plucked up courage to declare himself. Presented her with a posy of violets, because violets, according to my friend, symbolise affection. To, um, have her portrait taken now, she says, wouldn't be right.'

'Here, they're not hanging about with that bloke what topped himself, are they. Only fished him out yesterday. Burying the poor bugger this afternoon.'

Julia was too shocked to wash his mouth out with soap. Cyril —? 'The funeral's today?'

'Said so in the papers. Planting him in the Jewish boneyard, they are, three o'clock on the button.'

Any reply she might have made was drowned out by a hideous screech from the penny whistle and the slam-slam-slam as Bug opened and closed the shop door on his way out just to annoy her. Oh yes. There were some things she *definitely* wouldn't be sorry leaving behind.

The china dogs were another. It was a clever enough idea. Child spots doggie in the window. Mother caves in to screaming tantrums. Nice lady inside shop gushes over brat's photogenic qualities. Portrait booked.

Oh, Sam. If only you were here, there'd have been none of this to contend with. We'd have been taking portraits of self-important military types, po-faced couples, dead men in their Sunday best, and laughing about how long it took to keep that family of twelve stock still, scratching our heads over the best way to make Mrs. Brady look pretty for her *memento mori*, when her head had been caved in by a dray horse's hoof. And in between, you'd have been recounting your adventures in the Holy Land, the horrors you witnessed in the American Civil War, the women you wooed and won along the way, and we'd have sipped brandy —

Cognac, JJ. Would you call a lace wedding gown a white frock? Do you think of our dear queen as Vickie? For the same reason, you must never, never, insult the amber nectar by calling it brandy. It will take its revenge with the worst hangover mankind has ever known.

The pain of loss hit like a knife. He was gone. The only man she'd ever trusted, the only person who'd believed in her, and more importantly, made her believe in herself.

Regrets swarmed like hornets.

If Sam was alive, work wouldn't have dried up, because dammit not everyone was fooled into thinking he still ran this show. Then there'd have been no resorting to taking smutty pictures, and four girls would still have bright futures in front of them.

If only she hadn't assumed it was a handkerchief fluttering down in the churchyard. If she'd called louder, run after him, put him first instead of looking after her camera, Mrs. Strauss wouldn't be burying her son at three o'clock.

If only she'd been tougher when that grubby hand reached out to touch Flora's dress, a small boy wouldn't feel he'd been abandoned twice.

If only she hadn't kissed Inspector John Collingwood —

'Here you go, lovey.'

The nightmare of grief was broken by an explosion of jasmine perfume, accompanied by a rustle of bright yellow taffeta topped by a hat balancing half a lilac bush. The explosion held a sleeping baby in one arm, while the other gripped the hand of a small girl with an unfortunate pink bow in her hair that made her look like a rabbit.

'You left your comb behind.'

'Thank you, Rosie.' She hugged her. 'You're an angel.'

'I wish!' Rosie chuckled. 'It's because I'm a little devil that I'm up the duff half the bleedin' time! Not that I'm complaining, mind. I love my kids, every one of the little sods, isn't that a fact, sweetheart?' She tweaked the toddler's little plump cheek. 'Especially —' she mouthed — 'when they're at school and out my way.' Rosie's face crumpled like news print in the flames. 'Oh, the poor woman.'

Julia followed the line of her eyes, to Cyril's obituary folded open next to the violet. 'Reminded you of Charity?' she asked as tears splashed the yellow taffeta.

'There's times when the pain's so bad, it drops me to my knees, it really does.' Her expression hardened. 'No mother should have to bury a child. Not like that.' Rosie wiped her eyes and blew her nose. 'Well, now, look at me, screwing up my face, making a mess of this lovely frock! Bad as the nippers, I am. Which reminds me: you haven't seen my Olly, have you?'

'As a matter of fact, he dropped supplies off earlier.'

'Ships that pass in the night, eh? Well, if he pops back for any reason, tell him I'm looking for him, will you, love? It's Patience, see. I tried to make her wait until Sunday bath time before wearing her new frock, but oh no, not her. Now she's gone and ripped the bloomin' thing, and I need money off him to buy the horrid child a new one. Honestly.' She let out a loud, theatrical sigh. 'Patience. I ask you. What *were* we thinking of, when we called her that?'

Julia didn't think she was capable of laughing. Not with a fourth murder, Cyril's suicide, and Midge's sickening attitude so fresh and so raw. But she was still smiling ten minutes later when Collingwood strode in, locked the door and yanked down the blinds.

Oh no.

His eyes were cold, his jaw set.

Frozen with fear, unable to speak, unable to move, the only thing she could do was stand there and wait.

Then a miracle happened. Without a word, he pulled her into his arms and pressed his lips hard to hers.

Overwhelmed by relief, she surrendered to the hunger of his kiss, shocked by the instant response from her body as he pulled the pins from her hair and buried his hands in her curls. His mouth travelled downwards, caressing the nape of her neck. His breath was ragged, and his skin tasted of salt.

'Julia.'

A hand closed round her breast, teasing her nipple, and the world spun out of control. As he pressed her to the wall, she felt the unmistakeable outline of handcuffs in his pocket.

'You know, if you're not going to arrest me,' she said, 'I really think we should put these to better use.'

Chapter 25

'There's something I ought to tell you,' Collingwood said.

They were lying in Julia's big brass bed, sheets tangled, limbs ditto, the floor a confusion of frills and froths and worsted and cotton, spattered with collar studs, cufflinks and hairpins. Through the open window, he could hear children giggling in the park. The smell from the baker's two doors down reminded his stomach that lunchtime was approaching, while sunbeams searched in vain for any trace of the rug beneath the scattering of clothing. So why *did* women wear so many petticoats? Was it really about fashion? Or a ruse to drive men mad with desire as they teased them off, one exciting layer at a time?

'You're married. I know.' A chap could drown in the little dimple that danced at the side of her mouth when she smiled. 'Come on, Inspector. You can't think you're the only one who does their homework? And I'm sorry about your daughter. I really am.'

'Thanks.'

This wasn't the direction he'd intended to take, but dear God, he didn't want secrets, he couldn't face lies, and the relief that she'd entered this relationship with her eyes open was beyond indescribable.

He'd been dreading how to broach the subject of his marriage, because any decent man would have laid his cards on the table beforehand, and he couldn't argue that it was because he was a police officer, either. From the moment he first looked into Julia's affairs, long before confronting her with the photos, he'd been intrigued. And then, the second he saw her coming up the street — tendrils of hair escaping from her hat, dark and glossy like chestnuts on a woodland floor — his head hadn't stopped spinning.

Not an hour, not one, had passed when he hadn't pictured flashing eyes flecked with the fire of hell, or seen breasts raging against the indignity of their blue silk cage every time he closed his eyes. Hers was the last image he saw when he fell asleep at night. The first voice in his head when he awoke.

Swear to God, he only came here today to kiss her —

'Your hunch was right, by the way.' *This* was the intended direction. Not cowardice at not owning up. 'The victim by the canal was indeed Dickie Lloyd.'

Twenty-two years old, funny and popular, with his life barely started, he didn't deserve being found face down with his trousers round his knees, beaten to a pulp then pissed on. Nobody did.

'Any closer to finding his killers?' Julia asked.

'There are many motives for murder,' he said, wondering if any hair was softer or caught the light quite like hers. 'All I can say at this stage is, I've ruled out the top three.'

'Which is another way of saying bugger all.'

'With luck, that'll change shortly. I've held back from telling the press, so we could pursue any lines of enquiries, but...'

'Since you have nothing but nothings...'

He sighed. 'The announcement should make the midday edition.'

The mattress was feather. Almost as soft as the cloud he was floating on, as weightless as the waterfall of curls he could drown in. Not because passion was spent, not even because of the wild abandon with which she surrendered to him, giving and giving and giving. Collingwood had taken mistresses before. Too many to count, some whose names he'd forgotten, some whose faces were blurred, others who he remembered with fondness and warmth. But he'd never experienced this.

This wasn't sex. This was intimacy. The closeness of sharing. Of finishing each other's sentences. Of talking without being judged, being naked but not exposed, of giving and receiving pleasure in equal measure, and more critically, on equal terms.

'In that case, Inspector, we should toast Mr. Lloyd's memory.' She disentangled herself and reached into the bedside cupboard.

'Brandy, eh?'

'Shame on you, sir. Would you call a lace wedding dress a white frock? Young man, this is cognac.'

'With ginger biscuits,' he said, crunching.

'I thought you might want to spice things up.'

He pulled her mouth to his. Held the kiss. Ginger and cognac. If he died now, he would die happy. If he died aged a hundred, he would never forget this.

Words couldn't express the relief that his investigations had eliminated Julia not just from the murders, but from the pornographic postcard trade in general. He wasn't wrong about this. Her finances stacked up, two thorough searches revealed nothing, and it stood to reason a photographer would interact with other photographers and suppliers. Would he have been suspicious of one solicitor calling on another? A fellow bookseller dropping in on a colleague? Of course not. This was no different from any other trade, apart from the context.

Collingwood was no prude. Far from it. And he certainly didn't moralize. But dammit, Frenchies were more than some grubby little peep show. This was a greedy, cruel and (as many found out) vicious business, and the girls could style themselves as actresses and models all they liked. When pimps and drugs are involved, blackmail and beatings are par for the course, and with the factories, mills and refineries attracting more and more migrant labour, gangsters aren't far behind. Once these boys muscle in, there's no end to the lengths they'll go to, to retain control. Especially now there's a fortune to be made with moving pictures and slide shows.

He lay on his back, watching dust motes float through the air and sunlight bounce off the bedknobs. Was this what it was like, falling in love? How was that even possible in the space of just a few short days? Where did that leave Alice? Emily? His duty to them…?

'Don't suppose you'd care to tell me your real name?' he asked gently.

'Well, now.' She sipped. Nibbled a biscuit. 'Suppose I said it was Josephine?'

'As in Napoleon's wife? I don't believe that for one second.'

'Accusations of duplicity are deeply hurtful, Inspector.' She rolled on top of him. Slid her lips down his body, inch by very slow inch. 'But I can put up with them, providing *you're* not going to tell me "not tonight, Josephine".'

Given the right circumstances, there is evil in most people's hearts. Revenge, jealousy, anger, greed. All manner of motives can trigger it.

The flip book on the writing bureau showed a pretty girl with tumbling blonde curls, wholesome smile and big, wide, childlike eyes. Looking at her, you'd think butter wouldn't melt. Virginal. The white clothes that she was teasing off. The way her tongue pokes through her teeth as she strives to unhook a sticky button. The stocking that she accidentally drops, and has to bend over at the waist to retrieve.

An innocent, you'd think. Like the girl stepping out the bath, reaching for her towel. Until you remember that someone is staging every childlike move, every wide-eyed stare, every phoney little-girl pout.

They think they're clever. They think that, by faking innocence, they're not whores, and that's true. They're worse than whores. With street girls, men know what they're getting, and they're willing to pay. It's a business deal, pure and simple.

The flip book ripples the air, licking at any loose papers on the open bureau, again and again and again.

These girls aren't whores, they are spiders. Nasty, dirty, ugly little spiders, who drag unsuspecting flies in to their nasty, dirty, sticky little web by pretending to be sweetness and light.

Only there is no sweetness. No light.

Flip flip. Flip flip. Flip flip.

Tell me, what decent person can stand back and allow them to destroy more and more lives?

Flip flip. Flip flip. Flip flip.

No, a decent person does what everyone does when it comes to spiders. They squash them. Quickly and cleanly, because it's wrong to let a living creature suffer, even though these insects are lower than vermin. But squashed just the same.

Beside the flip book sat a British Bulldog revolver, with a fifteen-yard firing range.

It was already loaded with bullets.

Dressing was a challenge. Every time Julia laced her stays, nimble fingers untied them, then did things to her that reduced her willpower to dust.

'If you don't stop that,' she rasped, 'I'm calling for help.'

'And here's me, thinking I was managing perfectly well on my own.'

Oh, he was, he was. John Collingwood proved to be everything a girl could want from a lover. Experienced. Considerate. Passionate. He was tender and funny, unreserved, unperturbed. Satisfaction guaranteed, many times. Just the ticket to set a girl up, before embarking on a new phase in her life.

'What times were the girls killed?' she asked, as she finally managed to lace up her corset.

'Why?'

'Just curious.'

The scent of ripe strawberries wafted in through the window, along with the sound of children filing past, reciting their four times table, as the bells of St. Oswald's chimed twice.

'There has to be a connection,' she said. 'Since I was your prime suspect at one point, I assume you've ruled out delivery men?'

His whole body tensed. 'Why?' This time, there was an edge to the question.

'No reason.'

'There's never "no reason" with you, Julia. Even when I ask you your real name, you distract me.'

'Very well. The truth is, I was feeling pretty damned pleased with myself, being right about Dickie Lloyd, and — well, I rather fancied myself as another Sherlock Holmes.'

'Is that the best you can do?'

'Sod it, then. If you must know, I wanted details, so I can clear my name once and for all!'

'There's fire in your eyes when you're angry, and I like the way you plant your hands on your hips like a fishwife, I really do. Which is all very fine, and indeed quite arousing. Were it not for the fact that you're no longer under suspicion.'

'Maybe not, but someone's trying to frame me, so if I knew exactly where and when the girls died —'

'Jesus Christ, you know who's behind it, don't you?'

'Don't be silly.'

'Do you think I'm bloody stupid?'

'Please don't shout.'

He didn't even hear. 'You've had this information all along, and withheld it from the police? Give me his name, Julia. *NOW.*'

There are only so many lies you can tell detective inspectors. 'I don't have a name. It could be one of four people, maybe five, or none of them. All I have are theories —'

'Do you have any idea of what you've done?' Anger blazed cold in Collingwood's eyes as he pulled on his clothes. 'Because of — what? some stupid, selfish, pathetic little secret you've been keeping to yourself? — none of these men have been interviewed, time's been lost, resources have been wasted, and quite possibly Elizabeth Mansell died for nothing.'

Julia was wrong. It wasn't anger at all. That look in his eyes? That was disgust.

'If another girl dies, this is on you, and you were wrong. Very wrong. You bloody well are under suspicion, and if you don't give me those names now, and I mean pick up a pen and start writing this second, so help me, I will charge you with perverting the course of justice.'

Define self-loathing. Is it the humiliation of standing in nothing but corset and boots, feeling half an inch tall? Is it the knowledge that what's done is done, and can't be undone? Is it the belief that you were acting in good faith for all the right reasons, until someone shoves reality in your face? Or the fact that someone you respected, and who respected you in return, is staring at you in disbelief and contempt?

Sickness churned in Julia's stomach, and it had nothing to do with cognac and ginger.

With what little dignity she had left, Julia climbed into her clothes and pinned up her hair. Anything to keep her shaking hands busy, and stop him from seeing her cry.

'Then you will have to arrest me, John. It's as simple as that.'

'You're really this stubborn?'

'Are you?' She turned to face him at last. 'How do you think it would look, marching me down to Boot Street on the pretext of obstruction of justice? The woman whose — let's call it female intuition, gave you Dickie Lloyd's name, and which might well lead the police to Dickie Lloyd's killers? The same woman who's naïve enough to believe her — let's still call it female intuition, can do the same with the Purple Ink Killings. Oh dear, I do hope that reporter from the *Chronicle* doesn't hear me drop that nickname. Only I hear he hangs around the station quite a lot.'

'Jesus.' Collingwood ran his hands through his hair. 'Has there been one second, just once, since I walked into your life that you haven't been using me? Even today.' His lip curled as he lifted a tangled sheet with his little finger. 'You sold your body to wheedle information out of me.'

Julia swallowed. Counted to five. 'Sold suggests I received something in return.'

All you could hear in the bedroom was the sound of burning bridges. But what good could possibly come of giving him her list of suspects? Would it save her from the cells in the Boot Street? Not a single chance in hell. Once her involvement in the Frenchie trade became public, that would be it for Whitmore Photographic, and somehow the idea of bricks through her windows and having this lovely place looted held little appeal.

Then there was the emotional ripple. The wrecking of lives left, right and centre as the police tore the suspects' premises and reputations apart. What had Tobias Wood's wife, or his children, or his grandchildren done to deserve that? What of the slur it would cast over the church he so generously supported? Or the taint it would cast over every portrait, every wedding photo, every *memento mori* any of them — any of us — had ever produced? Mother of God, hadn't Flora's parents suffered enough!

Her stomach twisted. The models would no longer have the secrecy their photographer guaranteed. On the contrary. Their names and faces would be plastered all over the papers, the humiliation unthinkable. No employer would take them, and thanks to lack of income, the workhouse would be their only option.

On top of that, and despite everything, Julia had given her word to Midge that his secret was safe in exchange for Pandora's address, and her word had to count for something, surely? Because without integrity, a person is nothing.

Worst of all, far, far worse than anything, Oliver would be jailed and, with his assets confiscated, Rosie and the nippers would be turned out on the street. For pity's sake, all anybody in this game ever wanted was to make a better life for themselves, their friends, and their families. Julia wasn't ripping that contract up.

'I hope you can live with yourself,' Collingwood said quietly. 'Because if another girl dies, your finger might as well have pulled the trigger.' He smiled in a way that made her shiver. 'Oh, and please don't bother coming down, Mrs. McAllister. I'll let myself out.'

No, no, no, this wasn't how it was supposed to be. She was supposed to be helping. Making things better, putting things right. Instead, she was making them worse...

Should she alert the models to the presence of a monster? Scheherazade, the Swedish Princess, the Rose of Shanghai? Dammit, someone had a common link with the dead girls. Who the bloody hell was it? The problem there was, there had been no signs of a struggle at any of the crime scenes, suggesting they let their killer in — and the only reason they'd do that was because they trusted the bastard. In which case, Julia's warning could well have the opposite effect. Make them turn to the one person they knew they could trust...

She needed to think this through, and carefully, but right now, Cyril Strauss was about to be interred. Maybe "T" would show up at his funeral. Then at least one good thing would come out of this mess.

Chapter 26

What Julia knew about Jewish burials could be written on the nail of her little finger. It was a relatively small community, which kept itself to itself much of the time, and until now, she hadn't given any aspect of the process a second thought. Would she even be welcome?

'Mrs. Strauss.'

There was no mistaking the chief mourner, her face bloated from tears, her face twisted with grief, and Rosie was right. No mother should have to bury a child. Least of all, like this...

'Please accept my condolences.'

'I alvays take him his dinner round.' The words ran into one another. 'When he vasn't home dat first night, I knew somesink terrible happen.'

'I'm so sorry.'

'I vent to hospital, vork, nobody seen him.'

She tore at the rip in her black mourning gown, over the heart. Yes, of course. Julia had forgotten that the rending of garments was a Jewish tradition.

'Second night, I go straight to police.'

She buried her head in her hands, and Julia's heart thought it would break.

'You know my boy?' Mrs. Strauss asked eagerly. 'You come to give eulogy?'

Julia glanced round the little group gathered awkwardly round her. Mr. Newman she recognised from the baker's on the corner, also the old man second from left. Didn't he run a tailoring business? Other than those, the rest were strangers, and exclusively male at that.

'Mr. Whitmore from Whitmore Photographic sent me. With his compliments, he would like to present you with a commemorative photograph of the service.'

'So kind. Everyone so kind. You so kind.'

'When she read about the young man beaten beside the canal, the poor woman rushed to view the remains.' Mr. Newman leaned in. 'To think how happy she was, when she found out it wasn't Cyril.'

'To think,' echoed the man next to him, shaking his head sadly.

'It was accident,' Mrs. Strauss wailed. 'Accident.'

The men exchanged glances.

'I know my boy. If he mean to kill himself, he leave note.'

Damn. Should Julia tell her?

You can't choose who you fall in love with. That was the thought that went through her mind, when she waited for "T" in Willow Walk. Now those words whispered through the headstones. Whistled round his open grave. Cyril and his mother seemed loving and close, why leave a note for "T" and not her? Suicides, of course, are rarely rational. Julia suspected he'd reached the point where he only had the strength to pour his heart out the once. Or perhaps he wanted to spare her the shame? Or felt "T" could explain what he couldn't?

Wait. Suppose there was a second note? Realising he'd dropped the original and couldn't find it when he went back, suppose Cyril wrote another letter, and this time made sure "T" received it?

Ah, but these were fantasy thoughts.

No man about to take his own life sits down, pens another long outpouring of emotion, then calmly walks it round to the one person who might stop him. More likely, he was past caring about explanations.

Just end it, that's what he'd have been thinking. *Just let me end this torment.*

With a lump in her throat, Julia set to taking photos from every angle. There were no women close by or watching from a distance, veiled or otherwise. Damn. In fact, the only other female in the whole bloody cemetery was a widow, bent over and walking with the aid of a stick, who'd come to lay another stone on her husband's grave. Double damn.

The eulogies were few, and those there were, brief and rather vague. They praised his fine, upstanding character, but listed no specific instances, nor did they have any personal memories to narrate. Cyril Strauss, it seemed, lived the most private of lives, without friends or outside interests. Intense was the word that sprung to mind.

After the mourners had tossed soil on the wooden coffin, three spadefuls each, it was a sorry little procession that wound its way back to the house. Mrs. Strauss was never going to manage the traditional feast of hard boiled eggs. Supported by Mr. Newman on one side and the tailor on the other, she could barely stand, never mind swallow. It seemed she, too, lived the most private of lives without friends or interests. Unfortunately, like mother, like son.

Before the gravediggers came back to finish the work, Julia sneaked a pebble from the old lady's collection (the late Mr. Goldberg was in no position to miss it) and placed it on the pile of fresh soil.

Please God, Cyril, you have finally found peace.

'Her Ladyship says to give you this.'

Bug handed Daisy a kiss lock coin purse, clasp still intact but the leather slightly scuffed from where he'd rammed it in his trouser pocket then forgot about it when he fell in with some kids running a spud race down the tow path, and landed square on his bum.

'Didn't have no spuds on it when she give it me, mind.' He had a thought. 'You won't tell on me, will yer?'

He'd put up with another ducking in the tin bath, if he had to. Maybe even having his head washed with that soap stuff, or his hair cut, or that stupid brush put round his teeth. But s'pose she said no to the Music Hall. What then?

'Cross my heart and hope to die, Bug.'

The purse was heavy, and when she looked inside, her big blue eyes closed tight with relief. 'Talk about the nick of time,' she said. 'Bloody landlord. Just doubled my rent, he has, can you believe that? Says I'm giving the place a bad name, me and my loose morals.'

Bug had heard the neighbours. Rotten cows. Talking about her behind the backs of their hands, curling their lip like they was better than her, and Daisy were some kind of slime.

'Up yours!' he'd yelled at them, tossing in a dozen V-signs for good measure. That's why he brought her the tongue and digestives. Little presents, to cheer her up. Only he couldn't keep taking stuff from Her Ladyship's larder. Least, not without putting stuff back. 'She'll be crawlin' soon,' he said, pointing to Minnie.

'Oh, don't!' Daisy laughed. 'It's bad enough now. She slithers like a greased eel, Mrs. Mack says, isn't that right, my little elver?'

Something else that weren't fair. Bug only called Julia Mrs. Mack the once, and she said if he tried that again, he'd be wearing his teeth on the back of his head. Bug liked coming to Daisy's; it was a good laugh and she never threatened to wash his mouth out like Some He Could Mention. He liked bringing her things, too. Things like tongue and ham, and the last of the digestives, coz he knew what it was like, being poor. And it were all fine and dandy, weren't it, these lovely rows of terraced houses. Least, if you was lucky enough to nab a job in the factries.

Only took a fall, though, or a crushed ribcage or a foot caught in the machinery (like Some Others He Could Mention) and well, that was it. Curtains. He'd seen 'em, poor sods. Hands burned to the bone from hot metal. Eyes knocked out from all sorts of flying objects. That explosion last year. Lose yer job, yer lose the lot, and first you think, ain't so bad. I'll pop me watch, me coat and that rug in the parlour, that'll tide us over a bit. Next it's the china, then that clock yer Mum give us, and before you know it, it's the wife's wedding ring, and once stuff's in pawn, it don't bleedin' come out, ain't that the truth.

He'd lived with 'em. Whole families, huddled under the arches to stop from freezing to death. A lot took to crime. Couldn't get by otherways. But how many lasted the winter? How many of the poor mangled sods made it to spring?

Bug liked making Daisy laugh. That long hair falling over her face reminded him of his Mum, 'cept Mum's weren't shiny, and it was matted and darker than coal and had bits stuck to it, and once he saw something crawling.

'That's the demon drink for you,' the old bitch next door used to snarl.

Yeah. Like her and gin never met, eh?

Funny thing, though. Mum never laughed, never smiled, not once he could remember. Just sat with a bottle or got fighting with Pop. She couldn't half swing a left hook, could his mother.

'Beef and kidney, Bug.' Daisy lifted the tea cloth covering the plate, releasing delicious smells into the room. 'Still hot from the pie man, so eat up before it gets cold.'

'It's your supper,' he said. 'Yours and Minnie's.'

'There's enough to go round. Now tuck in, before I start to worry that you don't like it.'

He didn't need telling twice. He tucked in.

'How much does flowers cost?' he asked, wondering if gravy dribbling could be turned into some kind of career, coz he was bleedin' good at this lark.

'What sort of flowers?'

'Dunno. What sort is there?'

'Depends. How much money have you got?'

'Nuffin'.'

'Are they for Mrs. Mack?'

He nodded, because even for Bug there was too much in his mouth to reply.

'Take this sixpence; it's a gift, not a loan —'

'Uh-uh.'

Whoops. Crumbs and gravy all over his jacket, but he was buggered if he was taking charity from people what didn't have nothing to start with. That's why he wanted to pay Her Ladyship back. She didn't have nothing, neither. 'Cept he couldn't take her ham or stilton or pies, if he did she'd go bonkers, but she liked flowers, didn't she?

'Next time, p'raps.'

He'd nick some from the cemetery on the way home. Big bunch of lilies. There yer go, Her Ladyship. Whaddya think about that? No one'd notice. Even that rozzer watching the shop wouldn't think twice.

'*The banshee, the banshee, bejabbers, don't you hear?* I'm teaching Minnie a new song — you can join in, if yer like, Daise. *Its groaning and its moaning, begob it's moighty queer.* Good word, innit? Begob?'

'Tell me that joke from the Music Hall again. The one about the Prime Minister's dog.'

Bug wiped his mouth with his sleeve. 'Once me and Minnie's married, you won't have to live here, Daise, and the neighbours won't call you names behind your back, and you can tell the landlord to stick his rent where the sun don't bleedin' shine. But till Minnie and me's married, can I still keep coming round?'

Coz she was nice, and she was pretty, he was comfy here; it was like she was his big sister, and she didn't tell him to bugger off, neither. And he bet Minnie'd never, EVER have to duck from a cuff round the ear. Or get whacked with the buckle end of a belt till she bled.

'What's your name?' Daisy asked, pouring him tea in a cup. 'Your real name?'

Bug thought for a bit. 'Tom,' he said, tickling the baby under her armpits. 'Me name's Tom.'

And that's the thing, see. Now he had Daisy, and Minnie, and Her Ladyship back home, he didn't need to hide behind some stupid nickname no more. For the first time since his Pop left him with that priest in the long scratchy frock, he could — yeah, he could be himself.

Hee-hee. Wait till Her Ladyship heard *THAT*.

A British Bulldog revolver has a magnificent feel to it. The wooden handle fits neatly into the palm of a hand, and with the chamber well oiled, it works like a dream.

An instrument of death, but also an instrument of life.

Once these spiders were squashed, lives would be saved. Many lives. After that, the men whose lives had been saved would be free to live as God had intended. Respectably.

It was medical fact that masturbation caused epilepsy. Without these sirens flaunting their nudity, touching themselves, and inciting men to pleasure themselves, that would be the end of the disease. Imagine! No more fits, no more thrashing, no more foaming at the mouth, and because it would put paid to moral degeneration, the death of these spiders would curb mania and violence, and save even more lives by preventing murders in the future!

Crime would plummet.

Good would triumph.

First Oakbourne, then — once this made the papers and the evidence spread — London, then England, then the world.

Such a clever revolver.

The chief difference between what Bug so charmingly called the Jewish boneyard and any other cemetery Julia had known could be summed up in one word. Flowers. There were no flowers at a Jewish funeral, no flowers on the graves. Although beautiful when fresh, flowers fade, then wither, and eventually die. A stone, on the other hand, is the ultimate symbol of permanence. Testimony that memory will not fade, legacy will not wither, and love will not die.

In the cosy red light of her dark room, tears rolled down Julia's cheek that had nothing to do with the combination of sulphuric acid, carbonate of potash and bromide of potassium. (Having said that, not for nothing did the word bromide stem from the Greek for stench!) But as image after image revealed itself in the developing dish, it was obvious that every grave was adorned with its own pebble sculpture, unique and at the same time everlasting. Some people believed the weight of the stone stopped *golems* from gaining life from the soil wrapped round the dead. Others took comfort from fact that the stones, quite literally, kept the deceased grounded. Anchoring their souls to the world of the living, so that they might not wander and be forgotten.

Not forgotten. That was the point.

At the end, Cyril felt so worthless, that he *wanted* to be forgotten. To have his presence erased from human memory, even his mother's. Julia wiped her tears. She could not let that happen, she couldn't — but what was she supposed to do? Post his suicide note anonymously to Mrs. Strauss? Then "T" would never know the depth of his feelings. On the other hand, if she sent his letter to the *Chronicle*, "T" would undoubtedly take comfort from reading it — but how would this help his grieving mother? Learning that her son rated a lover she'd never met, or even knew existed, higher than her?

'My boy is dead in ground,' she'd wailed at his graveside. 'Me, I dead above ground.'

Once again, Julia understood what it meant to be literally laid low by grief.

Mrs. Strauss had sunk to the grass, hugging her arms to her body, in the same way Rosie slid down the wall at the news of Charity's death, rocking backwards and forwards, over and over, howling like an animal caught in a trap. Oliver slumped on the floor by her side, face waxy and white, too shocked and too grief-stricken to cry. No parent recovers from losing a child, but as Oliver said, there was comfort — if that was the word — in knowing their daughter died from natural causes, and Julia regretted being so harsh on John Collingwood, when his own child was slipping away. He had come to her bed, needing solace and escape. To find that he'd been manipulated would have holed his ego below the water line, and God knows he wasn't cramped by modesty to begin with.

But Mrs. Strauss had to live with the knowledge that her son took his own life, and Julia knew from experience that grief would soon turn to guilt. She would start to think his death was her fault — she hadn't been a good enough mother, she should have picked up the signs and stopped him. She wasn't to blame, absolutely not! But that weight would never be lifted from her. The poor woman would never stop feeling responsible, and Julia wondered how long it would be before the Angel of Death spread his wings over Mrs. Strauss, too?

Then there was the other question. Namely, how could splashing Cyril's innermost secrets over the front page honour his memory? Had he wanted his landlady, his mother, his bank colleagues to know the details of his private life, he'd have told them.

Damned if you do, damned if you don't.

Julia glanced at the clock. Her intention to call on Pandora before Mrs. McAllister vanished into thin air hadn't waivered, but it was important to catch the woman off guard, and the best way to catch someone off guard is during a meal. They're relaxed, they're happy — in other words, the perfect state to wrongfoot. In the meantime, she still hadn't quite found the perfect (if that was the word) picture to present to Mrs. Strauss. The majority of funerals that she'd covered had been commissioned from the wealthier strata of Oakbourne society, and a commemorative photo of a hearse drawn by a gleaming Flemish black adorned with feathers was a stirring sight in anybody's book. There was nothing rousing about Cyril's deal-wood coffin and a thirty shilling headstone.

Julia gently agitated the plates in the processing bath, then transferred them to the fixing solution. Around his new home, the names of his neighbours stood out clearly, and her heart ached to see just how many had been forced to flee the pogroms of Russia. There were Samilovs, Dikshteins, Manoviches and Gabinskis. Victors, Grigorys and Kadyas. Coming from all walks of life, rich and poor, these creatures had left everything behind, often family too, to start a new life in England, but many, too many, died young. Had there ever been such a wide range of occupations grouped together? Geologist. Ballet dancer. Journalist. Architect. There was even an opera singer buried next to a —

Wait. She snatched the plate from the bath. *There! That figure in the background!*

You can't choose who you fall in love with...

She peered at the image through her magnifying glass. *No, you bloody well can't.*

Shaking the drips off the glass plate, Julia pushed a wayward curl out of her eyes. If she followed up now, there'd be no time to trail out to the address Midge Belmont gave her. On the other hand, once she settled with Pandora, she couldn't hang around Oakbourne afterwards. Collingwood's net was closing in fast enough as it was.

For ten minutes she sat in the dark room, reminding herself that Cyril wasn't her problem, and certainly not her priority. Her priority was Pandora. Then taking the boat train to France.

Be who you are, JJ. No more, no less, no apologies.

*S*am, Sam, Sam...

Goodbyes were hard, but en route to London, the hansom would detour via Southolt Cemetery, where she'd lay white roses on Sam's grave and say goodbye forever.

Before that, though —

Julia picked up the telephone and placed a call.

Chapter 27

Dusk was falling over the canal. Low in the sky, the sun was a pale, almost white ball casting perfect reflections on the watery mirror, its pink haze making the smoke from the factories mysterious, and strangely appealing.

The narrow boats had tied up for the night and, for practical reasons, moored well clear of the bridge for handy access to the factories, for ease of loading and unloading.

Half the boatmen were independent contractors who owned their own barges, the other half worked for companies that ran fleets, but they all wore flat caps, corduroy trousers and braces, and clomped around in boots with steel tips. Some still used horses. Most these days ran on steam. They all led the same gypsy life.

Julia watched a heron flap indolently down the length of the canal. Shielded her eyes against the glare of the brass work on the boats as the sun dipped.

Expensive to build but cheap to run, there were nearly five thousand miles of these industrial waterways across Britain, carrying everything from coal to pottery to cotton to iron ore. But it wasn't just the hundred thousand water gypsies who made a living from them. By their very nature, canals have to be flat. The challenge of negotiating valleys and hills had given rise to some truly brilliant engineering solutions — tunnels, stepped locks, aqueducts, boat lifts — and since iron was cheap, everyone won: the architects, the engineers, the navvies, the people who manufactured the necessary construction equipment. With the canals needing a constant supply of water, reservoirs sprang up like weeds. More labour, more prosperity

— and in turn the canal network gave rise to more factories and more mills, drawing farm workers from all over, since agricultural wages couldn't compete. The population boom created a surge in house building, and of course the incomers needed food, heating, clothing, their souls needed nurturing, their children needed schooling, and everyone from bailiffs to beadles had to unwind. Hence the explosion in Music Hall popularity.

But it wasn't Oakbourne's rapid expansion or increased prosperity that preyed on Julia's mind. Obvious as it sounds, canals have to be waterproof. This was done by a process called puddling, in which the trench was lined with clay mixed with water. Basically an open clay pipe. How tragic that this clay base was the last thing Cyril Strauss saw. And that the canal, which brought life to Oakbourne, should be the instrument of his death.

The sun sank behind the sugar refinery, plunging the towpath into shadow. The coppery smell of smoke hung in the air. Bats squeaked on the wing.

Cyril, she'd argued, wasn't her problem, and it was true. She didn't know the man, had never met him, certainly hadn't caused him to drop his suicide note in the graveyard. No one asked her to play busybody, running after him with it then opening it to track down the addressee, rather than placing it on the seat where he'd been sitting, in the hope he'd come back and collect it.

Suppose, though, that was exactly what happened? Suppose he'd frantically checked his pockets, couldn't find the letter, returned to the cemetery, couldn't find it there either, and that was the last straw?

What if Julia pushed him over the edge?

Well-meaning or not, it was still interfering, and that's what had kept her awake at night. The reason she'd spent so much time sipping Darjeeling in the Willow Walk Tea Rooms. Why she'd taken her camera and tripod to the Jewish (thank you, Bug) boneyard. Why she couldn't leave without putting it right...

The boat people had closed their curtains for privacy. The only lights flickered from windows in the lock keeper's cottage, two hundred yards down the tow path. The cottage, like all lock keepers', was beautifully maintained, with gardens that rivalled Kew and whose fragrance kicked the factory stench into touch. Except Julia's route did not take her down that floral path. Instead, she picked her way carefully towards the bridge in the opposite direction, where a lone figure stood silhouetted against the white line of the steps.

'Thank you for meeting me.' She held out the envelope addressed to "T". 'I think you'll find this is for you.'

You can't choose who you fall in love with.

Grey eyes flashed into her mind. The grey eyes of a wolf. To hell with that. She crushed the thought like an ant under her heel.

But it's true. You can't choose who you fall in love with, and having ruled out waitresses and staff, she'd gone on to assume that "T" was either married or, when she discovered that Cyril was Jewish, not of his religious persuasion. Catholic, most likely. Or perhaps a Salvationist.

Yet who was in the tea rooms each time she'd been there, polishing his spectacles, over and over...?

A telephone call to the Cadogan Street branch of the West London Bank, directly opposite Willow Walk, revealed that one of the tellers was named Edward James Smith, known by all and sundry as Teddy. It also confirmed another hunch. That

Cyril Strauss used to work at that branch, until his recent transfer to Snowdon Lane, a mere three-minute walk from the tea rooms. Who'd think twice about two employees — friends and colleagues — taking their tea breaks and lunches together?

'I've seen you in Willow Walk,' Teddy said. 'You were taking pictures at the funeral, too.'

As gently as she could, Julia explained about the dropped note, the assumptions she'd made, and how she was terrified that it was her fault Cyril died.

'No.' Teddy's shoulders heaved. 'Nothing you could have said or done would have stopped him.'

Love like theirs had to be hidden, he sobbed, but true love it was, she had to believe that; they were soulmates. And as he poured out his heart, she envied people who could love unconditionally, give without reason and care without expectation. The true mark of friendship and love.

'Why didn't the two of you just run away, Teddy?'

'Where to?'

Fiji. Casablanca. What did it matter?

'What could we do? We're bank clerks, Mrs. McAllister. How could we support ourselves? We had no money. How could we live?'

Julia didn't see any of those as insurmountable problems, but it was too late and the damage was done. These quiet waters had become Cyril's shroud.

'It's my fault he died.' Teddy collapsed onto the steps. 'I killed him, Mrs. McAllister. I killed him, it's my fault, I killed him, I killed him.'

'Sssh.' She wrapped her arms around him and rocked him like a child. 'You can't blame yourself for another person's actions.'

Talk about hypocritical, given everything she'd just told him! But the poor man needed comfort, and there was no one else he could talk to.

'It seems to me,' she said, 'Cyril reached the point where he couldn't —'

'No, no, no, you don't understand.' Teddy's face was a picture of torture. 'I'm being married on Saturday.'

What?

'That's what drove him over the edge.'

We can't all be strong. In the face of what Teddy believed to be overwhelming odds, he caved in to respectability.

'You know where I work, Mrs. McAllister. It's a good position; people look up to us. If my secret came out...' He'd be ruined at best, thrown in prison at worst. 'I couldn't inflict humiliation on my family.'

'So you met a girl —'

'She's rather plain, but —'

'I know.'

Plain girls aren't snaffled up quickly. Plain girls are grateful. Plain girls don't ask too many questions.

Plain girls pose for erotic pictures to survive.

A hansom clattering over the bridge was a sharp reminder that Julia should be heading to London right now, going far, far away from this place. Away from Beryl, from Cocoa, all the other wretches sucked into the web of addiction. And she prayed to God she wouldn't regret meeting Teddy tonight, instead of calling on Pandora.

'Is this ... is this where he died? Is this where he threw himself in?'

She listened to the mournful hoot of an owl. Wished she was already far, far away. Anywhere else but here — 'No, Teddy.' She cradled him while he sobbed. 'This isn't where Cyril died.'

'Well, well, what *do* we have here, boys?'

Damn. Teddy's hacking had drowned the approach of a gang of youths slithering down the grassy bank.

'A sweet little courting couple.'

Within seconds, the yobs had surrounded the steps. Julia could smell ale on their breath. Sensed their hatred.

'And we all know what kind of coupling goes on under this particular bridge.'

'Filthy perverts.'

Fists slammed into the palms of their hands, an advertisement for what lay in store.

'P-please —' Teddy begged.

'Ho, ho, did you hear that? Pretty boy says please.'

'Want what's coming to you, eh, pretty boy?'

'Gagging for it, if you ask me.'

'What about this lovely little filly, then?' A rough hand jerked Julia to her feet. 'Wanna know how we deal with nancy boys who dress up as women?'

'The same way you dealt with the young man five nights ago?'

'Whoa, did you hear that, boys? This one's all woman.'

The same rough hand grabbed her under the chin. 'What you need to know, darlin', is we don't stand for perverts round here.'

A different hand whisked off Teddy's hat. A boot stamped on it.

'I say we show her what *real* men are like.'

'What would you know about real men?' Julia spat, pulling free. 'How many of you — five? six? to one nineteen-year-old?'

'Oh yeah. And what would you know about that?'

'I know you beat him, stomped on him, urinated on him —'

'Watching was yer, love? Like that kind of thing, do yer?'

'I doubt you meant to kill him.'

'Course we bloody didn't, but he shouldn't have fought back when we yanked his bleedin' drawers down.'

'Told him, we did. *We don't stand for no poofs on our turf.*'

'Well, that's the thing. He wasn't.' Just a young man with effete mannerisms, who took pride in his appearance. The sort they probably called Prissy Cissy at school. The sort who slotted in perfectly to the Music Hall world.

'You would say that, wouldn't yer? Cuddling this little perve in the dark, my oh my, what would your mother say?'

'Stop wasting time, boys. Let's get on and give 'em what they deserve —'

'What they deserve is a medal,' a voice boomed down from the bridge. 'What *you* get, my friends, is the noose.'

At Collingwood's whistle, uniforms swarmed out of the bushes, from behind trees, from the tunnel, quickly proving that fists were no match for truncheons. In the space of a minute, resistance was over.

Julia sank down on to the steps. Teddy had asked, is this where Cyril died? It wasn't. It was the spot where Dickie Lloyd died.

Chapter 28

'That was a gutsy thing you did tonight.'

They were lying naked in Julia's bed, moonlight streaming over the floor, and Collingwood was feeling satisfied on more levels than he ever imagined existed.

'Going to you about my hunch, Inspector, or setting Teddy up without telling him?'

He stared at the moon's disc, full and bright in the sky. 'Both.'

Contempt, she'd said that first morning in the tea rooms. Imprinted on his memory was the decisive way she'd spread her napkin on her lap, to emphasise the deduction. *Complete and utter contempt for the victim, which makes this crime personal.*

Also imprinted on his memory were the silly jokes they'd exchanged, the way that thick, dark curl on the left kept springing about every time her head turned when someone came in, and the passion (oh, the passion) when she talked about photography.

As for Mr. Lloyd, though...

Having established lucre wasn't the driving force, Collingwood quickly ruled out his other two favourites, lust and loathing. Given how the victim had been humiliated, it didn't take long to cross motives such as thieves falling out or the settling of grudges off the list, and vengeance is rarely a team sport.

'We need to go back to the beginning,' he'd told Kincaid. 'What the hell are we missing?'

True, Dickie was relieved of his valuables, but again, thieves don't run in a pack, and they certainly don't beat their victims to death in sustained and sadistic attacks.

Contempt. Complete and utter contempt for the victim.

Dammit, he should have given her opinion more weight at the time, because once he went back to square one, he saw she was right. For all its brutality, this was a cold crime, and emotions don't come colder than contempt.

An image had formed, of a gang of thugs using homosexuality as the excuse to perpetrate vicious acts of violence.

'I'm not sensing it's these louts' first square dance. Put the word out. See if there are any other men with … alternative lifestyles, who've been "taught a lesson",' he'd told Kincaid.

Kincaid reported back in what seemed like the blink of an eye. 'Surprising what the promise of anonymity and an oath not to prosecute can dredge up,' he said cheerfully. 'I'm already up to six assault and batteries, and climbing. So. Now we know there's a pack of vigilantes on our patch — how do we go about catching the bastards?'

The bridge was merely the latest in a string of ever-changing meeting points for men desperate to keep one step ahead of the law. After Dickie Lloyd's murder, the pick-up point changed. But the bullies hadn't known that.

'I *am* sorry, Julia. Under pressure or not, I said some terrible things —'

'We both did.'

'Not necessarily true, but I'm very glad you forgave me.'

'Who said I had?' She made light of it, tickling him when she said it, but it was true. At the moment, it was too raw to either forgive or forget, but after the relief of finally tracking down "T", along with knowing she hadn't pushed Cyril over the edge, then the fight — so much anger, so much blood, so much fear, so much hate — she'd needed release.

'Can't have been easy, picking up the phone to tell me you'd set a trap. Not with the way things stood when I left.'

That was an understatement. Because once Julia established that "T" was Edward Smith (was any love more forbidden or more hopeless?), she telephoned Teddy at the bank, arranged to meet him at the bridge — and only then, taking the deepest breath on Planet Earth, placed a call to Boot Street to tell Collingwood she'd set a trap.

'You exasperate the hell out of me at the best of times, Julia McAllister, but to put yourself in deliberate danger? Christ, woman, are you insane?'

He leaned on his side, propping himself up on one elbow. After all the mud, blood, sweat and sex, he still smelled of *Hammam Bouquet*, and in the moonlight, his eyes looked silver and unearthly. She desired him all the more for it.

'Insane would have been telling you my plan ahead of setting it up. Once the trap was set, you had no choice other than go along with it.'

'Damn right, but I'm as cross as a sack of rats about you walking into the lion's den.'

'Despite the fact you caught Dickie's killers red-handed?'

'Despite the fact I caught Dickie's killers red-handed. And tell me again why you dragged that weedy bank teller into it?'

What else could she say, but the God's honest truth? That the two of them had struck up quite a friendship over Willow Walk's jam roll, and when she happened to mention her theory about Dickie Lloyd's killers, naturally he was quick to volunteer assistance.

'Friendship. Of course. You and Teddy have so much in common.' Collingwood leaned over and kissed her. A long, hard, lingering kiss. 'You like men, he likes men...'

'You're not going to arrest him?'

'The courageous Mr. Smith, hero of the hour? Hell, no. The Mayor will probably pin a medal on him.'

'Then what are you complaining about?'

'What I'm complaining about is that if, in future, you have any more bright ideas, you come to me first, instead of putting yourself in the line of fire, worrying me sick, and making me explain to my Chief Inspector, my Superintendent and the Chief Bloody Constable why I risked the lives of two civilians in a midnight sting.'

All Julia could think of, as she nestled in Collingwood's arms in a tangle of bedsheets and moonlight, was her conversation with Teddy, after the dust had settled and the thugs had been led away. Specifically, the part where he asked *why*.

'Society can't have vigilantes going round, beating men to death, Teddy.'

Still under the bridge, well out of earshot of anyone else, she'd apologised for not telling him about the sting in advance (missing out any mention that, if she'd warned him, he might not show up), but swore, God's honour, that his co-operation guaranteed him immunity from prosecution. The inspector had given his word.

'No.' Teddy had stared at his feet. 'I mean why did you go to so much trouble to find me? You didn't know Cyril, you didn't know me.'

No, she didn't. But Mother of God, she knew her brother...

***

Charlie Kincaid poured himself a large tankard of porter and knocked half of it back in one swig. Rounding up villains was thirsty work, but by buggery, was it worthwhile. Five more toerags off the street, God willing at least two of them would hang, the others looking at a nice long stretch in pokey. Old men before they came out.

He hoped those beatings were worth the pleasure it gave them, because little men who think they're big very quickly find out otherwise once they join prison society. Boot on the other foot in every sense.

Kincaid took another guzzle and toasted a bloody good night's work, and also Lady Luck, for being on their side when the hunch paid off.

'Need anything else, sarge?'

'Not tonight, constable.' Kincaid had things pretty much wrapped up here at Boot Street. 'Go home, son, and tell the rest of the men drafted in to work the extra half-shift that they're dismissed, as well.'

'Very good, sarge. Goodnight.'

'Night, Harry.'

The mood in the cells was sombre. Exactly how it should be. One of the thugs, the beefy ginger one, was mewing like a kitten, which was also exactly how it should be. Kincaid actually heard the rib crack when his truncheon hit it.

'I need a doctor,' Beefy whined.

'And I'll call one,' Kincaid promised. 'First thing in the morning. Or maybe after lunch, once you boys have had a chat with the beak.'

Taste of their own medicine wouldn't do them any harm. Sweeten them up nicely, in fact, for what lay ahead.

'Oh, come on, mate! Show me sympathy here!'

'Fair enough.' Kincaid reached for the dictionary and leafed through. 'Ah, yes, here we go. Right between shit and syphilis.'

With a wink to the desk sergeant, he reached into the bottom drawer of his desk, drew out a flip book, took it and his tankard into Collingwood's office and closed the door.

Inspector Kincaid. Inspector Charlie Kincaid. Inspector Charles H. Kincaid. Had the right sort of ring to it, and he already knew how well the chair fitted. *Inspector Charles H. Kincaid.*

With a practised thumb, he flipped through the book. Mostly these girls were ugly or fat. Sometimes both. You don't see many lookers working the streets.

Not the Swedish Princess on the beach. Big wide eyes, long blonde hair, this was one lovely, lovely girl. Innocence written all over her. Yet in thirty flicks, this child-woman had shed every stitch of clothing in a manner that would arouse a dead man in his grave.

Not so innocent. Or the photographer behind the camera.

He finished his ale. Felt his pockets for — *Bugger.* Where was it? *Christ, don't say I dropped it in that bloody kerfuffle —*

'Lost something, sarge?'

'What? No. No, everything's fine, constable. Just, uh, looking for my pipe.'

'Can you sign this, please, sarge?'

Through the wool of his suit, Kincaid's panicking search felt the hard, reassuring wooden lump that fitted perfectly in the palm of his hand. *Thank Christ Al-bloody-mighty.*

'Course.' The signature on the report was unusually erratic. 'Now you go on home, son, before your wife learns the dreadful truth. That you prefer my ugly mug to hers.'

Alone in Collingwood's office, he returned to the flip book.

Ran through it again and again.

Chapter 29

St. Oswald's was chiming three when Collingwood finally hauled himself away from Julia's bed. Relieved that a bunch of vicious thugs were off the street, happy that Dickie Lloyd had received the justice he deserved, and with every square inch of her skin tingling with satisfaction, she pulled the bedsheets round her and snuggled down to sleep.

She should have known. Happiness is always fleeting…

They say beggars can't be choosers, but the same applies to widows. Especially when they're excited about celebrating their thirtieth birthday with their husband and two small children with a fine rabbit supper. The daughter answers a knock at the door. A man from the mine, a man in a jacket and tie that she's never seen before, takes off his cap and tells her mother, he's sorry to be the bearer of bad tidings, but her man fell from the ladder after shift. Never stood a chance.

'These are yours now,' he says, handing over her husband's tools. 'The men be bringing the body to you shortly.'

Oh, and she and the children can stay in the cottage till the end of the week —

The men lift the body from the barrow, lay it on the kitchen table, cover him with a sheet, won't let the woman or the children look at him.

'Hundred foot fall don't make for pretty viewing, my bird.'

The daughter can smell the clay the miners plaster over their skin to protect it from the arsenic in the shafts. It's a smell she will never, ever forget.

Falls are not unusual. In pitch darkness, with dust choking their lungs, heads pounding, chests feeling the effects of the pressure of the blasting, and with ears still ringing from the drill, tired feet often slip. And the daft part was, they usually slip right at the bleddy top. Just when they were nearly home and safe.

'What am I to do?' the widow asks his corpse. 'What am I to do?'

Women and children also work the ore. Bal maidens they're called, employed on the surface to break down the rock to a size where it can be put through the crushing machine. Only their daughter is still young, and boys have to be twelve before they're allowed down the shafts.

Women and children breaking rocks and pushing trolleys don't pay the rent.

The widow has no choice.

The only man who wants her comes from a fishing family on the other side of Cornwall. A man who's achieved the almost impossible feat of being thrown out of the army, and consequently is displaced, disaffected, resentful and bitter.

In short, a man who believes the world owes him a living, and the world has welched on its debt.

Beggars can't be choosers. The widow won't put her children in the workhouse. She marries him, leaving behind her tearful parents, sisters, aunts and uncles, friends and cousins, and of course the only life she's ever known.

And learns the hard way that her new husband's outlet for his anger is drink, violence, and a penchant for biblical quotes.

'The sun shall be turned into darkness, and the moon into blood, before the great and terrible day of the Lord comes'.

Like all bullies, he picks on the weak and the vulnerable, and homeless, penniless, grieving widows with two small children don't come more vulnerable than that. The man's a predator. It's the reason he selected them.

But small children grow. Their bodies change. The daughter is still young, barely fourteen, but already she's seen the way he looks at her when he is hitting her. The new light in his eyes. The bulge inside his trousers.

It's the son, though, who bears the brunt of the stepfather's viciousness.

'Thou shalt not lie with a man as with a woman. It is an abomination before God.'

The son is sixteen. He is scared. 'I haven't, I haven't, I swear —'

'Lying lips are an abomination to the Lord.'

Out comes the well-worn birch and the belt, along with quotes about how the works of the flesh are manifest. Adultery (thwack), fornication (thwack), uncleanness (thwack), lasciviousness (thwack, thwack, thwack).

'Stop!' screams the mother, who is punched to the ground for her troubles, and kicked. Kicked until her jaw breaks, and her cheekbone with it. Kicked until she is coughing up blood. Two days later, the mother and the son are still too badly injured to move from their beds, but the Devil is not.

He is sitting beside the river, a bottle in his hand, pretending to fish. The daughter walks up.

'I've been studying the Bible, too,' she says. 'Ezekiel 18, chapter 4 to be precise. "Behold, all souls are mine, sayeth the Lord. The soul of the father as well as the soul of the son is mine. The soul who sins shall die".'

'What's that supposed to mean?' The Devil's dark eyes are fixed on her tight little breasts.

The daughter shrugs. 'No idea. I picked it at random, because I knew it would get your attention.'

'Attention for what?'

'This,' says the daughter, emptying the chamber into his heart.

Julia had no regrets. She had not lost a single lost wink of sleep since she killed her stepfather. Her only sorrow was leaving her mother and Cador, but they understood and gave her their blessing.

'Tell them I've run away with him,' she said, replacing the shovel she'd used to dig the grave. 'Promise me you'll stick to that story.'

They promised, and she knew they would keep it with their lives. But no child's last memory of her brother should be his sobbing regret that he, as the older of the two, and the man of the family, hadn't stood up to the beatings and violence. Or of a mother, unable to do more than grunt, tears streaming down what was left of her face.

Julia never blamed her brother. Even as a little boy, Cador was what other boys called soft.

'I can't help it,' he'd tell Julia. 'I've tried to change. I don't know what's wrong with me.'

When, when, when would people understand? Psychiatrists, the clergy, the medical profession, the moralists. They found homosexuality abhorrent, something to be hypnotised, medicated, jailed or beaten out of a person, but you say to them, *fine. You think sexuality can change? How would you feel, if you were sentenced to make love to men for the rest of your life? No? A year, then? A month? What, not even a week?*

If that concept was repellent to them, what gave them the right to inflict the reverse on others?

Cador never stood up to their stepfather, because for him abuse came as standard. He'd been bullied and beaten his entire life, and had long forgotten how to fight back, or understand that his mother and sister should even try.

'So that's *why*, Teddy,' she whispered to the dawn, as it broke pale and pink over the Common.

She traced "T" out of compassion, and a fear that holding on to Cyril's letter was the last straw to him taking his own life. Compassion was also why she'd thought so long and hard about the young man by the canal, found beaten, humiliated and pissed on.

But when she saw Teddy's image emerge from the glass plate in her darkroom, it was Cador's struggle, Cador's terror, that made her reach for the telephone and set the trap by the bridge.

That young man could have been her brother. Any of them could have been her brother...

Chapter 30

With a shrill blow on the whistle and a cloud of white steam, the train pulled out of Oakbourne, chugging past farms and fields, cows and sheep, and cotton dresses hanging out on the line. Rabbits scampered in the hedgerow, bees buzzed round the hives, and by the time the train pulled into Bentley-upon-Thames, merely two stops down the line, there wasn't the faintest trace of the heavy urbanisation and industrial practices Julia had left behind. In fact, mass production might have been the moon, it was that far away, and as completely an alien world.

Handing in her ticket, Julia asked directions to the address that Midge had written down. Happy to oblige, the station master also told her where to find the bus stop and what time the next one was due. But the day was fresh, the sky was clear. A walk would clear her head.

Because for all the time that had passed, she would never — never in a million years — forget the way her mother held her father's mining hat the night they brought the news. Caressing the hardened felt, still sticky with his blood, comforting the lump of clay that held the candle in place, even though it had been battered flat.

One slip. One silly slip. And the whole world changed for ever...

Squaring her shoulders, Julia and her Brownie box camera set off down the street. Bentley-on-Thames was a pretty market town that had grown up around a broad bend in the river with an elegant five-arch bridge, and was dominated by the church of St. Giles with its sturdy sixteenth century tower and bells to match. Its biggest feature, though, and arguably its prettiest (especially if you were a photographer) was its water meadows. Different from grazing marshes, these fields were deliberately flooded then drained (in at a trot and off at a gallop) to force an early growth of grass in spring, improve its quality, and thus boost the crop of summer hay. Sadly, they were in decline. The industrial revolution put paid to the need for extra hay, thanks to machines taking over from horses.

But for now, today, Julia was content to stroll beside them, because it was by the water meadows, twelve years ago, that she was found by an itinerant photographer by the name of Samuel Whitmore.

These weren't the same meadows, of course. No, no, no. Her and Sam's paths collided in Winchester, in Hampshire. She'd made it that far from Cornwall on her own, but by the time he found her, she was weak and exhausted, easy pickings for all manner of vermin on the road, and for a long time she was distrustful of his kindness.

Sam being Sam, he never asked for anything in return except total honesty. That Julia gave him in spades.

'So then. You can't decide whether to stick with Jenna, or change your name to Julia.'

Two J's either way, he said, no rush, decide it later. In the meantime, he'd call her JJ. Neither Julia nor Jenna, neither male nor female, young or old, whatever she wanted it to be.

'The main thing is that it puts you on an equal status.' He shot her his famous lopsided smile. 'Everyone's equal in the sight of God, JJ, remember that. And never forget the essence of who you are.'

His stories opened up the world and Julia's mind. Back in the days when exposure times were long, plates needed developing straight away and professional photographers routinely travelled like gypsies with their mobile darkrooms, Sam stacked up more adventures than Julia could dream about. Visited more places than she knew existed on the atlas. The more they moved from place to place, the more he taught her and the more she learned, until one day he decided to swap horse-drawn wagon for bricks and mortar.

'I can't manage the business without an assistant. Will you stay?'

Sam, Sam. Such a terrible liar.

Of course she stayed. And of course she assisted. But the one thing she never expected was for him to bequeath it to her in his will. Then again, she never expected him to die. Men like Sam — they live forever, don't they?

But as he'd said so many, many times, *you can't change the past, JJ, you can only mould the future*, and the future now lay in confronting Pandora. The bitch who'd been feeding drugs to young girls, and turning them into addicts for personal profit. Confronting, then ending her filthy racket once and for all.

And dammit, she wished she could remember where she left that wretched flip book. The Swedish Princess on the beach. It wasn't in the shop, it wasn't in her bag. Must be at Mitchell Street, although she didn't remember going back there after —

Julia pulled up short. Who would have expected Pandora to be living in a mansion on the river? Eat your heart out, Oliver Blackstock!

The surprises weren't over yet. When she knocked at the tradesmen's entrance, swinging her trusty box camera, it was to discover that —

'Sorry, marm, Miss Pandora's not home right now. She's at the dressmaker's, for a fitting for her ballgown.'

Pandora was the lady of the house? Not the cook, or the housekeeper, or some lowly lady's maid? *Meow* went the cat among Julia's pigeons.

'No matter. It was purely a courtesy, to advise her that I'm here.' She handed the flunky her visiting card. 'She engaged Mr. Whitmore to —'

'With respect, marm, you don't look like a Mr.'

No fooling him, but her smile didn't waver. She was Mr. Whitmore's assistant, she explained, here to photograph the servants.

'Why?'

Julia bet St. Peter didn't operate this many security checks. 'Why? Dear me, I have no idea. Like I said, I'm simply the assistant, Mr. Whitmore doesn't confide in me. Shall I start with you? You have the perfect profile...' Blah, blah, blah, because if she could sweettalk the mothers of obnoxious children into having portraits taken, flattering coachmen was a walk in the park. And dammit, the man actually blushed.

From then on, it was easy. Once the Pearly Gates swung open, no saint could be more helpful. Snap-snap-snap went the little Brownie camera, as he hustled the hall boy, the tweenies, the kitchen, laundry and dairy maids around. Snap-snap-snap-snap-snap. But where was this getting her? At this speed, she'd never be able to keep up the charade until Pandora returned, and as obliging as he was, when the flunky spoke with the butler, the butler categorically refused to allow Julia access upstairs. Even though she photographed him from his best side, and promised him a portrait for free.

Another odd thing. The servants were being ushered to her, not the other way round, each and every one nervous and flustered. Because they were having their picture taken unexpectedly? Because when authority beckoned, they became unsettled? Or because they were scared of Pandora —?

There was no chance to chat. The second any of them opened their mouths, they were dismissed with a handclap and a curt *get back to work*. Time to change the balance of power.

'Right, that's that roll of film finished.' Would the flunky know the camera was loaded for one hundred pictures? 'I need a darkened room to change the roll.'

'Follow me, marm.'

'I'll also need a couple of girls to help me.'

'Maude! Beatrice! Quickly, please. Mrs. McAllister needs your assistance.' The cat among the pigeons stopped stalking. 'There's a cupboard off the pantry, will that do?'

'Perfect.'

Among the stone jars and glass bottles, rolling tins and salt cellars, the pigeons started to coo.

'Hang on, I'll light a candle,' Maude (or Beatrice) said, 'then we can turn off the electric.'

Probably why she hadn't risen above scullery maid, her words all slurring into one like a Saturday night drunk, poor thing.

'Not just yet, if you don't mind.' Julia pretended to fiddle.

'What d'you need us to do, Miss?' Beatrice (or Maude) asked, with the same speech impediment.

Of course. Same drooping eyelids, identical mannerisms, hopping from foot to foot — the girls were sisters.

'Must be comforting for you, to have found service together. Not many sisters are that lucky.'

Maude and Beatrice frowned at each other.

'We isn't sisters.'

The plump one wiped her runny nose with the back of her hand, and now she looked closely, Julia could see the girls didn't share any physical resemblance. What they shared were the same symptoms.

'You need a doctor,' she said. 'I'll get the butler to send for one at once.'

That's why they were giving her the bum's rush. The below-stairs staff were sick, and they didn't want word getting out. Why not? Was it contagious?

'Don't need the quack, Miss.' Maude (or Beatrice) was adamant. 'Need Miss Pandora.'

Oh. Dear. God. This was what opiate addiction looked like...

'She'll be back soon.'

'Better be. I need it.'

'She's gone a long time.'

'Too long.'

'I need another dose. I need another dose now.'

'I know, I know — she's not usually this long.'

'What's keeping her, Maudie? I need it. I do.'

Their anguish would haunt Julia for the rest of her life, but she was out of her depth here. Nothing she could say or do to Pandora would ease the girls' suffering. On the contrary. Without their "dose", their lives would be ten times worse.

If there was an alternative, she couldn't bloody well see it. She had to phone John, and she had to do it now —

'I don't want to die.'

'You won't die,' she promised Maude (or Beatrice).

'Feels like I'm dying.'

'Me, too.'

'I don't want to die.'

'I'm so scared.'

Julia's stomach turned somersaults for these girls. What Pandora had turned them into. Dammit, if she could just remember where she'd left that wretched flip book, it wouldn't be so bad. But once the connection was made between drugs, girls and Frenchies, it wouldn't matter that she'd handed him this case on a plate. Collingwood would tear her shop apart, and if he stumbled on that, she was done for. Please God, please, please say she'd left it in Mitchell Street and hadn't dropped it in the kitchen, beside the till, behind the bloody counter.

She daren't wait. With Pandora out, brewing fresh supplies, it stood to reason she'd come home, dose her needy victims, then do the rounds of everyone else on her list.

Julia wasn't putting her neck on the block just so this bitch could get away with it.

A trickle of sweat ran down her spine. How much time did she have?

To be certain of catching Pandora red-handed, Collingwood would alert his counterpart in Bentley-upon-Thames straight away. The counterpart would organise a raid with equal immediacy, which would close down her operation and ensure her servants received proper medical help. The trouble was, the whole thing would probably be done and dusted in less than an hour. By which time, Julia wouldn't even be in Oakbourne.

All she could do was warn him, and pray Collingwood wasn't waiting at the station. The only thing she needed was enough time to collect her case from Mitchell Street and vanish before the shadow of the wolf caught up. And hope to buggery she hadn't left it too late...

'I'm going for help,' she said. 'You girls stay put. You'll be fixed up soon, I promise.'

They were on the floor now, shaking, crying; they had cramps in their stomachs and were moaning in pain, worried about throwing up in the cupboard, but she didn't dare let them out in this state. The more they fretted about dying, the faster the hysteria built up, and if they weren't careful, they'd make themselves seriously ill. But the flunky couldn't get wind that Julia knew about the drugging. God knows what would happen then. No, she'd stay calm, play it straight, say her camera had jammed, she'd be back with a new one —

'I'm sorry, dear, you want me to give what to charity when I leave?' Julia asked.

'No, I'm scared Miss Pandora'll give us what she give to charity.'

'That's what killed her, see.'

Pandora's dead? Holy Mother of God, no wonder the butler wouldn't allow her upstairs and the servants were scared half to death! That's why Pandora had been gone so long, of course. She wasn't coming back! Was it murder? An accident? Natural — oh, no. No, no, no, no, no, no.

Julia's blood literally stopped flowing.

The girl didn't mean to charity. She meant to *Charity*. The apple of Oliver Blackstock's eye.

Chapter 31

No train had ever moved so slowly. No time had ever stood so still. Fields that seemed so wide and fresh and open just a short while before had become sad reminders of an agricultural boom that belonged to previous generations. Farmhouses, with their primitive sanitation and rickety roofs, were no more than throwbacks to the past.

Just as industry had transformed the face of Britain, so industry was also its future, and as the world looked to turn the page towards a brand new century, change hurtled with it. One of those revolutionary technologies, of course, was photography.

Oliver, Oliver, how could you betray me?

The one true friend she had. The only man she'd ever trusted, apart from Sam.

How could you look me in the eye, drink with me, sing with me, share, dammit, your deepest, darkest secrets with me, then break my bloody heart?

As the countryside passed by with agonising slowness, the pieces slotted into place. How Charity had begged and pleaded, whined and wheedled to have some kind of life and independence before she settled down. How happy Oliver had been that he'd given "his girl" a chance to spread her wings.

'There isn't a day that goes by when I don't thank God in His bountiful mercy that she found a decent job in service.'

Julia's throat clogged at the memory of sitting in his tiny office, him proud as punch that Charity had found "a nice, respectable house" in Bentley-on-Thames.

'At least, if you can say such a thing, she died comfy.'

With hindsight, the smell of fish was rank. Unexpected death from influenza? The fact that her parents weren't alerted to her illness, and only notified after the event? Pandora must have been spewing kittens when her dosage resulted in Charity's death. Give her credit, though. The bitch covered it well. Business as usual, as though nothing had happened, banking on the death of a child, especially when it was sudden, knocking logic off its feet. Because Charity died far from comfy. Charity died in unimaginable pain from some homemade mix of poisons, frightened and alone.

The sun shall be turned into darkness, and the moon into blood, before the great and terrible day of the Lord comes.

So it was true. The Devil doesn't die. It is simply reborn in a different skin…

At last, fields gave way to the tall, choking shadows of the future. Cotton dresses on the line turned into silks and parasols on the pavement, scampering fox cubs became horses clopping in blinkers, and the only rabbits here hung from a butcher's hook. If Collingwood was waiting at the station when the train pulled in, Julia would still have to give him the slip.

She would not be heading for Mitchell Street.

Was it possible, she'd asked herself, that she could trace "T", trap Dickie's killer, thwart Tarrant, stop Pandora, and wrap it all up in a big, fat, yellow bow in twelve short hours? Knocking on Pandora's door, she'd actually felt confident. Cocky, even.

Quite honestly, she hadn't expected to achieve half of that, but amazingly, she'd given Teddy comfort — Mrs. Strauss too, in a way, with the commemorative photo of her son's interment. She'd given the canal victim a name, and because of that, the police had been able to trace his family and notify them of his death, and she'd been instrumental in bringing his killers to justice. For pity's sake, if that wasn't enough to dance on air, holing Tarrant and Pandora below the water line bloody well was, and even before the train chugged out of Oakbourne this morning, Julia had stopped whipping herself about dragging her models into the business. Anything that kept girls out of the workhouse was good.

Oh, how a couple of hours changes everything! There was no confidence now. No purrs of contentment.

No wonder Oliver was so keen to give her suspects to follow. Everything made horrible sense.

'If my Charity died a natural death and it's eating me alive, imagine how their fathers feel, knowing they weren't on hand to protect their babies from a monster.'

Oliver, though, was not a monster. He was simply a man, a good man, and despite all that had happened, and all that he'd done, Julia still believed that. Believed it with all her heart. That's why his betrayal cut so deep.

'Whoever's framing you, Julia, this bastard needs to know we're in this together.'

Oliver, Oliver, how could you do this to me?

Deep inside, though, she knew exactly why.

'Not to be there, when your child passes, that's a bugger of a burden for a father to carry.'

Charity was his world. Her death brought him to his knees, because that's when he made the link with Pandora. He was aware of the drugging and the effect on girls (and boys) coerced into acts they wouldn't otherwise do. Was Charity coerced? Pandora wasn't wasting drugs on her servants without reason. Had Oliver seen postcards made by a photographer in Bentley-on-Thames? Discovered his daughter, the apple of his eye, was turning tricks to feed her addiction?

Julia was past caring. All she knew was that, unable to grieve openly, the pain became locked inside, twisting and hurting, until it turned into bitterness that needed an outlet in vengeance.

As the train pulled in to Oakbourne with a hiss of white steam, Julia understood why it was *her* card left at the death scenes, *her* models that were killed, *her* spare trade stamp that was taken. Who the hell else knew where she kept it? Who else knew she carried a Bulldog revolver? Who was out when Elizabeth Mansell was shot?

Questions, questions, so many questions.

Were they crocodile tears he shed in the name of the girls' fathers? Or was it genuine grief? In his dark twisted mind, were the models lice that needed to be exterminated? Or was he saving the girls from themselves?

Little round face on a little round body, they'd feel very safe with this caller with twinkly eyes and comic mutton chop whiskers. Especially when Mrs. McAllister had given him their address...

Oliver bore the girls no ill will personally, of that she was sure. That's why the shots were so deadly. So that the girls wouldn't suffer.

But somewhere along the way, in his addled heartbroken mind, Julia had become Pandora — and he wanted the world to know what she was like.

And to rid the world of her evil.

All the way from the station, Julia's heart raced. Her models were in danger, but who to warn first? There were ten on her current books, but Elizabeth Mansell proved that time was no factor. Where the hell did she start?

Then she remembered the missing flip book. She hadn't dropped it in the shop, or left it in Mitchell Street. The bastard had taken it, when he'd dropped by this morning.

Taking Daisy's stairs two at a time, she heard a gun cock. Heard the crack of the pistol. Crashed into a tableau frozen in shock.

Daisy. Eyes wide in horror.

Rosie. Eyes wide in surprise.

Bug. Little green eyes wide in death.

Chapter 32

'Why didn't you go around?' Julia screamed. 'Why didn't you go straight to Daisy's, like I told you?'

Eight hours had passed. Julia had not stopped shaking, but she was damned if she'd let Collingwood comfort her.

'This is your fault,' she yelled. 'Your fault Bug threw himself in front of Daisy and saved her life!'

She expected him to argue. Tell her, with respect, that was total rubbish, and point out that it was she who'd telephoned from Bentley in a panic, to warn him that Oliver was the killer. How he'd explained that, without evidence, the police could not arrest him, but that he'd have men watch Blackstock with immediate effect. Which he had.

'But I told you, John, I told you! When I rang from Oakbourne, I said Daisy was the target! If you'd been there, Bug would still be alive!'

Again, no contradiction. Instead, he let her howl and cry and screech, and didn't say anything about there being no time pattern with the killings — who could predict another quite so soon? He did point out, though, that the raid at Pandora's house was successful, if that was any consolation.

Her answer was unprintable.

And of course Bug's death was not his fault. Julia told him to watch Oliver. Not his wife —

And now she understood why the girls felt comfortable with their killer. Who's suspicious of a woman with a baby in her arms?

Because who could have imagined Rosie, distraught at losing her daughter and having no outlet for grief, visiting the house where she died in Bentley? Discovering, as Julia had done, that Charity had been fed drugs, lured into posing for pornographic pictures, then forced into prostitution before an overdose killed her?

Devastated at the revelation about her daughter's life, and the true cause of her death, Rosie daren't tell her husband. It would kill him. Instead, she takes matters into her own hands, because she can't stand back and allow these spiders to drag more unsuspecting creatures into their webs.

'She confessed everything,' Collingwood said.

They were in her studio, because the shop, the kitchen, even the bedroom held too many painful memories, and she wasn't strong enough to face them yet. Or the backdrop of the railway station, and its 1st Class bloody carriage. Like most women, she settled for the open park, fronted by stone balustrade and floral urns.

'Not because she was caught quite literally with a smoking gun, but because she genuinely believed that, in the long run, she was doing the world a favour.'

Masturbation causes epilepsy — it's a medical fact, Rosie said.

Unfortunately, the authorities weren't doing one damned thing about it, so if she could show how wiping out the cause wipes out epilepsy, hundreds — no, thousands of lives would be saved, and respectability restored.

I needed to kill them spiders quickly and cleanly, mind. I'm not a monster, Inspector Collingwood.

And she knew exactly how to do it, she explained. That day when Julia came round and left her bag on the settee? And Verity, bless her heart, emptied it out on the floor? That's when Rosie noticed the revolver.

'Elizabeth Mansell,' Julia said.

'What about her?'

'I should have realised, John. The day of Charity's birthday. Angus told me *Mrs. B's taken the bairns to the park.* So why weren't they with her, when she came rushing in, waving Edmund's letter? How come they were upstairs all the time?'

Possibly for the same reason Rosie didn't see that Faith was stealing items from her father's shop and selling them. You don't see what's under your nose. Not when you love and trust someone —

'What I don't understand,' Julia said, 'is why me?'

Everything was in the open now. There was no hiding her involvement in erotica, her secret studio — Charlie Kincaid had already made the connection between her and the flip book. It must have tangled with John's clothes, because he found it later in his pocket and placed it in his desk for safekeeping. That's where Kincaid found it, and if his inspector hadn't mentioned it, there had to be a reason.

The same reason he wouldn't arrest his chief suspect, despite the weight of evidence.

Mrs. McAllister.

Rosie, on the other hand, knew nothing about Oliver's peep show side-line. She was completely and truly ignorant of his involvement in the French postcard trade. Not her Olly. He wouldn't stoop to filth like that!

But she knew about the rooms on Mitchell Street, where he had signed the lease, and there was only one reason a man would rent a place and not tell his wife, and sure enough. Guess who had the key? Two and two quickly added up to four. Look at the amount of time he spent with Julia. The way they laughed together, the need for secrecy, the things he said sometimes. Like all the money coming in, but where was it going, eh? All this talk about mansions and fancy schooling, and that Percival Tarrant man being the fountain of wealth —

but what had she seen of any extra money? Oliver was supporting a mistress, that's what he was doing. Paying rent on Mitchell Street, and bailing out Whitmore Photographic unless Rosie missed her guess, and that meant one thing and one thing only.

He was in love with her.

Think she hadn't seen him kiss his fingers, then place that kiss on the camellia outside Julia's shop? That's love, that is. Like the way they went off singing the other night, arm in arm, like an old married couple. And yesterday. Think she didn't hear all them sex noises when she went to empty out the tea leaves on the roses? Him coming upstairs later, complaining about his collar being too tight and reeking of her posh citrus scent?

Killing her rival wasn't the answer.

'She was quite open about it,' Collingwood said. 'Oliver's love for you wouldn't die, if she killed you. Quite the reverse.'

'I'd forever be a paragon, his one true love in her mind.'

BUT. If it could be shown that Julia McAllister was a slut and a killer — up to her neck in pornography, prostitution and drugs — who would hang for her crime, Oliver would be so disgusted he'd come back to Rosie.

'So she framed me.'

Julia was too numb to feel bitter. Too numb to hate. But not too numb to feel the devastation and guilt Oliver would be feeling. Not too numb to put the pieces together.

Wheedling her way past the landlady in Mitchell Street, Rosie sneaks photos from the secret studio, steals the spare trade stamp from the shop and leaves the evidence beside the dead girls, in full view.

The irony, of course, was that Oliver was in the business far deeper than Julia ever was — and it never crossed his mind, not once, to be unfaithful to his Rosie Cheeks. His wife, the nippers, they were his life, his world, his reason for breathing. His reason for stashing the extra money into investments, so his children wouldn't need to go into service, to factories, the army.

So his wife would have all the luxuries she could only ever dream of.

There were no luxuries in the workhouse, which is where the Blackstock children were headed, and few dreams in prison.

Even fewer at the end of a rope.

Flora's house.

'I am going to take this girl's portrait, that's what I'm going to do, and you, sir, are going to help me.'

'Me? I don't know nuffin' about photographs.'

Her kitchen.

'For a small Bug, you have a precociously large appetite.'

'Man's gotta keep his strength up, else he'll die on your doorstep and you'll be stuck with the funeral.'

'Man's gotta keep his mouth closed while he eats, or his funeral will come sooner than he imagines.'

Her kitchen again.

'Thirsty?'

'Parched worse than Sarah Dezzard.'

'Sahara Desert.'

A scrawny shoulder shrugged. 'Parched worse than both of 'em, I reckon.'

And again.

'So off we goes, me and Pop, down to the canal, and all he's talking about is catching trout and cod and salmon for our tea. This big, he says, holding his arms wide. And how we'd fry them in best butter. Everythin'. Then he says, gotta call in here a sec, son, which was odd, coz us had never bin in a church in our whole lives. D'you go?'

Julia shook her head.

'Don't blame yer. Anyways, I follows him up the steps, little hand in big, yer can imagine, and there's this funny bloke in a long brown scratchy dress, who takes my other hand and squeezes it. Then Pop lets go, ruffles me hair, and the next thing I know, the gate's closing behind me with a clang.'

The banshee, the banshee, bejabbers, don't you hear? Its groaning and its moaning, begob it's moighty queer.

Chapter 33

'You can't leave.'

Six days had passed. Six nerve-wracking days, six tormented sleepless nights, and another funeral had taken place. Not a Jewish boneyard this time, though. Or a thirty shilling headstone.

'Julia, are you listening to me? I said you can't leave.'

Watch me. 'Why not? Don't you have enough evidence to arrest me?'

'You know and I know that it's not against the law to pose for pornographic photographs, or to take them.'

The crime lies in the possession and distribution of lewd material, although it piques my interest that you're aware of this fact. Collingwood's words — it seemed a lifetime ago — echoed in her head.

'How many times do I have to tell you? I've made it quite clear to Chief Inspector that you're not involved in the trade; in fact it's thanks to you that we put an end to it.' Collingwood moved to kiss her, but she pulled away. 'I've also put in a request to the Chief Constable that we take a leaf out of the Paris police book, and hire a crime scene photographer.'

'Good for you.'

'No, good for you. I put your name forward, and the top brass have agreed.'

'That's funny. I don't remember anyone consulting me on the subject.'

Other memories echoed back. To where this all started, in Flora's house, where to calm her nerves, Julia had followed the familiar ritual. That was exactly what she was doing now. Same order, same routine, because in habit there is order, and where there is order, there is calm. So she stood in her studio, running her hand over the Spanish mahogany case of her camera, inhaling the leathery tang of the bellows and fingering the beautifully crafted dovetail joints.

'Surely that's a good enough reason to stay?'

He laid his hand on hers. She snatched it away. Kept polishing away at the brass fittings.

'It'll mean financial security, independence — I'm begging you, Julia. Alice is dying. The doctor says she can't hold out much longer, and then … Julia. Please. Please don't leave me.'

You can't choose who you fall in love with.

Not John. Not the wolf in wolf's clothing, although that crossed her mind. But like the good Bug he was, he'd crawled into her heart and under her skin.

'I'm sorry, John.'

In any case, Inspector Collingwood might smooth this mess over, but it would only be a matter of time before he uncovered her past. That was what men who aspired to be Chief Inspectors did, wasn't it?

'Where will you go?'

'No idea,' Julia said.

It didn't matter. For premeditated murder, even the Devil's, you hang.

A NOTE TO THE READER

Well, Reader —

You can't see me, but I've got a grin a mile wide. After all this time, writing is still my #1 dream, and I can't tell you how chuffed I am that you're sharing it with me.

Especially since this series is a new departure for me! Until now, I'd set my thrillers way back, with a superbitch in Ancient Rome and a shrewd high priestess in Sparta. If you're familiar with my short stories, you'll know these bounce across all timescales and genres, but ancient history and myths were my passion.

Until I went to the Klondike Museum in Seattle. Its proper name is the Klondike Gold Rush National Historical Park. You can see why I shortened it. But on the wall outside, the plaque reads "...*adventure and hardship ... dreams made ... hopes shattered ... lives changed ... a city transformed.*"

Staring at the photos of the challenges, the suffering, the bones of the 3,000 pack animals who died on one trail alone and whose bones still lie there today, I knew, in that instant, that I had to write about someone who took images that would also change lives.

In 1895, there were no crime scene photographers in England. The Parisian police were applying the concept with sizeable success, but over here, the Home Office was barely getting to grips with mugshots, never mind fingerprints, footprint casts or photographic records that captured a murder scene before evidence could be trampled, contaminated or lost.

So was born Julia McAllister, taking saucy pictures to survive. Who said you can't rewrite history?

If you enjoyed *Snap Shot*, I'd very much value your review on **Amazon** and **Goodreads**. And if you fancy joining me on my journey into the unknown, buckle your seatbelt on **Facebook (Marilyn Todd–Crime Writer)**. It promises to be quite a ride!

Marilyn Todd.

www.marilyntodd.com

Sapere Books is an exciting new publisher of brilliant fiction and popular history.

To find out more about our latest releases and our monthly bargain books visit our website:
saperebooks.com

Made in the USA
Monee, IL
30 June 2020